Serving Up Secrecy

Published by H.M. Shander Publishing
Copyright © 2019 by H.M. Shander

Cover Design: Megan Parker-Squiers @EmCat Designs
Editing by: PWA & IDIM Editorial
Shander, H.M., 1975—Serving Up Secrecy

It's no secret,

I love my kids and husband,

And although things don't always go as planned,

I wouldn't change any of it.

It was meant to be.

~Chapter One

h, my throbbing head.

The second I woke up with a killer headache, I knew I was in trouble. Big trouble. Plus, I was so hot. I lifted the blanket off me and welcomed the cool rush of air over my aching legs, and my body. Oh my god, why was I naked? Pushing myself up into a sitting position, I cradled my head between my hands and moaned. I'd deal with the nakedness in a moment.

"Are you okay?" An unrecognizable voice spoke from behind me on the bed.

Instantly I jumped off the mattress, panic filling me as I yanked the twisted sheet around me. "Who are you?"

"James, we met last night," the heavy, husky voice full of sleep said as he shuffled in bed.

I backed against the wall and fumbled my way through the dark, my hand rubbing against the rough wallpaper that had been touched by what? *Eww...* The thought of a recent undercover bust on the cleanliness of hotel rooms circulated in my brain as I managed my way. Rounding a corner, I kicked something soft in

1

the process. My hand patted along the wall for another corner where I remembered the bathroom was, and I inched my way in, locking the door.

What was going on?

The lights blinded me, and I groaned out in shock, shielding my eyes to drown out the intensity. At least I was in *my* hotel room, the cheapest Hilton room available, as my personal items were tucked neatly into my overnight case on the counter.

My head pounded, matching the speed of my racing heart and quick breaths. Again, I cradled it between my hands, the bedsheet puddling at my feet as my stomach soured and did a back flip. A second later, I buried my head into the toilet bowl, trying to expunge the toxins from my body.

Feeling perfectly drained, I braced my naked body against the cool bathroom counter, the terrible lighting doing zip to hide the ginormous bags under my eyes, ringed with dark, smudged mascara and eyeliner. My pale blonde hair which had looked magnificent when I left last night, now won the prize for the worst bed-head look. I shook my head in disgust and a bobby pin fell bouncing off the faux-marble counter top.

Grabbing one of the wrapped glasses, I cringed from the crackling as I pulled the plastic off. Even though it was protected, I still gave it a quick wash under the warm running water and filled it to the brim. It touched my lips, tasting stale and hotel-like, and laced with vomit. Yuck. I spit it into the sink, ensuring it rinsed down the drain.

A knock on the door. "Hey, Josephine, are you okay?"

No. I'm in a hotel room with a complete stranger.

But I took another swish of the clear liquid and spit again. "I'll be fine."

"You sure? You don't sound it?"

Did he hear me retching?

I searched the bathroom, looking for my phone but it wasn't there. I had no idea what time it was. It could be the middle of the night for all I knew.

"Hey," I called out, secretly hoping he still lingered on the other side of the door. "What time is it?"

A pause. "Eight forty-three."

"Okay, thanks."

I dug through my overnight bag and pulled out my toothbrush and paste. As the brush scraped and cleaned my teeth, I tried my best to recall how I got into this mess. My hangover was rank… just how much did I drink last night?

Last night. My cousin's wedding. The most beautiful bride ever married the man of her dreams. So regal and elegant, she had the entire ballroom in the palm of her hands. That's right – there was a ballroom involved. A big, royal production with fancy chandeliers and a live band. My cousin's fiancé—correction, husband—was partner in a prestigious law firm and could afford to have a lavish event.

Drinks were free, and very likely, my greatest undoing. The liquor flowed like a river, hard stuff too. At least that much I remembered. And the ballroom dance floor? I believe I was the one who was out there the most, dancing in my bare feet, the hem of my silver gown dusting the hardwood floors. Gawd, it was so fun.

Lights and music replayed like a film played in slo-mo. It was mesmerising. My arms wrapped around a handsome stranger's neck, his body moving in time with mine. Was that the same man in my hotel room? It was hard to tell in the dark of the room, but I sincerely hoped so.

A knock again. "Are you sure you're okay? You've been there a long time."

I hadn't booked a fancy hotel room as the standard room rate with the bare bones basics was all I could afford, which meant one bathroom. Perfect for just me. Maybe not the guy standing on the other side of the door though.

"Do you need in here?"

"I wouldn't mind."

"Gimme a sec." I re-wrapped the beige sheet around my body and yanked open the door.

Mr. Handsome covered his face with his free hand as the bright light washed over him.

"Scuse me."

He side-stepped me in the narrow space, a pair of tighty-whities hugging his fine form, leaving nothing to the imagination. A dark pair of pants hung off his toned arm.

Nice.

I averted my gaze when he spun around, his features shadowed from the Hollywood lighting in the bathroom.

"I'm meeting my buddies for breakfast in ten minutes in the restaurant downstairs. You're welcome to join us if you'd like," he said as he shut the bathroom door, plunging me back into darkness.

"I'm good, thanks."

It was bad enough to wake up next to a stranger. No way was I going to join him and his friends.

The light leaking out from under the door was all I needed to make myself a single cup of java in the tiny space. It reminded me of work with its little sink cut into a counter with barely enough space for the coffee machine. I ripped open the single serve packet, inhaling deeply. I needed the jolt to truly wake me up. Within a short minute, a steaming mugful of nasty coffee barely warmed my lips as I choked down the bitter flavour.

I shielded my eyes from the mess in the room, stepping on soft material I could only hope was clothing and kicking a glass container with my toes. The path to the window lasted forever.

Still dressed like the Statue of Liberty, I cracked open the dark, heavy curtains enough to let a stream of freshly fallen snow-bright light to wedge its way in. It was time to see what kind of disaster I created.

Scattered clothes, all mine as I looked around, accounted for the mess on the floor. My lace undies dangled from the corner of the tv and as I glanced at my ridiculous self, behind me I saw several used condom wrappers littered on the side table. Blonde hairs whipped me in the face as I spun around.

Several? Oh, dear God. Guess I really had a good time last night.

The bathroom door unlocked with a click.

"Mind if I make a cup of coffee?"

My eyes travelled over the mess in the room, spotting at least a half-dozen empty Heinekens and a couple of Palm Bays. I tightened my toga.

"Fill your boots. It doesn't taste very good." I wasn't about to face my indiscretion.

"Never is."

Curiosity about my guest winning any weak debate, I turned my head. He was out of sight, no doubt making the world's worst cup of coffee.

His voice smoldered as he spoke. "Sure you don't want to join me for breakfast?"

"Honestly, I'm good. My stomach is not so well." No sooner had I said it when it did another fantastic flip, followed famously with a flop. Hiking up my makeshift night dress, I pushed past him into the bathroom, kicked the door closed and heaved again.

"Might make you feel better."

Exactly how much had I drank to feel this terrible? Wowsers.

"I feel bad leaving you like this. Maybe I should cancel."

"No, no, no" I said, the urgency in my voice. Last thing I needed was someone to take care of me. Especially someone I've known less than twelve hours. I spoke to the closed door. "I'll be fine, I think I've completely emptied it out now. Besides, I need to head home. I'm supposed to be at work by four."

Which gave me more than enough time to get there as it was an easy three-hour drive.

"You're sure?"

"Positive."

"Well, thanks for last night. I had a really good time."

I'll bet you did. Clearly, I must've too.

I'd let my inhibitions fly out the window and brought this man back to my room. But I stayed tight-lipped, leaning my wretched body against the counter.

"Can I call you?"

Why bother? It would never work.

"I don't live around here. I was just down for the weekend."

My home was three hours north in Edmonton, a place I'd lived all my life. I gave my pale face a rub, hoping it would perk up, and pinched some colour into my cheeks the way Grandma used to.

"I'll leave my number just in case." There was an edge of hopefulness in his tone. "Ciao for now, Josephine."

I nodded absently, knowing full well I wasn't going to make use of it. The less I knew of this guy the better. One-night stands were not my thing, so it was important to sweep this embarrassment under the rug. But I couldn't be rude about it.

"It was nice to have met you," I scrambled to remember his name. "James." I added when it hit me.

I pressed my ear to the door, listening. As soon as the main door latched shut, I tiptoed out of the bathroom. Relief covered me – I was alone.

Packing up my party dress and shoes, I tidied up the room

to a decent standard, tossing the litter into a waste receptacle and stacking the used dishes by the sink. No hotel maid needed to know the shenanigans I was a part of, especially since the room was registered in my name.

I glanced quickly at the note he left on my pillow, seeing it as I remade the bed.

There once was a man named James
Whose poetry jams were lames
The girl he just met
Was the cutest one yet
So Cupid please take your aims.
Last night was amazing.
Feel better and call me.
XOXO James

I stared at the note, rereading it several times over. This James was as sweet as apple pie, but it wouldn't work. He lived here, I lived hours away. Besides, sleeping with a guy on the first night was not something I did. Last night was a drunken-fueled mistake and it was best to drop this from my memory like a bad dream. As I packed up my bag, the note called to me as if a neon arrow were pointing at it.

Bag in hand, I held it and debated. To keep it or not. My eyes scanned the words and without a final thought, I crumpled the note, and tossed it into the waste can.

~Chapter Two

Eight Weeks Later

J scanned the want ads desperately searching for a new job. It's not that I didn't like waitressing, it wasn't working for me anymore. Lately, I've been blah about going into Westside as I've been there since I graduated high school, over six years ago. But I wanted something more. Wanted a 'real' job, a normal Monday to Friday job, working the nine to five. The Tuesday through Saturday evenings I currently worked were, well… I was ready for a change in my life. A big change.

Thing was, the more I scoured the online job postings, the less enthused I became. Did I want to sit at a desk all day and answer phones? No. One of the great things about waitressing was the movement – getting in 10,000 steps a day was easy. Warehouse positions were always available, but I had zero interest in working there as I was a person who enjoyed chatting with people too much. My options were limited, especially since I had no further education.

Sigh.

I closed the lid to my laptop and stood, stretching my back. Lately everything ached, and I battled a low-grade headache almost daily. It was irritating. I'd go to a party on the weekend and it would take me a day or two to recover. Seriously. What's up with that? I was a fresh twenty-four, not ninety. But after last month's raunchy hangover from a pretty kicking rave, I'd given up drinking. Didn't help me feel less stiff though. What a mess I was. Maybe I was dealing with some kind of low-grade flu, the kind that zaps your energy but yet, makes you ravenous. Seriously, it was strange.

My gaze flitted over to the bulletin board I'd hung up beside the door to pin important notices or take out menus on. New Year's Eve tickets – coveted New Year's Eve tickets to a sold-out event – reflected their golden edges at me. Thank goodness the event of the decade was less than a month away. It gave me time to completely heal so I could party like I wanted to.

Urban DC was calling it a night to remember, with guest DJs, lots of prizes – and Oh My God, Colby Sacks was attending and promised he'd play a set. He was the hottest new thing in Canadian pop music. The new year was going to be awesome.

After a quick daydream where Colby Sacks called me on stage and professed his undying love for me, I walked down the hall to my bedroom and hopped into my Zumba wear. Tuesdays were dance class at the main gathering hall, a nice little hub in the centre of my apartment complex. Every day something different was offered, but Tuesdays were the best. Nothing like dancing your butt off to good music.

Ninety minutes later, sweat soaked and feeling worn out, I clamoured into the shower lacking the energy to sing along to Ed and Taylor as they blasted from the speaker on the counter. I knew I worked out hard, but this tiredness was ridiculous. Perhaps I needed to go see a doctor. Maybe there was an issue with my thyroid or something. Or maybe I shouldn't have had such a heavy breakfast of eggs and cheese?

That wouldn't have done it.

I shook the bottle of shampoo, depositing a tiny little drop onto my hands. No matter how hard I whacked it against my palm, I wasn't getting any more. Wiping the water from my face, I opened the small organiser above the toilet, reached past the Tampax, and grabbed a small container of new shampoo, closing the curtain back up.

Tampax?

I thought long and hard. Shouldn't I have replaced that box already? Or had I? My mind drifted over the shopping trips as of late. Nope, no feminine hygiene products to speak of had made their way into my shopping cart.

NO! My eyes grew wide.

It's not possible.

I hopped out of the shower, shampoo still in my hair, and ran into the kitchen dripping wet. When the laptop fired up, I went to the period tracking website I'd been using since I was sixteen. For no other reason than to help me prepare. Painful cramps and wicked mood swings were no laughing matter. Day One was always the worst of my cycle and it was nice to have the essentials on standby for it.

My eyes scanned the online calendars. Nothing registered since September 29th.

What? Holy crow.

Impossible. I should've had a period at the end of October, and another at the end of November.

A blank calendar greeted me. How could I not have noticed? My phone should've synced with the desktop version if I had put it in there, so I checked the app… and it too lacked any data.

Cold trails of water rivered down my back. I hopped back into the warmth of the still running shower, quickly rinsing the soap from my body, and rubbed in a quick conditioner before donning a robe and returning to stare at my computer screen for a long, long time.

"It just can't be. It's not," I said to the air, shaking my towelled head. "Clearly I missed inputting it somewhere."

I thumbed through the standard calendar on my phone. Maybe I'd just been busy. Sure, that was it. My period was due Halloween, and I had a costume party that night, so I must've forgotten to add it to the tracker. It could explain one day, but what about the other four days always tagging along? What happened to them?

Skipped periods happened all the time, right? Maybe that's what this was. Still doesn't explain why I haven't had one in two months. Although... As I ran over the common pre-menstrual signs; I was having a few. Bloating. Nausea. Indigestion. Sore breasts. All great PMS signs. All signs of pregnancy too. I shook my head.

I can't be.

I haven't done the deed with anyone since Crystal's wedding. And we used condoms. Lots of them.

It's not possible.

Jagger, my boyfriend of the month as Ana called him, would be ticked if he knew I was pregnant, and even furious since I one-nighted with another guy while he's been waiting to score.

My phone buzzed in my hand. Incoming facetime call from Ana. Perfect timing as my BFF can zone in on my emotions from a million miles away. She's weird like that. I glanced at the clock. It's eleven our time which meant it was the middle of the night for her.

I pushed the accept button. "Hey, Ana."

"Jo-Jo," she whispered, her voice held a tinge of Australian dialect. She'd picked it up so easily, but I guessed living there for five months would help. "How's it hanging, matey?"

I felt as if I needed to whisper as well. "Counting down the days until you get home."

Only a few more weeks. She was coming home just before the new year.

"Aww, I miss ya too." She narrowed her gaze slightly. "What's wrong?" Those hazel eyes always saw right through me.

"Nothing. Yet."

"And your poker face totally gives it away. What's going on?"

"Where are you?"

Curiosity blanketed her, and she tipped her head. "I'm in Perth."

"I know that, silly. Are you alone?" I tried peering behind her to get a sense of her surroundings, but it was all darkness.

She flipped the phone around to prove she was alone. "See? No one's up at this hour. And it's very peaceful sitting here staring up at the stars, so different than there. Anyways, chicky, spill the beans."

I never beat around the bush with Ana as it angers her so, but I wasn't ready to vocalise my fear. It would just further cement the pregnancy as a real possibility. "I don't know. This isn't the kind of thing one says over the phone."

"Okay. Well now I've narrowed down to like three possibilities; you're either pregnant or about to run off with that new man of yours, or you're now batting for the other team because those would be the only things you wouldn't share over the phone." She snorted a little as she laughed.

"I'm definitely not batting for the other team."

"Hey, it's cool either way. Did you know it's totally acceptable here?"

I raised my recently plucked eyebrow. "Ana, it's completely accepted here in Canada too."

"I's just saying. My flatmates mentioned it." She cocked her brows. "So, it must be guy troubles, because I know y'ain't pregnant. You'd have to be in a committed relationship first, with a ring and a wedding behind you."

I hung my head. Completely proper, right? I was the poster child of a typical 1950's woman. However, my upbringing was about to get a good ole shaking.

"I'm sure I'm not."

"What? Damn girl." The tip of her finger came into view. I assumed she was wagging it at me, but it was hard to tell as I only saw a portion of her palm moving up and down. "Is it Jagger's?"

Nope. The only guy I truly did the full deed with recently was that guy from Crystal's wedding. Jagger was close but there hadn't been any in and out action, just a lot of mouth on special places, after a few parties. And I was smart enough to know you can't get pregnant that way. Which meant...

"Don't know. James something or other." My ballroom floor and mattress-mambo dancing partner.

"Ya had a one-night stand?" Shock rolled off her tongue. "When?"

It would've surprised me more too but was impossible to disagree. It was completely out of character. "At Crystal's wedding."

"That was like two months ago."

"I know." And I still thought about it when I fell asleep. How sweet he was, what an incredible dancer he was, and how he'd made me feel.

"Did ya take a test?"

I rolled my eyes. "I just realised this possibility less than thirty minutes ago. I'm still in shock it could even *be* a possibility."

"So, run down to Chang's and buy a test. Take me with ya." Her voice carried a pleading tone.

Chang's was the equivalent to a corner store. It stood beside the little complex where I took my Zumba class. Anything in there also cost twice what it would've at a grocery story. At Chang's you truly paid for the convenience, and that should be his slogan.

"I'm not going down, and I won't take you with me. Besides, I'm not even dressed." I pointed to the towel wrapped on my head.

"Aw, c'mon. It's been a while since I've seen Chang."

He was the little old Asian who ran the market. If you'd been in there even once, he remembered you. After a couple of visits, he knew your name. Ana said it was a photographic memory from seeing the name on a payment card or overhearing it, but I thought it was creepy. However, he carried the best chocolates—the kind you save for the first day of your period. He imported them from Switzerland, and they were worth every penny.

"I'm not going."

Clearly, I've missed out on buying the delectable cocoa creams and didn't need an inquisition into my neglect. Not that I'd get one. It was total paranoia.

"Do it now. I want to be the first to see ya take the test and see what it says." She smiled. "DO IT!" Her voice boomed through the speaker on my phone loud enough it should've woken up her flatmates.

I sighed, throwing on a quick outfit and tossing my hair into a sloppy bun. With my coat on, I grabbed my purse. "I can't believe I'm doing this."

She snickered. "Me either."

On the elevator ride down and the walk over to Chang's, she filled me in about her latest tour to Rottnest Island, and how she was falling in love with Australia. She was already talking about finding a way to live there which I thought was complete lunacy. Ana had lived with her parents right up until she graduated from college, when she moved in with me. When she said she was going to backpack around Australia, I had a hard time believing her, although she seemed to have managed okay. But living there? She struggled to find a job here, what was the market like there?

And not to be selfish, but what would I do if she decided to live there? I'd have to find a new roommate as I doubted Ana would continue to pay for an apartment she wasn't living in. And what roommate wanted to live with me, if I was pregnant? Which I couldn't be.

Three little bells chimed overhead as I opened the door into Chang's. He sat on his stool, eyes fixated on the daily newspaper while he shook his head about something.

"Say hi to him," Ana urged me.

I spoke through gritted teeth and lowered the speaker volume. "I will. When we get up to the counter."

Thankfully the market was quiet, and I was the only patron inside. Up and down the small aisles I went, stopping in the third one.

"Here they are," I whispered.

"Lemme see."

I turned the phone around to show her my very limited options.

"Get the blue one."

"Why that one?" I asked, turning the camera back to me, scowling at her.

"More accurate."

"How would you know?"

"See-mon," she said his name the way the French did, although everyone English called him Simon. "Year two of college."

Ah, right. That piece of work.

I nodded and pulled the lonely blue box off the counter. Should I get something else to cover it? Maybe a fashion magazine? I glanced around to see what would be reasonable, but there was nothing. When one purchased a pregnancy test, there wasn't much to go with it.

I sighed and inched my way to the check out, pushing the light blue box forward, avoiding all eye contact.

Chang folded the only newspaper to be delivered in Edmonton and set it to the side. "Ah, goo-morring, Jo," he said, keeping his own gaze fixed on the old-style register.

"Tell him I say hi," Ana's voice came out from the phone.

I turned it around, facing Chang. "Ana says hi."

He waved a little wave. "Aye, Ah-na." His gaze flitted over to me and his short finger pointed at the rack of specialties. "I bring new chocolate this month."

"I'm good, thanks." Shame had me looking away when he picked up the blue box.

"Ah, I see why."

Click, click and an old-style cha-ching sound as he announced the price, and tucked my purchase into a brown paper bag.

Embarrassment colouring me in bright neon colours, I paid and made good time getting out of there and racing back up to our apartment. Putting the phone on table, I started to walk away.

Ana yelled out, "Hey, where ya going?"

How her flatmates didn't wake, I'd never understand.

"I'm looking up at the ceiling. And it's not very pretty."

"I'm not taking you into the bathroom, Ana." I leaned over the phone and glared into the screen.

"Please. At least take me and leave me facing the ceiling in there." When I was about to protest, she played her trump card. "I'm your BFF, and I've been missing out on all of this. Please."

"Fine."

I dropped her on the bathroom counter as requested and opened the package, getting it ready to either destroy my life or teach me a very cautionary tale. If there was a God, it was an open promise to only sleep with someone I truly loved.

16

Pants around my ankles, I sat on the toilet. And waited. Nothing happened.

"I don't hear anything," Ana chirped.

"You're not helping."

C'mon. All I needed was a dribble. I could do this. But fear held me back as I didn't know if I really wanted to know. I mean I did, but only if it was negative. Then, I'd be able to relax, lesson learned. I didn't want to face the prospect of–

"Run some water," Ana offered up as apparently my inability to pee on demand was killing her.

Finally, I felt a little urge and directed the exposed end of the stick into the meager amount my body dribbled out. I hoped it was enough.

"Got it."

I placed it on the counter and cleaned myself up, sitting on the edge of the tub.

"I'm timing," Ana said.

I sat the phone up against the mirror, watching her face. "How much longer?"

"Two minutes."

The phone was quiet as we waited.

Please let it be negative. Please let it be another reason why I'm late. Let it be anything else… I promise if it's negative to never do the deed again until I'm married. You have my word. I can't be pregnant. I'm not responsible enough to grow and raise a human. I just can't be. There has to be another reason.

Ana whispered, "Time's up."

I swallowed, and with a shaky hand I picked up the stick and stared. The answer stared up at me clear as day.

"Jo-Jo?"

I flipped the stick around. "Pregnant."

Chapter Three

*T*en days later I had the unfortunate visit to the OB/GYN that came after a lovely trip to the ultrasound clinic. There I was blessed with an intravaginal ultrasound using a special wand, and let me tell you, it's not as fun as it sounded.

However, there on the imaging screen was a grainy black and white image of an alien blob, which the tech said was my baby. I was still in a little bit of shock, wrapped in a shroud of denial, but okay. I wasn't sure how the white mass was a baby, but whatever. Perhaps she was using someone else's images and trying to pass them off as mine.

After that, I met with my OB/GYN, the professional who'd deliver the little blob into the world when the time came. His hand thrust up inside me far enough to tickle my tonsils while his other pushed around my pelvis, informing me that everything was just great. Sure didn't feel that way.

In the span of thirty minutes, I'd had two different people all up in my business, and I got zero enjoyment out of it. At least Jagger, my boyfriend for the past three weeks which was a record for the year, made it interesting.

Oh gawd, what was I going to do about that?

Dr. Tonsil Tickler clicked on his keyboard, comparing his personal findings with what the ultrasound tech discovered. "It looks like you're about twelve weeks along."

I sat up, tugging the paper gown down and crossed my legs. "What?" How could I be that far along already?

"Everything looks good, and you're coming out of your first trimester, so you may have an increase in energy."

"Alright," I said, feigning excitement.

Twelve weeks out of what? There's nine months to a pregnancy, which has four weeks, so thirty-six weeks total. Jeepers. Another twenty-four weeks to go, which sounded like forever, however, the first twelve truly passed me by.

He listed a variety of symptoms, but none of them included shock or denial, because even with the grainy image and the lack of a period, it could still be something else. Right? Maybe it wasn't a baby at all, and it was a tumour, because that would stop my periods dead, right?

With a big fancy wheel, he lined up my last period and my likely day of conception, being that Crystal's wedding was the last time I had actual sex, and concluded I was due July 1 – Canada Day.

"Oh goody. Fireworks for the day my vagina gets ripped apart," I deadpanned, glancing at the giant poster of a huge baby head destroying the birth canal on its voyage out.

He cocked a cynical look. "I'm sorry?"

"Nothing," I muttered, my brain taking in the horror of something much larger than a man's dangler stretching out the delicate part of my body. No wonder women screamed in labour. A violent shudder rippled through me.

"I'll be right back." Dr. Tonsil Tickler excused himself to get the nurse to finish up for him. Guess he was more of a hands-on doctor, if you caught my drift.

Miss Lovely Nurse walked in carrying a package of presents for me. Nothing fun nor exciting. It was a giant stack of reading material, a list of prenatal vitamins I should be taking with some samples, and ways to keep fit and healthy. The latter wasn't going to be hard because I loved my Zumba.

"Do you have any questions?" Her voice was like melted butter.

"Yeah. How long does it take for someone to actually accept a pregnancy, because this," I covered my belly with my hands, "this could be misdiagnosed, and I'm really just having some weird hormonal imbalance because of a brain tumour or something, right?"

She gave me a quizzical look. "Do you have a brain tumour?"

I shook my head rapidly. "No, not that they've found."

"Is there a reason you think they would?" She stood closer.

I slumped under my paper covering and tacky gown. "No, it's just..."

She typed on the computer and scanned the data beside it. "Your ultrasound picture shows a definite baby, give it seven more weeks, and you'll be able to find out if it's a boy or a girl."

Her finger touched the screen, and she pointed out the head and spine and arms and legs. More typing and scrolling.

She paused and walked back. "Are you having a hard time with the news?"

"Yeah. I only found out last week, and now my whole future's changing."

A sympathetic look covered her face. "I take it this wasn't planned?"

For five to ten years into my future, but not now. I shook my head.

20

Unmarried, and wholly single. A waitress with no college or university degree, who's made nothing of my life, and yet, suddenly, I was growing a brand-new life. How was I supposed to provide for it? How was I supposed to nurture it and give it the best?

"I never planned on being a single mother."

Because there was no way Jagger would stick around, and I wouldn't want that anyway. He wasn't father material.

"No one does, but you make do. You find ways. Talk to your friends and family about it. Talk to the father. He's probably just as confused as you are."

Unlikely, since I haven't seen him since that night. At least not in person. My dreams were something entirely different.

"But the good thing is, you have lots of time to prepare. A good twenty-eight weeks."

I sighed and hunched over more. "Twenty-eight weeks? I thought I had twenty-four?"

The nurse scanned the computer screen. "No. Twenty-eight. You're only twelve weeks along. A normal pregnancy is forty weeks."

"Oh."

Well, you'd think I should've known but all I knew was a pregnancy was nine months. I sighed a long breathless sigh. Still… twenty-eight weeks wasn't that long in the grand scheme of things. There wasn't a lot of time to save and prepare and tell my family.

Oh dear God, what would they say?

"I'm going to get something else for you. It'll give you a moment to change."

Change? My whole life was about to change.

I spied my clothes hanging on the back of the door. Right those. That's what she meant. Slipping into my jeans and favourite sweater, I leaned against the wall, tipping my head back. What was I going to do?

A knock and the nurse entered. "Here you go."

I stared at the list of resources. It went on for two pages.

"You can start there. They'll be able to point you in the direction you need."

Blankly I tried to focus on the names and phones numbers for services like the food bank and shelters. I wasn't destitute by any means, I had asked in general about how I was going to make it work. She clearly missed my questioning but instead of correcting her, I nodded and thanked her for the list.

"See you next month, in the new year."

"Next month?"

"Yes. We recommend monthly visits until the 30th week, then every two weeks until the 36th week and weekly after that." She said it in such a way it sounded more gospel than a recommendation.

But what did I know? I just learned a pregnancy was forty weeks. Another sigh, and I left the room, chin tucked down.

I shouldn't be upset, but I was. Many women have walked down this hall to the front desk, excited or not for their pregnancies. I wasn't a teenager, and I wasn't a mid-lifer. Smack in between at the ripe old age of twenty-four. Old enough to be able to wrap my head around something of this magnitude.

After booking my appointment for next month, I fired off a text to Ana, giving her my due date. If anyone would be excited, it would be her. I laughed. Maybe I could convince her to have the baby for me too.

Knowing I was healthy and all that jazz, my next biggest conundrum was trying to figure out who to tell next – my boss, my parents, or my boyfriend? At least if I talked to my boss and got that all figured out, when I told my parents, I could show them how prepared I was. Then maybe, I wouldn't feel like I'd let them down by not being married and doing this on my own because the moment after I told Jagger, he'd be as good as gone.

Unmarried and pregnant. How that went against my good old Catholic upbringing.

Although my parents were liberal enough to know I wouldn't wait until marriage to have sex, this news would rock their world. It was wild enough news when Jeremy, my younger brother, moved in with his girlfriend. My parents still wait for them to announce a proposal, something that says they're committed. Never mind in the eyes of the law, they technically were after their first year.

I shuddered to imagine what they'll do when I announce my little secret.

It made my head spin just thinking about it. Perhaps it was best to talk it over with my boss—but only when I was ready. Just because I wasn't at the twelve-week mark and that's when most people announced, it didn't mean I had to, right?

My shoulder collided with a young man. A handsome guy. "Gee, I'm sorry."

"Watch where you're going, lady."

Lady? I was a couple years older than him, not ninety. My youth evaporated in the blink of an eye. I managed to walk out to my Jeep and climb in. The door had barely sealed when the waterworks started.

Later that day, I headed to Westside, dressed in my black pencil skirt and the gawd awful green polo top. I made sure my hair was brushed and my teeth clean and I smelled fresh, but no perfume. Strict work rule.

Since the management team had a shake up, and we lost our best guy, Niall, to a hotel chain, and my co-worker Audrina, who was nicknamed Evanora, got promoted to day-side manager, it meant the evening team got Meghan in the aftermath. She was stern and had the weirdest rules about what we could or couldn't wear. Plus, she didn't have the zest Niall did.

She sucked the fun out of work as she was more about pushing tables through, rather than letting the customers linger. Instead of refilling their drinks a couple of times when they finished, she insisted we only do it once and deposit the bill. What she didn't see though was how that affected our tips. Yes, we were serving more tables, but at what cost to the front-end staff? I won't even mention what she was doing to the kitchen staff. Let's just say there were a lot of grumblings and eye rolls.

When I stepped onto the property, my true identity of Josephine was gone, and Joy replaced her. The fake name was a safety measure implemented years ago, but it almost meant any anxiety and nervousness I had about my personal life, stayed out of Westside. I swallowed down my nagging disbelief at the way things had changed so abruptly and put on my happy face. My cheeks were going to hurt so much by the end of the shift from all the forced smiles, but I was okay with that. Every penny earned now had to be saved for later.

I was pleasantly surprised when I stepped inside the four walls of Westside and saw Audrina and Niall sitting at the staff booth across the restaurant. Both looked in my direction, and Niall waved me over.

He stood and gave me a hug. "Hey, Joy."

"Hey, stranger. How's the hotel life?" As was customary, I made sure to almost sing out my words. All the staff figured I was this happy go lucky person, and there was no point in changing it now.

"Fantastic." He slipped back down into the booth. "Have a seat. I was just talking about you."

"You were?" My ears burned suddenly, and my voice

24

dropped an octave.

They couldn't know, could they? Did I look different? Had this sudden pregnancy changed me already?

He laughed. "I was just telling Audrina here about the expansion they're already going to need at the hotel. She's going to see if Chad wants some additional winter work within the building. They just opened, but not everything was ready to go, and we need extra help."

I looked over at her, her smile growing larger at the mention of her boyfriend's name. It was so nice to see her happy. For the longest time, she had carried a dark cloud above her. It was even nicer seeing her and Niall acting friendly with each other, rather than her always biting his head off.

Whatever had gone wrong in their relationship, which could best be described as complicated, had been fixed. Over the past summer, they rekindled, but not in a hook-up kind of way. Audrina lost her brother, which was Niall's brother too, so I heard via the grapevine. It was all so weird.

"That's great. But what does that have to do with me? How did I get dragged into this?" I let out a little giggle. "I'm no handyman."

"I need extra help. On the dining room floor."

"Are you offering me a job?"

It would seem really out of place to do so in the establishment I was currently employed, in front of a manager no less.

"No."

I narrowed my eyes at him. "I don't get it."

"I was telling her," he pointed at Audrina, "how I could use some good, trusty servers. Your name happened to come up."

I shook my head, still confused. "Are you trying to get rid of me?"

Audrina snickered. "Hardly. I was telling him he needed to hire people who have as good a work ethic as you and Robin do, which he agreed and misses most about this place." She winked.

Niall nodded. "Indeed. Staff turnover is high. However, there's a hiring blitz going on the Monday after New Years, and Audrina was giving me pointers on what would keep an employee long term as I was picking her brain on why she stays here for so long. Usually only full-time employees get benefits, but I think I may be able to work something out so my part timers do as well. She said that was a perk."

My ears perked up with the word benefits. That could come in handy. If I were to go to the blitz and check it out. Although I put in full-time hours, I didn't qualify for the better perks like vision and dental. I got the very basic health care package, which, don't get me wrong was nice, but it would be sweet to receive the full deal. If I moved up the ladder to say a management position, that could change.

However, Niall's hiring blitz piqued my interest.

"So, what's new with you?" Niall asked me.

I shrugged and dug deep in me to bring my sweetest voice to the surface. "Not much. Things are going swell. Meghan is as charming as always. What's not to like?"

"Great," he said and glanced at his watch. "Shoot. I need to run. I just wanted to pop in and see how she's doing in her new role." He pointed to Audrina.

Audrina took to her manager's position like a duck to water. It suited her, and she was good at it. I only wished she could be the evening manager. Meghan was like a lightning storm. You never knew when she was going to strike. I understood she didn't pay us to stand around but taking a breather after a rush hardly qualified as a break.

As soon as I thought about Meghan, I felt her electrifying

presence approach. My head turned as she walked toward us, expressionless as always. Did the girl ever smile?

"Good afternoon. Niall, how lovely to see you."

"Meghan." With a tip of his head, he stepped away. "I'll talk to you tomorrow, Audrina."

"For sure." Audrina rose and smoothed out her skirt.

Meghan's gaze narrowed "It's after four."

The thing about Meghan was how she didn't fully need to say what was on her mind. Those three little words said enough. I was supposed to be *working* not sitting in the staff booth.

"Actually," Audrina answered before I could speak. "I needed to speak to Joy for a moment."

She did?

"Come find me when you're done, and we'll go over the day's reports before you leave." Meghan did a sharp 180 and walked back to the office, stopping to retrieve a spoon off the floor.

"I sensed you wanted to ask me something." She sat back down, gesturing for me to do the same. "What's on your mind?"

"Well…" I pushed back the cuticles on my left hand with my right index finger. "I was thinking ahead to the new year. Curious about job opportunities."

Audrina tipped her head to the left. "Like what?"

I swallowed my rising fear. It was hard to assert myself and ask for what I thought was fair. The fear of rejection, or worse the fear of being fired, scared me into keeping my mouth shut.

"I don't know. I've been here for six and a half years, and I was thinking like a promotion or a wage increase or a better benefits package." All my benefits covered was the basic health care premiums. No vision or dental or any of the other great perks like massage and chiro – something I figured I'd be able to use in the near future.

"I see." She leaned back against the booth and drummed

her fingers on the tabletop. "I can't offer you a promotion as there's nowhere up for you to go, sorry. All the management positions are full. You can transfer to a kitchen position, and it would come with a wage increase, but you'd lose your tips. However, I can look into when your last pay increase was and discuss it with Meghan. I can also inquire about bumping up your benefits, as you've most definitely earned them. I'd need to run it past Meghan first."

"That's fair." I nodded and took a deep breath.

No need in spilling any more beans until I had that covered. I had to keep mum. *Mum?* Dang it, what was wrong with me?

Her hand stretched out and covered mine. "You're a good employee, Joy, and I'll do what I can." She looked me over with a little more enthusiasm. "Are you okay?"

I nodded and pulled my happy smile back into place. "Yeah. Just been a long week."

"If you ever need anyone to talk to, my door is always open. And trust me, I speak from experience here, talking it out is truly helpful."

A few months back when she lost her beloved brother, the sorrow had consumed her in a way I'd never witnessed before, and even though she handled the situation as well as to be expected, it had taken a toll on her. Her support system wasn't much at all either, as only a handful of people showed up for the service, so I trusted what she said. I can't imagine how she handled it, someone must've been a good listener.

"When I'm ready to talk, you'll be the first to know."

"Okay then. Ready to clock in?"

I turned to see Meghan standing at the till, scanning the restaurant and making notes. A part of me wondered what new chores I'd have if it wasn't busy.

"Guess I'd better."

I laughed at Meghan's antics. Seriously, that lady needed to loosen up a bit. Take a yoga class or something. Or use her extensive benefits to get a massage.

I drove south to Calgary to meet up with Crystal. It was a beautiful Tuesday morning, and the drive had been easy. Thankfully the road conditions were great, as we were expecting a snow storm to blast in on the weekend. Crystal and Graham were going to come up, but I insisted on coming down. Besides, I needed the mini holiday.

The day before Jagger reacted exactly as I'd expected him to. The words barely escaped my mouth and he jumped from his seat, and as he was exiting the car exclaimed in no uncertain terms that we were over. Then like the idiot I figured he was, he got back into his car and I left. It was better that way. Besides, he wasn't the one. Every knew it.

I arrived at Crystal's place, this perfect and brand-new three-story townhouse. Even from the outside, it suited Crystal and Graham with its trendy colours and styles. After a huge hug, I followed Crystal upstairs to the spacious second floor, comprised solely of the kitchen and living room, and I swear downtown Calgary was on the horizon. It was an impressive view. The condo was bright and airy, with canvas wall hangings of flowers. They decorated it to resemble a show home and had pulled it off. However, I was afraid to sit anywhere for fear I'd wrinkle something.

"Sit, sit, sit," Crystal said eagerly and pattered off into the kitchen. "I'm so glad you came down."

I sat on the burgundy micro-suede sofa, running my hands over the soft, luxurious surface. A metal vase with three yellow gerberas sat on the reclaimed wood coffee table, beside a boxed wrapped with a yellow ribbon.

"It's just for the night, but it's nice to get away."

"Where are you staying?"

"Right by the airport."

"There's lots there to choose from." Crystal walked back into the living room and placed a tray on the other side of the table. Pastries and mugs, cream and sugar and a pot of tea engulfed the space. "Dress up your tea."

I added a splash of cream and a trickle of sugar and poured in the tea. It smelled heavenly. Like a bowl of my favourite kid cereal; Fruit Loops.

"It's Earl Grey." Crystal made up her own drink and sat back in a matching chair.

"So, how's married life?"

"So fabulous. We were able to decorate this home from the wedding gifts."

"You did a beautiful job, Crystal. Your home is gorgeous."

Even if it's lacking a Christmas tree.

Crystal had never had a tree, claimed they were too messy. Instead, she had a wooden cut-out of tree with a string of twinkle lights wrapped around it, like something off Pinterest. It was not the same thing.

She beamed and crossed her legs. "Thanks. Graham wanted to dial down the look a bit and make it more child friendly."

It would be cool to be pregnant together. At least it would take some of the fear away knowing I could confirm or deny symptoms with someone else.

"Are you thinking about starting a family?"

She laughed. "Oh god no. I'm not that crazy yet. Besides, I'm only twenty-eight."

Crazy. Is that what she thought having kids was? Would she think I was crazy because of my pregnancy? Mind you, it probably wouldn't be a big deal to her in the grand scheme of things. Graham made plenty of money, and I was sure their future was pretty secure. My insecurity with my own future had my hands twisting in my lap.

"This is for you." She pushed the wrapped gift my way.

"What's this for?" It wasn't my birthday, and we never exchanged Christmas presents, which was still two weeks away.

"It's your album from the wedding. I had one made for each of my bridesmaids." She wore her pride like a neon sign as she set her tea down and sat beside me on the couch.

"Thanks," I said, eagerly unwrapping the box and pulling out the leather-bound album.

I flipped the pages, taking in the beauty of all the stunning guests. Their photographer knew what he was doing. My fingers grazed a few of the pictures remembering the fun we had. When I got to the casual and candid section of the album, I slowed my scanning and stared hard into each photo, hunting through the crowds to see him. The stranger I woke up with. The father of my baby. Surely, I'd recognise him. *If* he was the guy I'd been dancing with all night...

That guy was taller than me, which wasn't saying much, a lot of people were. He had dark hair, a sharp contrast to my own, and I remembered the strong muscles under the soft feel of his dress shirt as we danced. James' silhouette matched what I remembered.

Eyes raked over guests in the background, and when I flipped the page, there was an adorable photo of me in the arms of my dancing hero. Sheesh, he was better looking than my memories recalled. I tapped my finger under the photo.

"James," I said, breathlessly and a million little memories of our one night together filled my brain. Most which were not PG.

"Graham thinks maybe he was the photographer's assistant. But you and he spent a lot of time on the dance floor." She flipped a couple of pages and pointed out the photos. "Did you two get together following the wedding?"

31

Heat seared across my cheeks and I slowly shook my head. So, this was James, eh? Fleeting memories danced in and out of my head like the beat of a drum.

"He was an amazing dancer but no, I haven't seen him since that night. We did grab drinks after the late lunch started."

Crystal laughed lightly. "Yeah, you left not long after."

"I'm sorry. I should've stayed."

"Why? The speeches were done, it was time to let loose and have a party. Which I think you did very well." She patted my thigh.

"Oh, I had a good time." I stared at the photo, and fuzzy visions of our own private party started to sharpen. "The photographer's assistant? Hmm." I breezed through the pics and he was in them quite a bit. "Did you pick the pictures?"

"Sort of. The formals were a joint process between Graham and I, and the photographer's suggestion. But I wanted something fun and sorted through 400 different casuals. Each bridesmaid got one tailored to her."

"It's lovely, thank you." I closed it and placed my hands over top. "Who was the photographer again?"

A knowing smile crossed her perfectly contoured face. "I'll see if I have his card." She stepped over to the kitchen and rooted through a drawer. "Found it." She waltzed back into the living room and presented me with a business card. "Going to see if you can snag another dance with him?"

"Maybe."

But how to go about it?

Hey, stranger? Remember me? Guess what? I'm pregnant.

Yeah, that wasn't going to happen. Until I knew more about this guy, I was going to keep mum on the subject.

Mum.

Sigh.

~Chapter Four

J stood outside the photographer's studio, breathing in the crisp winter air. Figured since I was in Calgary, I'd tackle this while I was here. But was I making a giant mistake? Was James the photographer's assistant? And would James remember me when he saw me? And then what? How would I move forward from there? Although I was 99% sure the James from the pictures matched the guy I bedded several times over, I wanted to make sure he truly was the guy before I blurted any life changing news to him.

After leaving Crystal behind, Ana and I texted about the whole going-to-find-the-assistant thing, and she asked if I was hunting down the father of the baby or a potential boyfriend. It had been a weird question to pose, but after mulling it over, I decided it was totally valid.

Was I on the hunt to locate and tell this stranger he was about to be a father? Or was I interested in meeting the man I'd had a one-night stand with and seeing if there was something more. After all, it had been an amazing night prior to falling asleep and waking up with the worst hangover ever.

Swallowing my fears down, I entered the studio, a doorbell chiming alerted my presence.

Immediately, a tall, thin lady, with black hair pulled back in a bun, wearing a tight leather skirt and four-inch heels stalked my way. Her eyes raked over me.

"May I help you?"

"I'm just looking for information."

"For what type of venue?"

"I haven't decided yet."

She cast a cold, silvery gaze in my direction. "I beg your pardon."

"What I mean is, I'm just checking things out. For the future."

Her perfectly manicured eyebrow went sky high. "Are you planning a wedding photographer?"

"Not yet."

"Need a trial with your engagement photos?"

"Haven't decided." I felt like lying would work to my advantage, but I couldn't muster the courage to do it. "My cousin had her wedding captured by one of your photographers, and I needed to speak with him and ask him a few questions. It's really important."

She stared at me for eternity. I was just about ready to turn around and walk away, when her lips parted and she spoke. "Who was the photographer? I can see if he's in."

"James."

"James?"

I nodded.

"I don't have an employee named James."

I stumbled over my words. "He's not the photographer, but the assistant."

"Our photographers hire their own assistants. We are not

liable for who they choose, nor are we in the know about it."

"There's no record on the wedding date? It was for the Lakey Wedding on October 12th."

She stalked over to a desk and typed rapidly on the keyboard. "And the photographer was?"

I shrugged and pulled out the business card. "Denny Durham." For safe keeping, I tucked it back into my purse.

An evil glare stabbed at me as her nails clicked on the keys. "There's no mention of a James on the listing."

"Really?" Darn, I expected this to be easy.

"Really." She deadpanned.

"Well, okay then." I stood there, wrapping my arms across my chest.

This wasn't going to be as easy as I thought. I secretly hoped if I strode in here, I'd see him waltz by and we'd gaze at each other while memories danced between us and like no time had passed between us, we'd fall in love.

Darn. Life does not imitate art. Those romance books had all been a lie.

"May I assist you with anything else?"

I shook my head, and quickly glanced around at the studios. If everyone who entered through the door had to deal with her, it would explain their emptiness. She really needed a training seminar in approachability and speaking to the general public.

"No, I'm good."

She rose and click-clacked away from me.

I wandered over to the door and let the frosty December air warm me up. It had been unpleasantly cold inside.

"No dice," I said to Ana over facetime. "They had no employee named James."

"And for sure that's what his name was?"

I stretched out on the queen-sized hotel bed, flipping through channels of bad tv. "That much I'm sure about. He told me and signed the poem with his name."

"You didn't tell me about no poem."

"Sorry." I kicked myself for having left it behind. "It was a rhyming poem like a child would write. Easy to do."

"But still. A hunky guy who writes poetry." Her face got all dreamy-looking.

"Ana, you're making this guy into some sort of god. For all we know he can be a serial killer."

She laughed, and someone behind her told her to quiet down. "Sorry, I woke a house mate." Her head turned and searched before filling my screen again. "She went back to bed."

I lowered my own voice and pulled the phone closer to my face. "And we both know, I've had wonky taste in men, so who's to say he couldn't be?"

"I don't buy it. Your choices in men have been interesting, but they've never been evil."

"Still."

"You worry way too much."

"Ana, my life is going to change. If I can find this guy, his life could change too."

"His life *will* change, if he's an upstanding guy."

"Maybe."

"So whatcha going to do now?"

I shrugged. "I don't know. What would you do?"

"Well... ask Crystal for a guest list and see if anybody named James shows up."

That made sense. Would be a little invasive of privacy though.

"What about the guest book, the one that was at the entrance

36

of the ballroom? I could see if someone signed in as James. Maybe see who he came with? If he was someone's plus one…"

"Maybe you should just tell Crystal the reason you're looking for this guy. She'd be able to help."

"Yeah, and Graham would somehow get involved and probably sue him for paternity rights when they find out."

"But at least you'd know."

"I suppose."

It didn't make me feel any better though. I wasn't out to make James pay for a mistake, that wasn't the reason I was searching for him. I was just super curious about who this guy was so someday down the road, I'd be able to tell my baby who their father was. Or maybe it was best to not know and then I'd never have to worry about saying something untrue. But then I'd have to explain the whole one-night stand thing. God this was a nightmare of epic proportions.

"Jo-Jo, are you even listening to me?"

I blinked a few times and looked back at my phone. "Sorry, I was just–"

"Thinking… I know." Only my best friend could know and understand. "Listen, it's really late here and I'm getting sleepy. Email me later when you've got the guest list."

"Sure thing."

"Hey, this is kinda fun. It's like we're going on a quest."

"A quest for what?"

"A curiosity quest." She glanced around her. "Don't worry. We'll find him. I'll be home soon, and I'll help you hunt in person."

"'Night, Ana."

"G'nite, Jo-Jo."

I blew her a kiss.

She returned it with a little more finesse and sent the phone flying, at least I assumed so, as the image went black and a loud whack came out of the speaker. "Whoops," she said, coming back onto the screen. "Love ya too."

I hung up and flipped it over and over in my hands. Did I call and ask about a guest list, or just give up? It clearly wasn't the photographer's assistant.

I opened the album and flipped to the adorable photo of us. We were close, but not intimate close, however there wasn't much air between my chest and his. His gorgeous face, healthy and tan, his hair dark and styled nicely. It was long enough, and soft enough too, to run my fingers through. Judging by the rosy tint in my cheeks and the glassy look in my eyes, I was feeling the effects of the alcohol, but wasn't bombed. Yet. That much I knew. I remembered dancing with him and the feeling of being lighter than air.

It was well past the speeches and dinner, and the first few important dances. Crystal had said once that was over, we were free to enjoy ourselves, and that's exactly what I had done. I didn't remember sitting much, always out on the floor, cutting a rug with whoever asked. This guy asked a lot. And he was a great dancer, with whom I'd had a natural rhythm.

I covered his face with my finger, trying to see the outline, to see if this was the James I partied privately with in my hotel room. At least if it had been in his room, and I knew the room number, I could've called and asked. But that's not how it went down. I squinted at the picture, trying to earnest to verify if was him. It was so close and so hard to tell.

Grabbing my phone, I called Crystal.

"Heyyy," she sang into the phone. "Changed your mind about coming for supper?"

"No," I said. My plans were to order room service, sit in a bubble bath and enjoy some private time. "But I have a question. In the book the guests signed when they entered the ballroom, was there a James listed?"

"I don't know. I could check. Whyyy??" Curiosity laced her voice like sunshine on a bright day.

I sighed. "I don't want to jinx anything yet." I covered my lower tummy with my free hand.

"He wasn't at the studio, eh?"

"No, but we had a really good time together and we parted ways before we could exchange numbers. I'd like to reconnect."

"Oh, just like that movie?"

"What movie?"

"With John Cusack... umm... umm..." Her fingers snapped. "Serendipity."

"Never heard of it."

"Oh my gawd. You have to watch it." She ran over the basic premise. It was sort of familiar, except not once did she mention a pregnancy.

"Sounds intriguing."

"Let me go and check. I'll call you back as soon as I find out anything." She hung up before I said *thanks*.

I passed the time channel surfing, internet surfing and basically pacing the room. Finally, after forever, my phone rang.

"So... what did you find out?"

"I went digging through the signed guest book. There was one James, but he was signed as Bethany and James Dominico, so I don't think that's your guy."

My heart plummeted into my gut. "Don't think so."

"He's an old colleague of Graham's anyway."

I sighed, silencing the tv with a flick of the remote. "Anything else?"

"There were two Jay's. One sighed Jay S, and another signed J. Wilder."

My voice held hope. "Maybe he goes by Jay to his friends?"

"Maybe. So, I pulled out the acceptance cards and went

through them. There were a few *and guests*, which didn't help. I checked our email responses and there was no mention of any Jay. He must've come as someone's plus one."

I stole someone's date? How big a homewrecker was I?

Crystal continued, "I'm sure he was with the photographer though."

"Tried that. They don't keep records of the assistants. Those are hired independently. Besides, I don't remember him at the photoshoot."

"Speak with Denny personally, and find out. You want to find him, right? This would solve your little mystery."

"Yes, it would, but…"

"Then it's settled. Call him. Otherwise, I can post a picture on social media and we can track down this mystery-man that way."

My chin touched my chest as I hung my head, my hair falling like a lacey curtain on either side of my face. The horror and humiliation. My parents would see, the rest of my family would see. Crystal had a huge following, as she shared everything. Nothing was sacred.

"Can I ask you not to do that just yet? Give me some time to see if I can track him down. Plus, I should talk to my parents first."

"You think one of them would know?"

"Maybe. Dad knows a lot of people." I was grasping at straws, but I wasn't ready for a public outing. The image of us splashed across Crystal's social media page screamed desperation to me. "I'll search out a J. Wilder and see what I can find. It's a start."

Perhaps having a sit down with my parents was on the next to do list, if I couldn't easily locate this guy. I dialled the photographer's direct number and reached his voice mail. I hesitated to leave my information and hung up instead.

<h1>Chapter Five</h1>

*I*t was my sister Cecelia's twenty-seventh birthday, and my immediate family gathered around the round table at the back of Amici Cibo, our favourite Italian restaurant on the west side. There were seven of us today; my parents, my older sister Cecelia and her fiancé Victor, and my younger brother Jeremy and his long-time girlfriend, Narina, and me.

Cecelia was a year old when my parents adopted her from China. A year later, the Edmonton-based list they were on called and said they had a newborn baby girl (me), and fifteen fast months later my brother joined us. They say you never choose your family, and I would argue profusely. My parents picked me and my siblings, and we couldn't be happier. We're a pretty tight-knit family and met on Sundays for brunch, and birthdays, anniversaries, and any other reason to get together. We enjoyed each other.

Drinks had been ordered, but I politely declined. Now that I was expecting, I had removed alcohol from my diet. Not that I was a heavy drinker at a Sunday supper, I saved that for parties. But sometimes, on our family gatherings, I'd indulge in a glass of white wine. But that was before those lines on the stick appeared.

My mom, a beautiful red-head I've always envied with her grace and charm, sat smiling as her children laughed and chatted. Since finding out *the news* I've been watching all the little things she did. If I became half the mother she was, I'd consider myself successful.

CeCe, sitting nearest our mother, dinged her knife against her wine glass, capturing everyone's attention. "Since we're all here, I'd like to make an announcement." Her dark eyes smiled at each of us. "Victor and I have set a date. We made a lot of phone calls first to make sure we could secure the places we wanted, and well… we're getting married on Canada Day."

Holy crow. Of all the dates in the summer to have a wedding on… I swallowed and glanced around.

"Oh, that's wonderful." My mother clapped and kissed my father. "A summer wedding, how delightful."

"That's splendid. Congrats." My father stood and shook hands with Victor across the table.

"That's a long weekend. We'll be able to visit with all the extended family, and we can have a few guests stay with us. What do you think, Jefferson? Perhaps the McLaurens or would the Sokoloski's be better?" My mother was already in full planning mode, judging by her lit up face and excitement in her voice.

Since Crystal's wedding, she had hoped CeCe would be the next one, as Jeremy had yet to ask his girlfriend, Narina.

As thrilled as I was for my big sister, that was also not the best day, however, since I had yet to say anything about the bean growing within me… "Why'd you chose Canada Day?"

CeCe beamed at Victor. "It's kind of cheesy, but we wanted fireworks on our anniversary, so what better way?"

Victor squeezed my sister's hand. "She's already called and booked a wedding venue and hall."

I threw a glance to my parents. Both devout Catholics, this could prove interesting if they went against marrying in the church.

My father swallowed, the Adam's apple bobbing in his throat, but maintained a smile on his face. "And? What did you decide?"

"Well…" CeCe hesitated. This wasn't going to be good.

My focus volleyed back and forth between the growing concern on my parent's faces and the utter fear rolling off CeCe.

"In keeping with both our faiths, we decided not to shun either family." Victor was Jewish. "And we're going to have an inter-faith ceremony."

A quizzical look crossed my mother's face. "How does that work?"

"I've talked with Father Bobby, and he's agreed to say some things, and Victor's Rabbi will also say a few words."

"So, it won't be in a church?" my father asked, eyebrows pushed high enough to touch his receding hairline.

CeCe looked at Victor and back to my parents. "No, it will not. We've rented a beautiful hall outside the city, and with any luck, it'll be an outdoor wedding."

Victor leaned closer to my parents. "It worked beautifully when my sister got married last year. Both faiths were equally represented."

"That's what inspired us to do the same. Neither family complained about a lack of their religion and the guests didn't feel it was too much either."

My sister was waving her hands around, something she does when she gets really excited. If she had to sit on her hands, I doubt she'd be able to carry on a conversation.

Victor moved his wine glass to the side as a precaution. "We have a meeting set up with both in the new year. We'd love it if you attended, as they can answer all your questions."

43

"Please say you'll come," CeCe pleaded.

Both my parents took in the scene, neither as agitated as I expected them to be. Were they mellowing out? Would this mean that my own news wouldn't rock the boat?

My mom nodded first, followed by my dad. "Fine," she said, "we'll go, right, Jefferson?"

"Of course."

"Yay," CeCe said, relief blanketing her. Shoulders relaxed, she folded her hands together on the table after dramatically wiping them across her forehead. "Whew."

"Were you that worried?" my mother asked.

I certainly would've been.

"Maybe just a little."

And I understood that. I sensed she was afraid of disappointing them, something we all grew up with. Hearing the phrase *I'm so disappointed in you* was worse than any punishment we could've been dealt. It was something I was horribly afraid to hear when it was time to make my big announcement.

"Now that that's settled," Victor turned his full attention to Jeremy, seated on my father's left. "Would you be one of my groomsmen?"

My little brother, by a mere fourteen months, proudly responded, "Damn straight!" He stood and reached across the table to shake Victor's hand. He leaned over too much and Narina's glass tipped over, red wine quickly advancing across the pristine white tablecloth.

"Oh no," CeCe said, drawing the attention of our waitress.

Quickly, she came over and sponged up the liquid. With another cloth and a spray bottle with clear liquid, she soaked the stain and dabbed at it. Within minutes, the stain faded away.

"Wow, miracle cleaner," Victor said to our waitress. "I need to get some of that for home." I didn't miss the wink he sent in his fiancée's direction.

"I'll write down the recipe." The waitress didn't look up. "Whose wine glass?"

"Mine," Narina stated.

Jeremy explained, "It was my fault."

The waitress stood with the wet rags. "It's all good. I'll bring you out another."

Glass and tableware made their way back to the rightful place settings and everyone sat back down again.

"So, now that Jeremy has continued the weekly tradition of spilling a drink," CeCe said jokingly and faced me, "I wanted to ask you if you would be my maid of honour."

Oh wow. And oh no! Her wedding date was the same as my due date. I'd either be as big as a house, or if I just had the baby, would still be unfit to be parading around in a bridesmaid's gown.

The weight of a dozen eyes focused on me, all expecting an answer and wondering why the delay. I wasn't ready to say anything about my one-night stand yet, I hadn't even found the guy. I swallowed and took in the faces that stared at me.

My gaze skipped over Jeremy and Narina. My father inched forward on his chair. Not a good sign as it meant he was ready to diffuse a situation. Apparently, his ability to read and assess things hadn't stopped with his police retirement. My mother had a loose grasp on her grace and bordered on the edge of anger and sadness.

My gaze locked onto CeCe.

Trepidation creeped into her voice. "I know, it's a big deal, right? Parties and showers, and dress shopping. It's a lot to ask, and I know you are ridiculously busy." But she still wore a smile and a faint hint of hope.

"I am busy, but never too busy for you. You know that. Truly, I'm beyond honoured to do it." All honest words, and I kept my tone nice and even.

"Yes!" CeCe said, her face splitting in half as she clapped her hands and settled back into her chair.

"I hear a but in there," Jeremy said, interrupting CeCe's little celebration.

I shot him a look that silenced any further comments.

"You don't want to do it?" CeCe's face contorted. Oh no, she was going to start crying.

I put my hands up and waved them around. I was very much like my sister that way. I would most definitely die if they were tied down. "Of course, I want to do it. Nothing in the world would please me more than to be your maid of honour. It's what we've dreamed of since we were little girls playing Barbies."

Her eyes were glassy. "I know."

I inhaled sharply; this wasn't how I'd planned it.

"But in all our playtimes, did we ever imagine the bridesmaid being pregnant?" I hung my head as the gasps rolled out.

"You're pregnant?" CeCe's voice had a distinct ring of annoyance to it.

I was sure it was because as the oldest, she should've been first. Or because she worried I'd upstage her special day. If I had a choice, I'd rather not have to push a watermelon through my lady bits.

I couldn't bear to look up and instead twisted in my seat, a deep feeling of doom washing over me.

Everyone was quiet. Too quiet. Uncomfortably quiet.

My father broke the deafening silence with a good, solid throat clearing. A robust man, he reminded me of a thinner Uncle Vernon from the Harry Potter movies, complete with greying hair and a bushy moustache. "Go on, dear. You were about to answer Cecelia's question."

I slowly lifted my gaze from the table, sweeping it around to rest on my father. His expression hadn't descended into disappointment, but it was hovering very close. It seemed wrong to apologise for this and yet, it's what I felt I needed to do.

"Yes. Yes, I'm pregnant. I'm sorry."

My mother covered her gasp, and whispered, "Not my girl."

Not quite as close to that unique phrase of *I'm disappointed in you*, but it circled the block. You'd think I was fourteen and not twenty-four.

"Yes, your girl."

"When?" She breathed out, unable to look at me. Her gaze went in CeCe's direction.

"When did I get pregnant, or when am I due?"

"When are you due?" CeCe's heartbreaking voice beckoned me, and I shifted back into her view.

"July first."

"You're going to ruin your sister's wedding." Leave it to my father to over-react just a tad.

I wasn't planning on ruining anything except my own life and possibly the father's. But that was up to him, if I could find him.

"Really? July first?" The edge in CeCe's voice worried me. Either she was going to snap, or she was going to burst into tears. Either way, a scene was forthcoming.

"It's not like I picked the date." Because really, if I could, I would've avoided being pregnant to begin with. Remembering the condom wrappers littered around the hotel room, I thought we had.

My father cleared his throat once again. "And who's the father? It better not be that Jagger kid."

"Jagger kid? Really? He's older than me, Daddy."

"It's him, isn't it?"

A slow shake of my head as I inhaled sharply. "It's definitely not him but I'm not ready to share any more information."

"Why not?" His fists were clenched and I half-expected him to bang them on the table.

"Now, Jefferson, settle down." My mother's voice still carried a hint of calm, although the flushed cheeks were a dead giveaway to her burgeoning anger. "Our little Josephine is a grown woman. Maybe she and the father are working out their own marriage details."

I kept the eye-rolling to a minimum, but the restraint nearly killed me. She honestly still thought of me as a child. Regardless, I focused on my sister.

"I'd always planned on having you by my side on my big day," she mumbled, shaking her long, jet-black hair.

"What about changing the date?" my mother questioned. "You could move it to the long weekend in August. It would give Josephine time to work off the baby weight."

Tears over-flowed as CeCe shook her head, but she didn't look at me. She focused on mother instead. "The venue had a cancellation minutes before we called. Clearly, this venue was meant to be, it's what I've always dreamed of."

"And I'm in Europe in August," Victor added.

My mother composed herself. "I'm sure there's a way we can make this work."

Six pair of eyes lasered in on me. Maybe it was best for everyone if I backed out.

"Will you still want me there when I'm out to here pregnant?" I gestured to the edge of the table and around. I really hoped I wouldn't be that large, but it was a possibility.

"Of course, you're my sister. Besides, you'd look beautiful in a paper bag." Another tear streaked down her cheek.

I wasn't sure about that, but I nodded.

"If we can make it work and have a stand-in just in case you're busy giving birth, will you do it? Will you be my Maid of Honour?"

Once again, all eyes weighed on me. I rose from my seat

48

and walked behind Victor to my sister.

CeCe stood and wrapped her arms around me, while she still could before my expanding midsection made it impossible. "Does this mean yes?"

I leaned over and squeezed her tightly. My big sister was also my little sister as I towered over her. "If you'll take me like that."

"I can't imagine you anywhere else. Except, I may have too now." The corners of her eyes tipped up with a smile.

"Thank you," I whispered into her ear, relief blanketing me. Of the two of us, I always thought CeCe was the more diplomatic one, and she proved it again.

She broke away and wiped her cheeks dry. "On July 1, not only will I become a wife to the most wonderful man alive, I could also become an aunt. What an exciting day."

"Let's hope the little one either comes before or later, and not actually on the wedding day," my mother said, her grace and charm flooding their area.

But it hadn't touched father yet. He looked deep into my soul. "I don't like how you're in trouble and you hadn't told us about it. We're going to talk later."

I nodded, praying to God he'd cooled down by then.

~Chapter Six

With the big news announced unexpectedly, I set to work doing what limited research I could on this J. Wilder. Facebook didn't prove to be of any assistance as there were about 1000 listings for the name. Other social media searches led nowhere. At the behest of Ana, I even searched through LinkedIn, but found nothing at all familiar. None of the pictures matched the one I kept open on my dresser. By now, I was certain he was the James I searched for.

He showed up in my dreams, dressed so eloquently in a form-fitting pair of pants and a nice button up. I knew from the pictures it was grey, but it appeared white in my mind. The tie's still the same, black and white diagonal stripes. And his face, so handsome, with a warm sun-kissed glow and dark, wavy hair. But it was the expression that did me in. That sweet way he looked at me and tipped his head for the photo, it was as if we'd known each other all our lives, and yet, we introduced ourselves for the first time on that dance floor.

Sigh. It wasn't meant to be. If it was, I would've grabbed

the number and note he left for me or he could've called me. As a bridesmaid, it couldn't have been that hard to track me down. But, if he lived in Calgary and I was three hours away, could it be a detriment to any effort on his part? Had he even tried? The distance between us would be too much of a commute, and I wasn't willing to move away from my family. I couldn't speak for him, but I couldn't see him giving up a career to re-locate here, either.

There were other things possibly preventing James from finding me. Maybe he was in jail, or had been in an accident, or gulp, he could be dead. Morbid I knew, and Ana chastised me for even thinking it. I tried not to focus too much on those possibilities, but they did appear from time to time. Mostly I just stuck to the truth. I'd been a notch in his bedpost.

Instead of focusing on the fruitless and endless hunt for him, and the lack of any further communication between us, I hung out in pregnancy forums and groups. I managed to find a group of ladies who were expecting in the same month as me and it was comforting to know I wasn't alone. However, they all seemed to be on top of what they were going through and were a wealth of information. It was high time I did the same.

I drove to our local library, a place I hadn't visited since I was in high school. Even after all this time, it still amazed me as I walked through the glass doors how I was instantly transported into another world.

The architecture was incredible. The ceiling was peaked, but with glass inserts, allowing the natural light to flood in brightening the space better than any florescent lights. Children laughed in the kid's area, and as I walked deeper into the library, all the computer stations were in use by a mixture of people; old and young. At the very back, the fireplace was lit, a simple gas one, and stepping closer, its warmth and cosiness beckoned me. Unfortunately, the two comfy chairs on either side were occupied.

I'd forgotten how much I'd enjoyed being here. My afterschool hideaway. I looked through the glass wall at the school I attended not so long ago, back when I knew everything and had plans for world domination. Or success, at least.

How I laughed now. I was a pregnant, unmarried waitress at a mid-level restaurant. My future held no world domination. Now it contained diapers and feeding schedules. Which was what brought me to the library in the first place.

Pacing through the bookshelves, I ran my fingers over the titles of romance books, followed by sci-fi; my two favourite genres. I grabbed a couple of interesting titles and crossed the floor to the reference area, reading the displays until I came across the section I was most interested in: pregnancy and childbirth.

There were so many titles, each offering up an array of choices. Pregnancy in your teens, pregnancy for the over forty crowd, holistic pregnancy, pregnancy for dummies, pregnancy in the first trimester, and so on. There was even a pregnancy in the fourth trimester, which I didn't bother looking deeper into. Even I knew there were only three trimesters.

The decisions were overwhelming. Eventually, I settled on just one I felt I could handle. It was a beginner guide and sounded like something right up my alley with weekly changes in the baby and my body, tests to expect and a great Q&A section.

I tucked it under the two novels I'd selected, lest I run into someone from work, and meandered through the remaining bookshelves, making my way over to the kid's area. I stopped at a shelf at the back, and after placing my books on the ledge, I just watched. There were children of all ages, from babies to those old enough to jump off the wooden train engine onto a cushion on the floor. Moms sat together on the benches along the wall, sipping their coffees, laughing.

None of my friends were pregnant, none of my extended

52

family either. Not even my colleagues were. Did these women grow up together and all enter that phase of their lives around the same time, or did they meet someplace else? I couldn't live on a forum forever, interacting with people, I needed face to face contact. How did one go about doing that? How did an adult go about making new friends? Were there support groups for clueless pregnant moms?

All the wondering caused a headache to spring into the forefront of my brain, and I pinched the bridge of my nose to counter it. Usually it worked.

I spun around and stepped without looking, right into a metal cart. The accidental encounter caused a few of the books on the trolley to spill, sending a couple flying across the floor.

"Holy Doodles, I'm so sorry," I said, grabbing the farthest books. When I righted myself, I was staring into the deep, dark eyes of James.

"I remember you," he said, his voice like a fine whiskey; smooth and pleasant.

I was sure my heart tapped out a double beat as it took a second or two to catch my breath. It was going to be hard to play it cool, but I tried. This was the man of my dreams… literally.

"James, right?" I shifted my weight to one side.

"Yeah, that's me." He put some distance between us. "Josephine?"

I inhaled sharply and nodded, unable to speak as my tongue weighed a thousand pounds. The father of my unborn baby stood before me like a GQ model in beige pants and a navy-blue button up with long sleeves. In person, sober and not hung over, he was hot enough to make me sweat in unladylike ways. I fought the urge to fan my shirt to cool down, figuring it would give off the wrong impression. Seeing him sober, I realised why I couldn't keep my hands off him. He was the epitome of yummy and handsome, and by the way my heart pounded and a lightness ebbed out from my chest, my body remembered the fun times we had.

I searched for something clever and interesting to say, but my mind stopped working the moment I saw him. "You work here?"

Well, that was foolishly dumb.

"Clearly." Thank goodness he laughed. "You here to take out books? Or are you here for the Resume Writing workshop starting in ten minutes?" He tapped his watch but kept focus on me.

I needed to break the intensity. It was a bit surreal to run into him here of all places as this was the last place I expected him to ever find him. My eyes fell to the stack of books I'd tucked onto the shelf. Why couldn't those have fallen and mixed in with the ones on the floor?

"I… I was just looking for a good book to read."

He eyed me, not in a suspicious way or in a way to make me feel uncomfortable, it was just the opposite. It warmed me up all over and it didn't feel like the dead of winter, it felt like summer and endless sunshine with lilacs blossoming and robins singing.

"What do you like to read?" His head dipped a little and the slight grin on his face garnered my attention. "Josephine?"

I snapped back to him.

His tone had a hint of interest woven through the huskiness. "What do you like to read?"

"Umm… Something science fiction like but fun and entertaining." I was stretching a bit.

The sci-fi books I've read had been way out there with aliens and distant planetary systems we've yet to discover. It was the best kind of escape to travel across the universe and meet the most interesting characters.

His fingers grazed across my arm as he gently pulled out the books I'd collected from the floor. He set them on the trolley and led me away. "This way."

A last glance back to my three books. I needed to come back and pick them up – when I was positive he wouldn't see me.

We were tucked behind some shelves, out of the main area when he stopped walking. His voice changed from cheerful and friendly to one with a touch of annoyance.

"How've you been?"

Pregnant, surprisingly pregnant.

But I didn't spill. Not yet. Maybe not ever, I wasn't sure yet. I softened my voice in hopes it would soften his and with a nonchalant shrug, I increased the distance between us. "Good. You?"

It worked. He calmly asserted, "I've been busy." His firm, muscled back leaned against the edges of the shelf and he crossed his arms over his chest, covering up the lanyard he sported. "I must say I was a little disappointed you didn't call me."

What? Really? Why did that surprise me so much? We had a good time, but in all honesty, I suspected his leaving his number behind was because he was being polite, not because he was truly interested.

My hands flew as I spoke, "I'm sorry. I was in a rush to get home, and I left your number on the bed."

"Likely story. I was hoping there'd be a chance to get you know you better." The pitch in his voice filled with hurt.

Dang, I never wanted to hurt anybody, and suddenly shame coursed through me. "If I even thought for a moment you lived here... I thought you lived there and the commute..."

The dark eyes holding mine fell away. "Anyways, the sci-fi books are over here." He squatted down to the bottom of the shelf. "I recommend this one."

I took the book from him, not really interested in rereading the doomed Martian story, but oh well. It gave me something to hold on to which would stop my hands from flying about. "Thanks."

"You come here often?"

I narrowed my eyes at him. It was a strange question, but I gave in. "No, not really."

"Then the chances of you running into me again are low."

There was a change in his tone, but I didn't know him well enough to figure out if it was sarcasm or something more sinister, but he turned away from me, so I took it for what it felt like. For the second time that day, my heart did a double beat. It was pure fluke I found him and now that I had, he was upset with me, and maybe, rightfully so. I stood in silence as he walked away without looking back. I needed to know more about him, if for no other reason than so I could tell my child all about their father.

"James, wait," I called out as I clutched his recommendation and increased my pace to catch up to him. "You know, you never tried to get in touch with me either. You're just as guilty about this as I am."

I held back the urge to poke him in the shoulder. Even though we'd been intimate, it seemed a strange thing to do to someone I couldn't call a friend.

"All I knew was your first name."

A smug look crossed my face and I snorted. "That's all I knew about you. I was a bridesmaid, it wouldn't have been too hard to contact the bride and groom."

He yanked the book trolley and caught a couple of books before they fell. Without a word, he pushed it back towards the main desk at the entrance of the library.

I wanted an answer. If he was going to be upset with me over not phoning him, then I had every right to give him the Spanish Inquisition over his lack of communication with me. We were equal partners in this.

"Why didn't you contact them?"

He stood there silently staring at anything but me.

I raised my voice. "Listen, if you really wanted to see me again, then you could've made the move." I wanted to move closer and get right into his face but that may seem aggressive, and others may interfere, which I didn't need. All I wanted was a conversation with this man.

He stepped toward me, the distance between us closed in a heartbeat. "I'll make it up to you, let me show you the best space we have. We can discuss scheduling an activity in there."

"What?" I narrowed my eyes at him, confused at the sudden turn in conversation.

As I glanced around, a couple of librarians at the desk stared hard in our direction, likely assessing the situation. It's what I would've done.

James stood a foot in front of me. "This way."

Trying my best to ignore the questioning looks from the staff, I pushed my chin up and set my shoulders straight, marching behind James. Once we were in a cosy room with plush couches and a giant tv screen, he closed the glass sliding door and the noise and atmosphere changed. The low hum circulating in the library with the children's laughter and people's whispered chatter disappeared. Even the sound of my rapidly pounding pulse seemed diminished. We were in a sound-proof room

"We use this for our teen gaming events. Then the noise they make doesn't disturb the other patrons, but the glass wall behind you allows staff to see inside and make sure there's no hanky-panky going on."

"No one out there can hear us?" My voice didn't echo at all, in fact it completely absorbed into the air. It was the strangest room I'd ever been in.

"No."

"Wow, that's cool."

"That's not why I brought you in here." He planted his

hands on his hips, a questioning expression on his face.

"Sorry." I threw my shoulders back and lifted my chin. "Where were we? Oh right, why *you* didn't contact *me*." My hand flew in his direction as if to say *your move*.

"It's complicated."

I fell into one of three available couches and crossed my legs, tossing the book beside me. "I have time. Well not too much as I'm due at work in a couple of hours, but you know what I mean. I searched for you, I'll have you know."

"Was it hangover guilt, or were you truly interested?" He stood with his back to the dark walls but facing out towards the library.

"Morbid curiosity."

"Interesting." A smug smile tickled the edges of his perfectly formed lips. "And what did you find out?"

"Absolutely nothing." If there was wind in my sails before, it had completely died down. "My cousin had a couple of Jays attend her wedding, but nothing that matched up."

"There shouldn't be."

"Why is that?" A ribbon, a tiny thin ribbon, of fear settled in my gut.

If he wasn't a Jay or a James, then who was he? Why had he lied and scrawled out that name on a piece of paper. Maybe the phone number wasn't even legit, maybe it was his buddy's and they'd have a good laugh afterwards. It was a good thing I didn't call. I didn't need that kind of humiliation.

"I told you that night."

A snort blew out of me, and I sent my focus out into the library as people walked by, no one paying us any attention in here. "Memory of the finer details eludes me." The other more intimate details did not.

Movement from behind me caused me to turn back in his

direction. He walked over to the tv and gaming console, and retrieved a controller, checking the battery compartment first. "Here. Take this."

"I'm not interested in playing games," I said, pushing it away.

"My boss is walking by. Please," he pleaded.

"Fine." Not one to get someone into trouble, I yanked the controller out of his hand and twisted so my back faced the wall of glass. I even pushed a few buttons although it was pointless as the system wasn't even on.

"At what point did you stop remembering?" He stood beside the tv and silently pointed to things while I thought. His tapping along the console was highly distracting to my memories.

I closed my eyes. What was the last thing I remember? It was all so foggy, like a dream. A sweet, sexy dream. "I remember dancing."

"We did a lot of that."

With a flush to my cheeks, I opened my eyes to see him watching me. "We danced in the hotel room." Naked. To country music. A Patty Loveless song, I thought.

"You said some amazing things that night."

"I was drunk, I wouldn't believe everything I said. In fact, I wouldn't believe anything."

Ana once told me I nearly convinced a tall, dark stranger that I was distant royalty from Belgium in Canada for a month and was rather enjoying the nightlife. I wasn't sure if I was that convincing of a drunk liar, or if the guy was hoping for his own personal party, but Ana said he ate up every word. Thankfully, she dragged my posh butt back home, no guy in sight.

A gentle nod, and a sly smile appeared. It lightened the mood just seeing it. "I would. Alcohol reveals people's truths and personality."

"Trust me, I'm no distant princess from a far away land."

He gave me a questioning look. "What?"

"Never mind."

The tv turned on with the push of a button and he muted it. We were probably being watched.

My stomach flipped. How many lies did I spin out that night? What kind of web had I created? Details were sketchy at best even if it was easy to remember how much I wanted him, and how well we tangoed together, but as the night ticked on, my sensibility waned. Clearly. I eagerly bedded a strange man; this handsome stranger. I dropped the controller into my lap and twisted my hands.

He walked closer and lowered himself down to my height, a sweet smile pushing on the corners of his lips. "It wasn't bad. It was charming, and part of the reason I wanted to get together with you and see you again. I wanted to know more about you, sober and real."

"Wanted? You say it like you're no longer interested." Leave it to me to latch onto one word in that whole string of words.

He shrugged, and his lips thinned. "That night was over two months ago. I'd given up since you never called."

"This can't be all my fault, James." I stood, anger boiling in the pit of my stomach.

Why was he mad at me for this? The anger swirled a little more. Things never turned out well for me if I got too angry. I needed to pace off the energy.

He straightened. "You told me– Ah, it doesn't matter. You don't remember the finer details, so it's unlikely you'd believe me anyways."

"Try me."

"Look I got to get back to work."

"No," I said with strength. "You're not going to dangle the carrot in front of me and pull it away."

"And you just told me I shouldn't believe everything you said while you were intoxicated."

I threw my hands up in the air, hoping to disperse the anger. "If you tell me what I supposedly said, I could tell you if it was truth or me just being ridiculously drunk."

He walked over to the door and slid it open. Noise filled the space instantly, flooding in like a wave on the beach.

"It was good to see you again. Take care." Back turned to me, he walked away.

Inhaling sharp currents of air, I waited until he was out of sight and inched my way through the children's area, back over to the shelf where I'd left my books. I could make my way back to the check-out computers and be gone before he even spotted me, however when I stopped at the shelf, my books were gone.

Had James already picked them up? And if he did, did he connect them to me?

Chapter Seven

"Honey, why aren't you coming to lunch tomorrow?" My mother's sad voice dripped through the phone. "Because father thinks I'm an incompetent idiot." There I said it.

Father and I'd had a very heated discussion over the phone about my lack of 'keeping my legs together' to which I laughed out loud at, claiming it was people like me who gave him the very children he called idiots. After that he hung up on me and we hadn't spoken since. Which admittedly, stung a little.

But until he saw me as a grown up, capable of owning up to her responsibilities, I had bigger things to deal with. One of those was to not surround myself with people who called me an idiot. The other? Find a way to connect with James and prove to him I was interested, and not the total idiot my father thought I was. Yeah, it was a tough pickle to be in.

"You know he wants to see you."

"I'm sure he does."

"I heard that eye roll."

It didn't surprise me she had. It's a gift. She claimed it was part of being a mother and one day I'd understand. I doubted it.

"Say you'll come. We're going to Amici Cibo. It's the last one of the year."

As if that would make me cave. There was less than ten days until Christmas. I could wait to see my father again. And as much as I craved good, wholesome Italian food, preferably the rigatoni with fresh parmesan, I wasn't interested.

"I'm working on a project."

"For work?"

"No," I laughed, "it's a personal project."

"Ooh, that could be fun. Can I help?"

It wasn't anything wedding or baby themed, so I doubted she'd be interested. Still, there was no point in offending her. "Thanks, but I've got it under control."

A long pause crackled between us, but I shrugged it off.

"So, how are things with the guy you won't tell us about?" I'll give her ten points, she's good at giving guilt trips on the sly.

"We had a bit of a fight yesterday." Total truth.

"Oh, I'm sorry. Anything I can do to help?"

"No, it's me that has to do the mending. Apparently, I'm the one who messed up." I wasn't sure I truly believed it as the lack of communication fell to the both of us. However, I was willing to accept most of the blame.

A soft, motherly sigh tickled against my ears. "Well, take him his favourite cupcakes."

"That's lame."

"I'm serious. It worked every time on your father. We'd get into a tissy, and later I'd show up at the office with four special cupcakes and all would be forgiven."

This time I did roll my eyes. "Just like that?"

"Yes, dear. Your father could never stay angry with me for

very long, he loved me too much. I think it was because the bakery put extra love into each cupcake, but I could be wrong." Her voice drifted off in what I could only imagine was a wonderful memory.

My parents had a dream marriage. Always lovey-dovey with each other, and as rarely as they fought, I never remember them going to bed angry.

Hmm... maybe there was something to the cupcake thing. I could show up at the library with something like that. Isn't the way to a man's heart is through his stomach? Maybe, it wasn't as lame as I first thought.

"I'm just putting this out there... Maybe if you brought your father cupcakes..."

"Ugh, for one, no. You just said that was something *you* did. And for two, in this instance, he's in the wrong and he knows it. I'm a big girl and a mistake happened. One I'll pay for the rest of my life. But I'm owning up to it, and planning for our future."

I wasn't yet sure how, but I'd figure it out. I'd been waitressing for six years, what's another dozen or so? It had been exhausting job hunting online, and I'd pushed my laptop away as I had zero skills for anything. The switch in conversation caused a dull ache to form at the forefront of my brain. I laid my aching head against my arm on the table.

"Well, dinner still stands, dear. We'll be there at one, and we'll save you and your boyfriend a seat."

"Don't hold your breath. Not tomorrow. I need time to work things out."

"If you need help, just ask."

"I'll be fine." I hoped that was true.

"Love you, dear."

"You too." I hung up and tossed my phone into the middle of the table.

Needing a stretch, I rose and extended my hands up as high

64

as I could and bent down to touch my toes. Yes, I could still do it. Read online it wouldn't be much longer and I'd be unable. Not only would my life be changing, so would my body. I sighed and headed down to the communal gym for a quick jog on the treadmill.

The next day, I shopped at the best bakery in the west end of the city and with the baker's assistance, selected four of the most perfect-looking cupcakes, each a different flavour. Having found James, my quest had changed into one of getting to know him, and since I didn't know his tastes and preferences, or allergies for that matter, I grabbed a gluten free, a nut free, a red velvet and an ordinary everyday type of cupcake, like the kind you'd have at a birthday party. Each was exquisitely designed, and the baker put them into a beautiful box and wrapped it in brown twine. Giddy with excitement, I couldn't wait to give it him. Let's see if Mother's plan worked or not.

I walked into the library, eyes scanning through the people and shelves of books. My heart skipped a beat when I spied him, placing a book on the bottom shelf. I needed to watch from a distance, if for no other reason than to calm the rush of my pulse and the flutters in my belly. If his genes were stronger than mine, I was going to have a good-looking kid. He stood and smoothed his navy pants, and oh how they fit him so perfectly. His button up was a lighter shade of blue but worked well with what he wore. As he turned around, he searched the area, stopping as he spotted me.

"Busted," I said, walking over with a gentle swagger, which was the total opposite of the running straight to him and jumping into his arms that I wanted to do. However, his sullen not-pleased-to-see-me expression held me off. The edge of the package buckled slightly under my grip. "These are for you."

He peered into the plastic window of the box. "Cupcakes?"

"Yeah."

"What for?" His dark eyes roved up my body and settled on my face.

Oh dear. My pulse dropped lower than my stomach and heat pooled in my happy place. He was so easy on the eyes, and his voice was as sweet as the icing on the cupcakes.

"An apology of sorts. I feel like we got off on the wrong foot a couple of days ago, and I wanted to make it right."

He nodded, and the edges of a smirk came into view. "I agree."

"I want to get to know you better. It's important to me."

So that someday I could tell my baby what a great guy their dad was, and how tragic it was that it didn't work out.

Because he was a prince from a far away land.

A laugh circulated in my head at the absurdity of my story. Seriously, I needed to get a grip. I wasn't out to ruin his life. Ruining my own, according to my father, was enough.

"Oh yeah?" He took a half-step back. "Why's that?"

I swallowed and pressed on. My voice fell to a whisper as people shuffled by a few feet from where we stood. "I don't do..." I looked around. "One-night stands."

The warmest laugh greeted and tantalised my ears. "Nor do I. Thus, the reason I wanted you to call."

Touché! Relief settled over me knowing that he wasn't seeking me out for a quick thrill either. At least, he claimed he wasn't, and for now, I'd take him for his word. "So, your work schedule. Do you normally work days?"

He cocked his head ever so slightly to the left. "I'm typically the one to nine shift. But this week I'm on days until four."

Well dang. I was on evenings, always have been. That's where the bigger tips were. But I had two days off a week – Wednesdays and Thursdays. Hmmm... "What about Wednesday?

Are you free?"

"Let me check." He retrieved his phone from his shirt pocket and thumbed through something. "No plans after four."

I swallowed again. It was tough being the lead for this. How did guys do this all the time? Nerves jingled and jangled in my insides like the Christmas music playing overhead.

"So... How about I pick you up at four-fifteen on Wednesday and we'll make it a date. Try to smooth things out."

"A date, eh?"

A little giggle escaped me as if I were a schoolgirl. Sheesh, what was wrong with me? "Yeah, a date."

"Okay. Fine. Four-fifteen. Where do I meet you?" His fingers grazed against mine as he removed the box of cupcakes. It was a promising start.

If I was going to be the one in control, all the details fell onto my lap. I sighed and cleared my throat from the giant frog that had settled in there. "Remember, I'll pick you up."

"From my place?" A quizzical look crossed his handsome face with the golden glow.

And as much as I wanted to say yes, I didn't. If that's where we started, it could be hard to leave. My quest was to get to know him, not wrap my arms around him and do the deed until the sun rose.

"I'll pick you up here?"

"I promise, I'm not a threat."

I shifted on my feet. "I sensed that, otherwise I wouldn't be trying to locate you."

Still he stood and stared. "I can pick you up, you know."

"This will be easier."

A gentle nod came my way, but his eyes never left mine. "Okay. It's a date. You'll pick me up here on Wednesday."

It felt so weird being the date maker as opposed to the date accepter. "Yep." My cheeks pushed up sky high as a smile broke out and a relaxing sigh rolled out of me. I pointed to the box clenched in his hands. "Since I didn't know which you'd like, there are four kinds in there. Next time I see you, tell me which one you had first."

"Is it important?"

"Very." I gave him a wink.

He raised his brows. "I'll tell you on Wednesday." The distance between us evaporated as he whispered, "Thanks for the treats."

My knees weakened at the close proximity. I closed my eyes and took the opportunity to inhale him. Spicy and sultry. Figured. "I need to go."

My eyes popped open, and his face was right there. If I didn't have any control, I probably would've reached out and threaded my hands through his dark, wavy hair, throwing caution to the wind, but we were in a public place. Where he worked. I needed to exert more self-restraint than normal.

"Wednesday," I said breathlessly.

Without so much as looking back, I sped to my car and drove home.

I'd never dreamt of living someplace else, although the warmth Ana was experiencing in Australia would be welcome as I huddled under a heavy quilt. Would she be up? It was after one my time, which put it in the dead of night there. Yeah, she wouldn't be up, not normally anyways. Instead of facetiming her, I sent her a quick email asking her to call when she woke, or to call when I finished up working.

Not sure why it surprised me much, but my phone rang with an incoming facetime call a minute later.

"Shouldn't you be sleeping?" I clicked the answer button.

"Actually, I'm slowly trying to adjust back to our time. Reset my circadian rhythm or something. If I stay up later here then when I get home I shouldn't be that far off."

"And who suggested that lunacy?"

"Oliver." The glow ebbing off her phone in the middle of the night surrounded by darkness couldn't hide the fresh flush of blush crawling over her cheeks.

"Oliver?"

"My flat mate. He's so swell, Jo-Jo. You'd love him."

"Hopefully not as much as you do."

She waved her hand. "Hope not." She showed me the side of her head and pointed to her ear. "Can ya see that?"

I stared at the phone, her ear growing bigger in the display. "Is that an earring?" She had a little stud in the flap of skin covering the ear canal.

"Got it done yesterday. It was part of a bet. Told Ollie that if I screamed during a bungee jump, I'd get my tragus pierced and he'd get a tattoo. Aces, eh?"

I sat up straighter. "You went bungee jumping?"

There's no way it happened. Ana was terrified of heights.

"Yeppers. Twice now. It's exhilarating and freeing. Y'ought to try it."

Umm, no thanks. "I'll pass."

"Besides, there's probably no place there where you can jump."

"I'm sure there is." But I didn't know. It wasn't even on my radar for something fun to do. "I'm glad you are living large. Only eight days until you come home."

"Yeah, and two days worth of travel." She rolled her eyes. "But Ollie's going to come visit me in the new year. Do you have an issue if I let him bunk with us for a couple weeks?"

"Can I think about it?" I wasn't a fan of a stranger hanging out in my home for two weeks, especially unattended. You never know what they'll get into when unguarded.

"Spill, chicky. What's going on with you and James? Did you find lover boy yet?"

I nodded, and filled her in on the details of our run in.

"No shit. What are the odds?"

"I know, right?"

My stomach growled loudly, and I thought Ana heard as she tipped her head. I pushed myself off the couch and rummaged through the kitchen, searching for something to eat. The browning banana sitting all alone was the most appetising, so I went with that.

"And…"

"I'm taking him out on a date on Wednesday."

"You asked? You're brave."

I laughed as her eyes bugged out. One time she waited and waited for a guy to ask her out, but she never sucked up the courage and the guy went out with another girl. Totally angered Ana, but she said she wanted to feel important enough to be asked, and clearly that guy didn't think her worthy. Then she downed a pint of ice cream to bolster her self-image.

"Yep. Do you have any ideas? I need something fun, and yet quiet. I really want to get to know this guy."

"Why is it every time you say that, I keep thinking it's only temporary for you?"

"I don't know what you mean."

"Like you're just getting intel on him for the baby. Like you're expecting him to not be around for that."

I cocked an eyebrow at her and pursed my lips together. "Think about that, Ana. If you were James and I dropped that bomb on you, would you stick around?"

She shrugged. A voice called out to her in the background. "Come say hi."

The camera moved all over, enough to make me queasy. "Ana, hold still."

"Hey, meet Ollie."

A man's face popped into the side of the camera. He was charmingly cute, and had a surfer look to him.

"G'day." He turned to Ana. "This Jo?"

"My bestie."

His chin rested on Ana's shoulder. "Ah, the three am caller?"

I waved. "Guilty."

"Ana talks ya up non-stop." Even in the dim lighting, he lit up with Ana's name.

I had to admit, they looked super cute together. "I hope she's not spilling everything."

"Not ev'rthing."

Had she told him about the baby? I wasn't ready for it to be public knowledge. But since he didn't say anything and continued to stare into the phone, I remembered what we were talking about before he arrived. "Anyways, Ana. I need date ideas."

Oliver spoke up. "Go to the beach."

Which was ludicrous. It was the start of winter and everything was bone-chilling cold.

"It's twenty below there," Ana said, twisting to look at him. She turned back to me. "Go ice skating."

"And if I fall?" I scrunched up my nose and waited for the secret to present itself.

"Good point." She tapped her chin with her finger while I munched on the banana. "I've got nothing, other than the standard dinner and movie. It's too cold to do anything there. That's why I can't wait to move here."

"You're still considering that?"

"Yeah." She nodded, and her smile increased in size. "It's

71

warm all year long. No snow. No minus frigging cold. Beaches a plenty. Pretty much the same laws as back home. I'd just need to get some documents."

I had hoped she'd help me with the birth, it was scary to think about it and I knew I'd need someone. But it would take a while to secure whatever she needed, so maybe there's time.

Ana yawned, but thankfully covered her mouth. "Hey, Jo-Jo, I should go to bed. It's late."

"Of course. If you get any ideas though…"

"I'll email them over. Promise." She blew me a kiss.

"Later, Jo," Oliver said and disappeared into the darkness behind him.

"Love you."

"You too, Ana."

The line went dead, and I was no further ahead in my ideas.

Chapter Eight

My reflection in the mirror wasn't pretty. Dark circles jumped out from under my greenish eyes and there was a pallor to my skin I hadn't seen since those all nighters from high school. Whoever said you catch up on sleep when you're pregnant, lied. Thanks to non-stop worrying, I haven't had a decent night's sleep in a long while, and it showed. Even my freshly washed hair looked as limp as it felt. Where was that luscious glow? Maybe it only came to those who were violently ill in their first trimesters, I didn't know. I was lucky that way. Aside from a bit of breast tenderness, I wouldn't even know I was pregnant. My clothes still fit as my figure hadn't changed, which I checked each day certain it would just suddenly stick out, but there's no bump.

The past two days I'd mulled over what Ana said. Was I only wanting to know more about James for informational purposes? To explain to my baby what their daddy was like, or was I hoping for more? More would be nice, but I was definitely not expecting it. The only thing I truly expected was for him to high tail it away from me as fast as his feet carried him. Like Jagger had. So, for now, I'd enjoy it for what it was. Fun, no-strings-attached dating. Although I used the term loosely. *We weren't really dating, were we?*

With my blond hair straightened and a setting powder applied to my makeup, I'd just slipped into a pair of black skinny jeans and a tank top when a knock sounded on the door. Grabbing a warm and cosy grandma-knit sweater, I pulled it on and padded lightly to the door. Through the peep hole, I gazed out into the hallway and opened the door.

"CeCe? What the heck?"

"Sorry, someone else was leaving and I slipped in." Her shoulders rolled in and a dark cloud hung over her. "Can I come in?"

I needed to leave in twenty minutes and pick up James, but my sister's body language suggested whatever was on her mind would take longer. I opened the door wider. Family always came first, right?

"Victor and I had a fight." She shrugged out of her jacket and kicked off her shoes, making her way over to the couch.

"That sucks." I closed the door slowly.

Should I phone the library and put my plans with James on hold, or worse cancel? If I did that, the likelihood of him accepting another date would be like snow falling in the middle of July.

My sister curled up on the couch. I couldn't just kick her out either. Clearly, she needed me, as her sister that was an obligation. It was such a pickle to be in.

I planned out my route—if I made the lights to the library, it would probably take about ten minutes, but I'd like a buffer. Could I hear CeCe out in fifteen minutes and send her on her way? Asking what they fought over would only prolong the time she was here, so I skipped that.

"Are you okay?"

"No. Do I look okay?" She burst into tears.

Well, this was going to take a while.

I walked over and slumped beside her. "What's going on this time?" I tried to hold back my irritation. It was always something with CeCe. One might say she was a bit of a drama queen.

"He wants steak and potatoes for our wedding supper." She sobbed again. "Steak and potatoes. Can you believe it?"

"Wow, I'm speechless." And a little relieved it wasn't actually something serious. "And you were hoping for?"

She wiped her eyes. "I wanted a nice turkey dinner with all the fixings."

"That's different." I pressed my shoulders into the back of the couch and crossed my legs, bouncing it quickly.

"Different wrong?"

"No, just different."

"A turkey isn't a specialty item, needing to be cooked correctly depending on each person's taste. Having steaks means we need to have another caterer there, and the price goes up."

And there it was, it always came down to money. I loved my sister dearly, but she was the cheapest person alive. If she could get away with it, I was sure she'd add BYOB on the invitation and insist dinner was a potluck.

"Okay." I glanced at the clock; there was still time to make this work. "If you insist on the turkey dinner, you need to give him a free pass to something else, like the dessert menu or the drinks for the bar."

"But we've already selected that."

I shook my head. "You're not hearing me. Compromise. Work this out between the two of you. If he's strongly for something, and the only thing holding you back is price, then reach an agreement. Tell him you'll give him that, but you want… I don't know, whatever it is you're feeling strongly about."

"I… I suppose."

I scooted my butt to the edge of the couch, the pace in my voice ran a little faster. "What's something you absolutely want?"

"I want our colours to be lavender and petal pink."

"So, tell him that."

"I have. He says it would look awful."

Yeah, Victor wouldn't necessarily concede on that. I don't think there were many men willing to wear pink or purple on their wedding day.

"Well, you need to find something to compromise on. Either that or let it slide about the steak dinner."

"But the cost."

"Let me tell you something. I've been to many weddings, and I can't remember one where the meal was so standout it was the highlight of the event. You could serve burgers for all anyone cares. They're there to celebrate your love and happiness and have a wonderful party. Trust me, the meal will not be the focus, and if it is, then they're attending for all the wrong reasons." I sighed and checked the time. Fifteen minutes until the meet up with James. Tick-tock. My legs stretched out before me, anticipating a quick break.

"You think I should have the steak dinner then?"

"I think you need to have this conversation with Victor. Honestly, sit down with him and work it out. I'm here to listen of course, but I can't make this decision for you." My hands twisted together, and I stole another peek at the clock.

CeCe's head rested against the top of the couch. "Oh, Jo, I don't know what to do." She wasn't leaving.

My heart fell into my stomach and soured. I pushed myself off the couch and padded over to the table, hunting for my phone.

"I need to make a phone call. Give me a couple of minutes." I opened a new page on google and looked up the number for the branch of the library James worked at and hit call.

The phone rang twice.

"Hi, can I speak to James please?"

I paced in the kitchen. I hated having to break this date, but my sister needed me more than I needed to connect with James. It was like karma or something, except I couldn't remember doing anything bad. It was definitely an intervention of some sort though.

The lady picked back up. "Sorry, James has left already. Can I leave a message?"

Crap. "No, no message, thanks." I hung up and banged my head against the fridge. Little splinters sprung up across my heart. I hadn't realised until this moment how truly geared up for this date I was, and now it wasn't going to happen. I had no way to get in touch with him. He'll think I've stood him up and may never speak to me. Of course, he'll have every right to do that. So much for getting to know him. I banged my head again.

"You okay?" CeCe joined me in the kitchen.

"I'll have to be."

"What's going on?"

"Nothing." I tossed my phone on the counter and pulled the edges of my sweater across my body. It was seven minutes after the top of the hour. In eight, I'll be officially late and not long after that, I'll be a deadbeat. Crap. Crap. Crap.

"Is James a new boyfriend or is he the father of …" Her eyes fell to my belly.

I grabbed a box of herbal tea and set it on the counter and proceeded to fill my kettle. "Want a tea?"

"Were you supposed to meet with him?"

The kettle slammed onto the counter.

"If it's that important to you, then go." Disgust clouded her features as she snorted.

Shame filled mine. "It is. But you need me now. It can wait." I patted her arm.

Like she'd been snapped, she pulled back. "No. You go. Whatever it is, you're very upset that I'm keeping you from it." She grabbed her jacket and pulled it on. "You should've said something when I got here and saved us both the hassle."

With a slam of the door, she was gone.

I glanced at the clock. Five minutes until I was supposed to meet him. Could I make it? CeCe would be at the elevator and I wasn't in the mood to ride down with her now, would I be able to take the stairs? It's only seven flights. The longer I stood there debating, the more time I wasted. I wanted this. To see him again. Pulling my coat from the hanger and grabbing my purse, I raced down the stairs as fast as my legs could carry me. Nothing ventured, nothing gained.

I slammed my Jeep into park and in a mad dash ran inside the library, hunting around to find James. I half-expected him to be at the entrance since when I called earlier, they said he wasn't here, and it was too cold to be out wandering the parking lot. At a brisk pace I walked the length of the library, searching and scanning between shelves but came up empty. The digital clock flashed in my face, screaming I was ten minutes late and he'd already gone home.

"Dang it," I said in defeat and slumped into a nearby sofa chair.

Family came first, it's how we were raised and what we were always told. If your family needed you, you dropped what you were doing and helped. It's the way it was and would always be. CeCe knew that, and even if I thought her problem was petty, I still should've made time for her. I added her to the list of people angry at me. First father, then CeCe, and now James.

I buried my face into my hands and rested my elbows on my knees. Someday, things will work out for me, just not today.

"Can I help you with something, miss?"

I lifted my head and trailed my gaze over the figure before me. "James." I quickly hopped out of the chair. "I thought you... I thought you'd left."

"I just used the washroom and was about to head home when I saw you." He was dressed in his winter jacket, a fashionable length that looked dashing on him. "Everything okay?"

"I'm sorry I'm late."

"Tsk, tsk," he said, but he wasn't as upset as I expected. The sparkle in his eyes said otherwise.

"My sister came by to unload about her wedding problems and disagreements."

"Say no more. Are you ready?" He tipped his head toward the entrance, a soft smile slowly stretching across his whiskery face.

"You still want to go?"

"I'm here, aren't I?" He pointed to the main door. "Shall we?"

A spring in my step, I walked beside him until we got outside. "I'm over there. The blue one."

Unlocking the Jeep with a click of my remote, I slid in.

"Where are we off to?"

"Well... I've given that a lot of thought. Since it's friggin' cold outside, that eliminates anything outdoorsy. I want us to be able to talk, but the dinner-movie combo is so overdone."

He shrugged. "There's nothing good playing anyways."

"Exactly." I put the vehicle into gear and backed out of my stall. "Which made finding something fun and different a bit challenging."

"I imagine it would."

We exited the parking lot, and I headed in the direction I needed to go, hoping he'd never been to the destination.

As we stopped at a red light, he blurted, "Oh, red velvet."

"Huh?" I stared at him. What an odd thing to drop into conversation.

"On Sunday, when you dropped off the cupcakes you told me to tell you which one I ate first."

Right, that sounded familiar. "And? How was it?"

"The best damn cupcake I've ever had."

Sweet relief, so he's not a vegan which means we can enjoy hamburgers and steaks together, and he's not one of those that needs to avoid gluten for health or peer pressure reasons.

"And the others?"

"I ate the regular one and sampled the vegan and gluten free. Neither were what I was expecting."

"Edible?"

My experience with both was that they were gross. I tried a vegan 'hot dog' once and thought I'd throw up. And the gluten free bread I sampled? Sawdust in my opinion. I was thankful I didn't have dietary restrictions keeping me from my favourite foods.

"Not in the slightest." A sweet smirk filled his face. "Sorry, but I had to toss those two."

Not a biggie, I would've too. "So, you like red velvet? Good to know."

"It's my fav."

The small space became even tinier as the conversation came to a halt. I chanced a peek at him, and he whipped his head to stare back out the window, hands sitting on his thighs, his elbow sharing console space with mine.

It was a different type of date already with me taking charge, making decisions, and playing the traditional male role. I rather liked it, especially since the toughest part of actually asking him out was over. So far, any way.

"Music?"

"Sure." He turned his head to the radio.

My finger was poised over the buttons. "Classical, country, top ten or Christian."

Those bushy eyebrows pushed up into his forehead. "You have each of those pre-set?"

I pushed each one to show him. My musical tastes varied with my mood. Some days I just wanted to sing along with whatever was current. On more melancholy days, I preferred country. But there were other days, especially when I'd finished a gruelling shift at work where I needed to zone out, and classical really did the trick. Christian music only factored in when I was feeling a lot of pressure on my soul and need some spiritual guidance, so it's not one I pushed a lot. Something to be grateful for.

"I'm impressed." He selected the top ten button. "Sometimes you just need to hear a good Maroon 5 song."

I nodded as Adam Levine belted out his latest hit. "Agreed."

A few minutes later we parked outside a strip mall, littered with many mom and pop shops.

James exited and glanced down the street. "Well, this should be fun." He headed towards the Eastern Food Experience restaurant.

I'd heard the place was quite risqué with sultry music and tantalising food. Maybe it would be a good date down the road, if anything were to happen between us, but not on our official first date. "Not there, but here." I pointed to the sign above us. Checkers.

He tipped his head in deep thought. "A board game café, eh? Interesting."

"I needed a place that wasn't too out there. Here we can

talk, eat, and enjoy an atmosphere of fun and excitement." We entered the establishment, and I strode over to the counter. "Hey, Lindi."

"Nice to see you back." She gave us a friendly wave.

I wrapped my jacket around a chair, and James did the same. "What would you like to play?"

Ana and I frequented Checkers, or had before she left. It's fun, the people were good people, and the food was pretty decent too.

"I don't know most of these." James whistled as he checked out the wall of games, pulling out one and after reading it, put it back into its slot. "I haven't played a board game in years."

"May I make a suggestion?" I stepped close, and reached across his chest, getting as close as I could without actually making contact. "These four are easy to learn and plenty of fun to play." I tapped out the ones I thought I could teach him without too much difficulty.

"Easy and fun; two of my favourite combos," he whispered into my ear. It tingled and sent a line of fire straight to my core.

Unable to focus on proper thoughts, my fingers tightened around the game closest to me, pulling it free from its slot. I held it in my outstretched hand, blinking rapidly and picturing his hands on my body. I could show him easy and fun again. I already had. Several times over.

"This one, eh?" The box became lighter as he lifted it away.

"Uh, yeah." I gave my head a little shake.

My body reacted strongly to this guy and he hadn't even done anything, however, I blamed the baby. Perhaps it knew the father stood just inches from me, breathing me in the same way I was breathing him in. It was intoxicating on a whole other level.

"What would you like to drink? There's tea, lattes, milkshakes and pop."

A sly little grin surfaced. "Do you always give people choices?"

"What? What do you mean?"

"You gave me four different cupcakes. With the music, you selected four different genres. Same with the games and now with the drink selection."

"I'd never thought about that before." Weird. A force of habit from work? I didn't know. But I'd have to watch and pay more attention. I stepped back to our table.

"It's interesting. And cute." He tapped the tip of my nose with his finger and my legs turned to jelly.

Well, maybe I won't pay too much attention to it.

"What'll you have?" I managed to carry myself over to the counter.

James spoke to Lindi. "I'll have a chocolate milkshake."

I snickered, moving to stand beside him. "You know it's fifteen below outside."

"Yep, I do. But it's really hot in here." His voice a teasing sound of sex and sultriness.

We weren't going to make the night, I was sure of it.

"I'll have a diet coke. No, make that an herbal tea."

Can I have tea? Herbal has no caffeine but are the herbs safe? Better not.

"Sorry, Lindi. I'll have a chocolate milkshake too."

"Good choice," James said as a twinkle appeared in his eyes. He waited until I sat down before he took his own seat. "You're a regular here, I take it."

Snuggling into the leather chair, I raised my hand. "Guilty. My best friend Ana and I came here quite often. It's been a while."

"Why's that?" He shook out of his jacket and folded it before placing it on the back of the other chair beside him.

"She's in Perth, but she'll be home for New Years."

He pushed the game box off to the side. "Do you have plans for New Years Eve?"

"Do I ever." I smiled, moving my gaze from his eyes to the game on the table. Lifting the box lid, I lifted out the game board and spread it between us. What I really wanted to do with it was fan myself; it really was hot in here. "I managed to win tickets for Ana and me to Urban DC."

"You're going to that?" He leaned in closer, his eyes lighting up with enthusiasm. "That's the ultimate party in town."

"So I've heard. Colby Sacks will be playing, up close and personal."

"You're so lucky. I tried to get tickets, but they sold out within minutes. How did you win?"

"Radio station."

"Not the classical or Christian one, I take it."

"No. Definitely not." I let a small giggle out, dealt out cards and set up our tokens. "So, what are you doing for Christmas and New Years?"

He repositioned his token, so it stood shoulder to shoulder with mine. "Nothing much. I fly out to Vancouver in three days for Christmas."

"Family there?"

"Yeah, my mom and younger sister."

"Are you from there originally?"

Wow, Vancouver. One needed to be fairly well off to live there, especially in the core. The area had pricey homes and a higher debt, at least according to a recent study discussed on the radio late one evening.

He nodded. "I moved here a few years back to attend university."

Really? "Forgive my ignorance, but you need a university degree to work in a library?"

84

That couldn't possibly be true. How hard was it to shelve books? You follow the alphabet. B came after A, W came after V. It wasn't difficult. It must be for another job he wanted.

"You need a degree to work almost anywhere."

Well, that was only partial truth. No piece of paper was required for me to work at Westside.

"So, you have a library degree?" It sounded odd to even say it and I fought the ensuing giggle.

"Actually, I am finishing up my MA dash MLIS."

"Your what?"

He leaned in a little closer. "My Master of Arts in Humanities Computing and my Masters of Library and Information Studies."

"You're going to have two master's degrees?" Sheesh. I had none. I didn't even hold a college diploma.

He leaned back and grabbed his five cards and placed them into whatever order he needed. There was a lot of rearrangement going on. "Sort of, it's a joint program."

"Wow, you're really smart then." Would an uber smart guy like him be interested in a waitress like me?

"Just passionate about a few things."

He lifted out the instructions and scanned the four-page manual. It was an easy game to learn, and even easier to play. I wasn't one for the complex three-hour long games like Ana tried to rope me into.

"Are you in school full-time?" I tried to wrap my head around this.

A double degree, while working? Where did he find the time?

"A couple evenings a week I attend classes and the rest I do online."

"When will you finish?"

"If I stay focused, like I'm planning, I'll be done mid April."

I continued to set up the game board.

"Wow, that's really amazing." And I was in awe.

"Where'd you go to college or university?"

I dropped my head a little and sorted the quest cards after a solid shuffling. "Didn't. Never had the desire. There wasn't anything I was passionate about."

"That's too bad."

Was that a shot? My voice pitched a half octave. "Well, maybe because we were given such wonderful upbringings and were shown a little bit of everything that it made it hard to focus on something so passionately."

James threw his hands up in a sign of defeat. "You don't have to defend your reasoning for not attending post-secondary. I'm not attacking you."

I stared, willing myself to breath and calm down. "Sorry, it's always a sensitive subject. I started waitressing right out of high school to help save for tuition as the few scholarships I had wasn't going to be enough. Then I decided to take the first term off and make sure I had really saved, but I'd also moved out on my own. And... well... six months became a year, which became permanent."

"You almost sound like you regret your choices."

Was that what it was, regret? I wasn't so sure.

"It's never too late to go back. Have you considered taking a couple of courses and changing your path?"

"Oh, I've thought many times about changing my path."

Before I'd slipped and said something I'd really regret, my eyes jumped to the counter when Lindi set down two tall glasses of thick chocolate shakes. I stood, pulling my top down over my tummy. There was nothing showing but I didn't want to potentially give anything away. I wrapped my hands around the chilled drinks and gave James his.

"Thanks."

Sitting back down, I took a long sip, and reviewed the playing instructions with James. I gave him credit though as we played through the first game—where he kicked my butt—he kept the conversation on trivial things like weather and sports and the latest Marvel movie. Preferring to stew a little bit over the fact I was playing with someone who was clearly not my equal in academics, I kept my mouth mostly shut.

Someone as smart as him would surely see me as a gold-digger or something similar if I mentioned I was carrying his baby and wanted some kind of a future with him. There's no way a baby wouldn't ruin his life, it would utterly derail it and keep him from pursuing his higher education. Besides, I was merely a waitress. It was just another reminder how I was going to be a single mother, and I had no formal education to keep me from slowly sinking. My life was not where I thought it would be.

Chapter Nine

fter dining on Checkers uber delicious paninis and fries, and playing another game where I lost – again – I decided to call it a night. Clearly, he was superior in the gaming department as well.

"Well, shall I drive you back to your car?"

He looked rather stunned. "For real? It's not even eight o'clock?"

Truth be told, I was getting tired. Not of James or his company, but just sleepy in general. And the thought of stretching out on my couch in a pair of pajamas sounded wonderful, even if actual sleep would prove evasive.

"Did you have something else in mind?" Nasty thoughts sprung to mind.

"Maybe." I didn't know what he was thinking, but a mischievous smirk appeared. "Do you have mitts and stuff?"

"I have mitts," and I pulled them out of my pocket for good measure, "but I'm not sure what *stuff* you have in mind."

"There's this wonderful little place I like to go and think. It overlooks downtown and it's very pretty to see it at night. I just want to make sure you'll be warm."

Ooh, romantic. Snuggled together, gazing out over the city. I rose after I tucked the last piece back into the game box. "My jacket has a hood, and I always keep a blanket in the back of the Jeep. For emergencies."

His voice rose in pitch. "What kind of emergencies?"

"Like the Jeep being ditched, and I need something to keep me warm until help arrives."

"It won't do you much good if it's in the back, will it?" He cocked an eyebrow, and I couldn't help but smile.

Hmm… never had it put to me that way. Growing up, as soon as we got our own vehicles, it was strongly encouraged to have emergency supplies; an empty can, a candle, some matches, a blanket, and extra mitts. I never thought about actually needing to reach them from the front seat in the event of an emergency, but they were always there, tucked into the back.

"Are you game for what I have in mind?"

The romance part I could handle without batting an inch, but being outside? "Sure, as long as we're not out for too long. I'm not a fan of the cold."

"And yet you live here." He pulled on his coat and zipped it up.

I mirrored his actions and sealed myself up inside my own jacket. "It's a beautiful city."

"Yes, it is."

I cleared our tab, after vehemently protesting to James I would take care of the bill. As the date planner, it was my responsibility.

Shivering in the cold vehicle waiting for it to warm up, I asked James, "Where's this place?"

"Are you good with directions?"

"Very much so."

Jeremy, my brother, couldn't find his face in the dark but I had zero issues with directions. North, south, whatever. Directionally challenged wasn't one of my faults.

"Good, because I'm horrible with street names and such. I'm more of a turn right at the big rock kind of guy."

"It'll be an adventure then." I put the Jeep into drive and followed his directions.

He was better than I expected, although turning at the green street sign threw me, and I had to take the next right turn and loop back.

"Park here," he said, pointing to the side of a residential road.

Beyond the snow-covered field lay a ravine where the frozen river snaked through in the warmer months. A bench sat on the boundary, and the most impressive view of downtown I've ever seen lay beyond. It took my breath away.

"Grab your blanket."

I popped the back door and tucked the wool blanket under my arms.

"We'll use this too." He reached for some cardboard I kept in there in case I needed to start a fire or something. "It'll keep our asses warm."

The door slammed shut, and I zipped up my jacket right to the top and slipped on my mitts. The cool snow crunched under our boots as we walked thirty feet away from the Jeep.

"Was I right?" He extended his hand to show off the view.

I nodded. The buildings were on the other side of the river but lit up with lights from the inside. Similar to how I felt.

He brushed the snow off the bench and set the cardboard down. "Have a seat."

I did as instructed and fanned the blanket over our legs. It made such a difference – I honestly hadn't thought it would be as warm and cosy as it was. Suddenly it didn't feel so cold, only chilly.

James snuggled a little closer, wrapping an arm around my shoulders. "Is this okay, me being this close?"

"Yes."

His mitted hand grazed my thigh, and a wave of warmth that had nothing to do with the blanket covered me. In this moment, I was perfectly content to sit here all night long.

My mittened hand covered his. "Do you come here often?"

"Not as much as I'd like."

"It's peaceful." It came out as a whisper. Anything louder would've broken the tranquility.

It was so quiet I heard the soft inhale and exhale of his breathing. I was sure it was my imagination, but I thought I also heard the pounding of my heart beneath the layers of my shirt, sweater, and winter jacket. There was something wonderous about this guy, as I was completely comfortable, despite the cold, the dark and a strange place.

That feeling took over, and I rested my cheek against his shoulder.

"Are you cold?"

I shifted closer for good measure. "Not in the slightest."

"Good."

We stared out in the distance, the lights from the core of the city flickering in the cold air.

The clouds released their captives, and the snow began to fall. It was magical to be in the big city when it snowed. The flakes were great at being sound absorbers, so much so that passing cars became silent, and people naturally whispered. It was like waking up in the stillness of the night. And the fat, falling flakes were the most enchanting of all. There was an amazing beauty in watching them dance and float to the ground.

In a moment like this, winter wasn't so awful.

I tipped my head back and opened my mouth, hoping to catch one.

From the corner of my eye, James stuck out his tongue and with luck, one landed on the tip. "Got it."

One got caught in my lash, and with each blink, a ghost appeared in my vision.

"Wait," James said, pulling his hand free of his mitt.

Tenderly, he stretched out his finger and the flake melted with his touch. His other fingers caressed my cheek, leaving a trail of heat in their path. His thumb rubbed the tip of my nose and over my lips.

My breath warmed with each gentle stroke as the fire roared within. I closed my eyes to the falling flakes and the sweet expression on his face, breathing in the closeness between us.

"May I kiss you?" There was an innocence to his words and question.

"You'd better," I said, twisting my body towards him.

Like a snowflake, his lips grazed across mine, touching and teasing.

I wrapped my mittened hand around his neck and pulled him closer, giving him permission to kiss me harder. He did not disappoint.

Firmness replaced tenderness, and heat warmed the air between us, turning the snowflakes into rain. I parted my lips in heady anticipation. With a little tease, his tongue danced into mine, and for a heartbeat we were joined together.

Instinct took over, and I groaned in pleasure. It had been a long time since I felt so desired and alive, not including the night of Crystal's wedding. But I understood why my body responded to his. He was good. A firm yet gentle kisser. And he had lit me on fire. I swear the bench warmed and glowed under me.

It had lit him on fire too. "Should we go to my apartment?"

I pulled back slightly and looked up into his expectant face. Every bone in my body screamed out yes, but something in the back of my mind whispered to really think this through.

"Are you okay?" His eyes searched mine, flickering between my left and right.

"I… uh…" Words failed me as much as coherent thought apparently did. "I…" My hand pushed against his chest and even with his layers on, it was a brick wall. "No."

What would that do to the baby? If he made love to me, would it hurt the baby? Would he be able to tell I was pregnant? And if he did, how fast would he leave me?

"No, you're not okay?"

Rational thoughts once again eluded me. "No, we shouldn't go back to your apartment. I have to work tomorrow and so do you."

"So, what?"

I shook my head but firmly held his gaze. "I just can't. It's too fast."

His laugh was gentle, but it also instantly annoyed me. "Too fast? May I remind you–"

"For the record, I prefer to take things more on the slow side. I'm not a slut, you know."

"What? I never…" He pulled his hand away.

I put a couple of inches between us and tried to read the expression on his face. It was like reading the mechanics of rocket science, nothing made any sense.

"I really enjoy your com–"

"Just stop, please." I allowed my focus to shift from him to over the river valley. The falling flakes obscured the view. Figured. Everything was fuzzy. "I need to think. I know we hooked up the night of the wedding but what if it was all the enchantment with the music and the drinks and the stars being lined up to bring us together? We're so different."

This whole finding him thing was only an informational quest, and yet, my heart was taking hold of the situation, something my mind said wasn't a smart idea. My head ached, and my chin tipped down as I scooted away from him just a little bit more. I had to put the brakes on us.

"I can't. Not right now. I'm sorry."

A small huff blew warm air out his mouth. "Don't be sorry."

"It's been a real nice evening," I said, trying to change the tension between us. It had all been so easy and carefree until I slammed on the brakes. I was attracted to him, and I thought he was to me, but I didn't want *just* a physical relationship between us. There needed to be an intellectual one as well and there couldn't be.

More snowflakes piled up on my blanket. Things between us hadn't warmed up enough to melt them.

A few minutes of tense silence cooled the air between us to Antarctic conditions. He rose and folded up his blanket.

With one easy swipe, I'd ruined the date.

Feeling deflated, I whispered, "I'll drive you back to your car."

"No thanks, I'll walk."

"What? No. I can drive you." We were a long way away from the library. Had to be a good hour long walk at least.

"Forget it, okay? I said I can walk. I thought you were different."

"Different how? Like easy?"

His boots crunched across the hard-packed snow, leaving footprints as he increased the distance between us.

I didn't know what to do, so I let him go.

~Chapter Ten

"What a jerk!"

"Ana, stop."

"Well, he is. Because you refused to go to his apartment, he turned all huffy?"

When I got home from our date, I immediately emailed Ana, who had just woken. I couldn't wait for her to be home; the time change between us was getting to me. My life felt like it was falling apart, I needed my bestie in the here and now.

"I think he had every right to. I did put the brakes on full."

"Yeah, and why is that? I gathered he was really hot."

Hot didn't even cover it. James was the whole package. "He really is, but what if he notices the change in my body?"

Ana gasped. "Are you showing?"

"No, and believe me I'm looking, but I think it's too early. I just feel I look different."

Making love would probably feel different too. I cupped my breasts. Surely, they looked as uncomfortable as they felt -- heavy and full and achy.

"You look beautiful, just need to work on getting more sleep. Aren't preggies supposed to sleep like all the time?"

My hands moved from my breasts and prodded around my eyes. They changed too, tired and withdrawn, despite the layers of mascara and eyeliner. Everything on my body was changing but the obvious. No protrusion from my belly yet, which was a good thing. My secret was safe for now.

"If I could shut my mind off, maybe I'd get more."

"Always with the worrying. You need to let some things go."

"Yeah, yeah, yeah." Ana always accused me of worrying enough for two people, but now, I actually needed to worry for two: me and my baby. "I need more than a sexual relationship, there needs to be an intellectual one as well. What if I'm not smart enough for him?"

She scrunched her nose. "Is he a part-time rocket scientist?"

"No, he's a full-time librarian and a part time student. He's working on his master's degree, that means he's smart and dedicated."

"So?"

My job was always slapping me in the face. "I'm just a waitress, with no degrees or diplomas, aside from high school."

She growled. "Gawd girl. You graduated in the top of your high school class and weren't you a valedictorian?"

"Only because Josie Switzer got mono three days before."

"You're so much more than that. You bring people food and smiles and sometimes, you change their day around. They can be miserable and foul when they come in and by the end of their meal, they're laughing and enjoying life again."

"That's the food doing its job, not me."

"No, it's all you. Why do you have so many regulars?"

I shrugged as my lips turned down. "I don't know."

"You need to get out of that head space. Being a server is a hard job. I should know, I quit after two weeks. And you've been doing it for how long?"

Six and a half years. Six and a half long years. With nothing to show for it. Not even a manager's position or something.

A change in topics was needed. I didn't need another reminder how making some quick money waitressing to help pay for university tuition turned into a full-time career. "So, do you have your flights confirmed? Just a few days more to go."

Her face fell. "I know."

"You're sad to be leaving, aren't you?"

"You've no idea how wonderful it is here. I think in a past life I was an Aussie."

"Judging from your emails and plans, I'd say your future life too."

Ana planned on coming home for six months only - enough to file the paperwork she needed, pack her things and head back. It came as a hard blow since I'd need to find a new roommate as there was no way I'd be able to pay for this place on my own, and I highly doubt Ana would continue to pay a portion if she was truly gone.

With the baby coming, I couldn't see a long line of roommate applications filling my inbox. Or I'd have to move into a new place with less amenities and no Chang's because there was no way on God's green Earth I was moving into my parent's house.

"Ready for Christmas?"

I paced down the hall to the bathroom. "Almost. Have a few stocking stuffers to get."

"Your dad speaking to you yet?"

I set the phone beside the sink and put my hands together in prayer formation. "No, and I've made no attempt to speak with him. I'm sure he's lit every candle in church to pray for my wayward soul."

Ana laughed at my eye roll. "Your mom must be beside herself."

I tossed a washcloth into the sink and wet it. Squeezing it out, I held the heat against my cheek. It was soothing. "With which part? That her husband won't speak to his daughter, or that she's going to be a grandmother?"

"Isn't she excited?"

"No, she is. Between CeCe's wedding and this birth, she's over the moon. She texts all the time with baby room ideas, so I can only imagine what she's doing with CeCe and the wedding. But she's conflicted and doesn't think she should be as happy about being a grandma as she is, you know, because I'm having a child out of wedlock." Thinking of CeCe reminded me to call and check up on her. See if she's still angry at me as well.

"Hey, Jo-Jo, I need to go. Ollie's beckoning me. We're meeting his family at the zoo for a Christmas party."

"Oh wow. Have fun!"

"Love you, Jo-Jo."

"You too." I ended the call.

Too tired to have a one-sided conversation with my sister, I finished washing up and went bed.

I went to work in a bad mood, which was awful. But I was doing a lot of hating lately and it was giving me the worst pain in the neck. A crick I couldn't get rid of despite a hot shower and heating pad. Maybe Ana was right, maybe there was such a thing as too much worrying. It was all taking up residence in my shoulders.

I just returned to the serving station, from hanging up my jacket and changing out of my boots when I spotted Chad— Audrina's boyfriend—hanging out near the front.

"Hey." I stopped at the hostess station to wipe the menus.

"How's it going?" He walked over and leaned on the podium.

I shrugged. "Can't complain, and no one would listen if I did." But I laughed as I said it. After all, my nametag said Joy and I really needed to live up to it, even when I felt light years away from it. The whole fake it until you make it philosophy usually worked.

"Now that's not true. I'd listen."

Chad was a pretty cool guy. He suited Audrina perfectly. When the two of them were together it was like a puzzle with its missing piece finally in place. Besides, he was easy to talk to and always helped out when Audrina worked the odd evening shift. Meghan would never let that happen.

"Really? You want to hear about my man troubles?" I wiped off the daytime server names and wrote on tonight's staff list, outlining who had what section. It made it easier on the part-time hostess we hired for the supper rushes.

"That depends, how severe of troubles are we talking here?" Chad straightened and his brows knit together.

I sighed and put my hand on the podium. "He's upset with me, and I want to make it up to him. Find a way to say I'm sorry."

"That's easy, Joy." Chad never did know my real name, and if he did, he kept it to himself. "Have you thought about sending flowers to his office?"

"Wouldn't that be weird? A guy getting flowers?"

"On the contrary. Because it happens so rarely, it's kinda sweet when it happens. All the attention that comes with it. Makes a man blush for all the right reasons."

I leaned closer, resting my arms on the table map, effectively wiping it free of the nice outline I highlighted a moment ago. "Has Audrina ever sent you flowers?"

"Hard in my line of work."

Chad worked in construction, and every week he could be working someplace different.

"I suppose."

The seed had been planted and the idea of sending James a gigantic bouquet to his work nagged at me. It could be fun, but I wasn't sure if James was the type of guy who enjoyed that kind of attention. I'd hate for him to be uncomfortable.

"But what if you're not sure what kind of a relationship you want with the guy?" I pulled the marker out of the drawer.

"Well, now you've lost me."

"I'm not sure if I want a serious relationship, or just want him as a friend, or if I just want to know about him for later."

"In case you change your mind?" He scratched his head.

I laughed and redrew the outlines of server sections. "It's complicated."

"If there's one thing I can tell you, and I speak from experience on this, time doesn't wait. If it's something your heart wants, you need to strike while the iron's hot. Swallow whatever fears are holding you back and go for it. You can talk to Audrina about that."

I suspected there was a deeper story there, however, I wasn't one to pry and if it was something she wanted to share with me, she'd have to instigate that conversation.

"Are you talking about me again, Chad?" Audrina said as she sauntered closer to us.

"Always." His face lit right up when she came into view.

Audrina faced me as a small grin formed. "You chatting his ears off?"

"Hardly." I grabbed a few menus and wiped them down before I spun around and headed for the server station. "Thanks for the tip, Chad."

"Give the flower idea some serious thought. A little

attention goes a long way."

"Will do." I nodded and looked around.

Always best to look busy and be busy, even if the place was dead. The coffee was empty, so I began making a fresh pot.

Robin walked in and grabbed a tray, giving it a solid wipe with a damp cloth. "Did I hear correctly, are you having man troubles?"

And this was why I never shared anything about my personal life. The little bits I did, staff always found a way to gossip

He gently pushed me on the shoulder. "I didn't even know you had a man, let alone one to give you grief."

"Oh, stop it," I said, playfully and tossed the empty package of grounds into the trash. "It's not even a thing. I think."

"What's going on?" The new server, nicknamed Celeste as she was a huge astronomy buff, waltzed in.

Robin nodded in my direction. "Joy's having boyfriend issues."

"Oh, is he afraid of commitment? I hate it when they get like that." Celeste shook her head, her ponytail of curls flying all over.

Robin tucked the clean tray into its slot and leaned against the counter, crossing his arms over his chest. "Yeah, that tends to happen when you propose to someone after the third date."

"I didn't propose. I simply told him we were perfect together, and he got all flighty and left. Dumbass."

"I wonder why." Robin rolled his eyes. "And what about that other guy? Didn't you like profess your undying love for him after a couple of weeks?"

Celeste's cheeks pinked up. "Maybe. But I tell you Matt was amazing, and I think we could've made beautiful children together."

"You do hear yourself, don't you?"

A faraway look landed on her face. "I'm a hopeless romantic."

"You're hopeless alright." Robin stretched out and pushed the start button on the coffee machine. "You forgot to do that."

I'd been so wrapped up in their back and forth conversation, I hadn't noticed. Watching them interact was interesting; they seemed to have a very easy nature with each other.

"Did you ever win them back?" I asked Celeste.

"Hell no. They obviously weren't worth it."

Robin looked at me, after shaking his head. "Are you living together? The guy you're having troubles with?"

I shook my head. "No, we're at the very beginning of our relationship, as in two dates." If I included the wedding. "We're still checking the other out."

"Checking each other out, fun times indeed." Robin wiggled his eyebrows. "Try sex," he whispered as he walked by and rinsed out his cloth in the sink.

Inside my head, I laughed. That's what got me into this mess.

Celeste was a little more helpful. "Write him a romantic love letter."

Yeah, 'cause that wouldn't scare the guy off at all. "I need something a little less heavy and maybe a bit flirtier and fun."

Robin backed into the space, sincerity etched on his face. "Yeah, don't send him a letter until you've moved into serious territory. Take him to a movie he wants to see, something with a lot of action, and lots of blood and guts."

I cringed. "That's something *you* would like, and I'm not dating you."

"Try something scary then. He should enjoy putting his arms around you and protecting you."

As much as I wanted to believe him, the snicker and tone

said he was saying it in jest.

"Dating's so hard," I said, grabbing a pad of paper and pen, stuffing them into one of the pockets of my apron.

"That's why I'm a firm believer in casual flings. No strings. No attachments." He nodded at the door. "Incoming."

"That's quite the life you've got set up for yourself, Robin," Celeste countered as she smacked him on the shoulder and walked out onto the floor.

Audrina stepped closer. "I didn't mean to overhear but if you are serious about this guy, a little affection really does go a long way. Leave a note on his car. Show up when he's finished work with a picnic lunch. Little things like that. Take an interest in what he's interested in and go from there."

That's sort of what I'd been doing. I was trying to find out as much as this guy as possible, so I could tell my child all about his or her father. My parents had very little info on my heritage, and I didn't want my child to be without that knowledge. I wanted, and needed, to get as much as I could. Maybe even his blood type and ancestral background.

I laughed. Was that too much?

~Chapter Eleven

hristmas came and blew by in a flash, and I found myself waiting alongside Ana's parents at the airport the day before New Year's Eve. Mr. and Mrs. Shapiro were giddy with joy, pacing back and forth as they checked and re-checked the monitors, hoping for no further delays. Their only child had already been delayed once on the long trip home.

"She's landed," Mrs. Shapiro said, a squeal in her voice, and she grabbed the arm of her husband.

These two were cute times ten. Always holding onto each other, the body contact was very high. Aside from a quick trip to the bathroom, they hadn't separated. It was sweet. They were also old school. Very old school. From what Ana's said, her parents didn't even kiss until their fourth or fifth date. I've highly suspected Ana was a honeymoon pregnancy.

I readied my sign.

Two days ago, Ana insisted I not come because she would spend the night at her parent's and come home to our apartment the next day. But with the change in her flights, she was no longer landing in the middle of the night, it was broad daylight out. Besides, it had been so long since I saw my bestie in the flesh that waiting any longer would surely be the death of me.

A throng of people burst through the door, and I held my sign high, hoping to catch Ana's attention. Weary travellers pushed past us, heading to the baggage carousel.

"I see her," Mr. Shapiro said, and with his wife's hand tightly gripped in his, they advanced through the people.

I held back a bit – Ana should see and greet her parents first. And she did. I heard her screams over the crowd as she ran straight to them, wrapping them in a hug.

The Australian sun had done wonders for her complexion, her skin tanned and her hair sun-bleached enough to make it appear almost white, instead of the bombshell blonde, but it suited her as she could almost pass as my sister. She'd also put on a few pounds, and her face was a little rounder. Clearly living down under had a magical effect on her, she looked amazing and healthy and so happy.

"Jo-Jo." She ran over and gave me a big bear hug and planted a kiss on each of my cheeks. Stepping back, she ran her hand over my belly before I could push it away. There wasn't anything for her to feel, I was still flat as a pancake. "How's my baby?"

Stunned and slightly embarrassed, I stepped back, eyes growing wide with each passing second. My gaze flickered between Ana's and her parents, who both stood open mouthed staring at my belly. I've known the Shapiros since high school, and I've never seen them look so surprised.

Mrs. Shapiro's gaze remained on my belly. "You're pregnant?"

"She's due Canada Day," Ana said, smiling as wide as the Grand Canyon. "I'm going to be an aunty."

"Where's the father?" Mr. Shapiro asked, wrapping his arm around his wife's shoulders.

"Who's the father?" Mrs. Shapiro asked, clearing her throat, and finally moving her gaze up to my face.

"He's working right now. Just got home from Vancouver where he spent Christmas with his family." I said it with as much confidence as I could. Besides, it was all true.

A rumble of a voice came from behind me. I turned around and recognised the guy as Ana's flatmate, Oliver.

"G'day, matey." His accent was much thicker than I remembered. He stuck out his hand and shook Mr. Shapiro's hand first, and then Ana's mom's. "I'm Ollie."

Ana cuddled up next to him, placing her hand on his chest. He was wearing a sweater, but it wouldn't do much to keep him warm, not in the sub-zero temperatures waiting outside. Maybe all that hair would help trap in some heat?

"Mom, Dad, Jo-Jo, this is Oliver... my fiancé."

"Your what?" Mr. Shapiro's voice was a little on the loud side.

A couple passersby stopped and looked in our direction.

Mrs. Shapiro clutched her husband and held on tight. "Oh my god, Gerald."

Guess I wasn't the only one capable of stunning the Shapiros, and I felt a little relieved. But not too much.

Ana's dad's face was filling with blood and a touch of rage. His brows knitted together, and his mouth formed a thin line. "Your fiancé?" He took a step toward Ollie but kept his focus on his daughter. "You couldn't tell us until now?"

I faced her, wondering the same. "Yeah, Ana, what's up with that?"

"This isn't the kind of news you tell someone over the phone." She kept her hand splayed on Ollie's chest, and I spotted the ring. It sparkled in the light.

Sure, my news had been discussed, but not hers? "But I told you about the baby…"

"Nah, I coaxed that outta you."

Mr. Shapiro advanced on the young couple. "Are you pregnant too?"

"God dad, no. Never."

Ollie retreated a step. He was much taller than Mr. Shapiro, and a good deal thinner, borderline lanky. However, I'd hedge my bets on Oliver winning any kind of physical fight. But this wasn't the place for that.

I stepped between the men, and my stomach grumbled at the intervention. "Hey, let's be civil here."

"Gerald, let her explain."

Mr. Shapiro spun towards his wife. "What's there to explain? I told you her going to Australia was a bad idea. She moved away for six months and now she's engaged." He faced his grown daughter. "I suppose you plan to marry him here and have him come into our country to live as your groom?"

I flipped my gaze over to my best friend. I knew what her plans were, but clearly, she hadn't yet shared them with her family.

"Actually, the reverse is true." She squared her shoulders and linked her fingers through Ollie's. "After we get married, I'm moving there."

"Oh, Gerald." Mrs. Shapiro lost her colour and gripped on to her husband.

I reached out for her, afraid she was about to pass out.

"We'll talk about this in the car ride home." He stepped back. "But he's not staying at our place. No way. I'll not have you having sex under my roof."

"Daddy, I'm twenty-five years old, I'm not a child. Besides, I can just stay at my apartment with Jo-Jo. With the delays and everything, and she's here…" She pointed at me.

Mr. Shapiro's voice lowered and the sound of it sent chills through me. He wasn't just angry, he was hurt. "Not happening. After everything your poor mother has been through, you can spend the night at our place."

I looked at the two of them, a happy reunion crushed by Ana's verbal diarrhea. I wondered if she thought this was the best way to tell them, and then I worried how the ride back to her folk's place would be. It wouldn't be any fun being a fly on that wall.

"Where do you reckon I shack up, doll?"

I sighed. It wasn't ideal, not in the least. "Oliver, since you were going to apparently stay at our place anyways…" I glanced at Ana, shooting little arrows at her. A little heads up would've been nice. "You may as well come back with me, and I'll get you set up in Ana's room."

The pair stared at each other with googly eyes until Ana looked at her parents. Her happy expression fell from her face.

"Ah, mate, I reckon it'll be swell. Enjoy your mob." He nodded towards her parents.

"You're sure?"

"No drama."

She reached up to kiss him, whether it was for show or for another reason, but it took a while for them to break apart.

They grabbed their bags from the baggage carousel, and we split up. Ana followed her parents like she was a young child and knew a lengthy lecture was waiting for her. I felt bad, however, at least her dad would yell and scream and then it would likely be over with. Mine was still raging with disappointment.

"Do you have something warmer than that?" I asked Ollie before we stepped out into the cold.

"Nah, I'm tough."

"Have you ever been to Canada before? In the winter? It

can be brutal." I shivered inside my own jacket and I'd lived here all my life. This was normal for us. A stranger, from a warm country? This would be torture.

"I lived in Toronto until I was ten, then we moved to Perth." He shrugged.

"Not the same. Tell you what I'll go get my car and come back to pick you up."

"Nah, mate, trust me, I be fine." He hoisted his rucksack over his shoulder. "Lead the way."

The drive back to our apartment was a boisterous one. I anticipated Ollie would be quiet as he was riding with a stranger in a strange land to an unfamiliar place. Turns out he was quite the chatterbox and hardly shy at all. He spilled about how he came to meet Ana and how he proposed to her in front of his parents at the zoo. Apparently, they had completely taken her in like she was one of the family, even though they'd known each other less than a few months, and only dating for a few weeks.

Sounded like my outgoing bestie found her place in the world, and it was on the opposite side of the Earth. But hearing how sweet Ollie was, and how he described her, well, it made it okay. Tolerable. He worshipped her, and she needed that. She'd had enough bozos in her past.

I showed him Ana's room, a very girlie room with lavender walls and yellow accessories splayed over the double sized bed I was pretty sure Ollie's feet would hang over. "Make yourself at home."

He dropped his bag beside the bed. "Are Mr. and Mrs. Shapiro always like that?"

I laughed. "No, tonight was unusual. They got a double whammy, with my baby news and then your engagement." I leaned against the frame of the door. "They'll come around. They're pretty cool people, they just need to get over the shock."

A soft nod came from him. "She's gonna get a gobful, ain't she?"

I shrugged trying to figure out what he was saying – the slang threw me. "Maybe. But Ana's tough. She can handle it." Pushing away from the door when my tummy squawked quite loudly, I asked, "Are you hungry?"

"I can eat, as should you." His eyes fell to my midsection. "You're too thin."

A small laugh eased out of me as I gave him a skeptical look. "Right where I should be."

"Nah, ya need meat on yer bones. Mum's an OB, ya need to eat more, the babe needs the nutrients."

"I'll keep that in mind." I headed to the kitchen. Rifling through my fridge, the only appealing thing was yogurt. I grabbed it and tore off the lid.

Ollie joined me but just stood there.

"Help yourself." I spooned some into my mouth and shuddered. It didn't taste like strawberry. My eyes roved the container. Not expired, but on the fence.

Ollie rooted through the cupboards and found a loaf of bread. He disappeared, reappearing moments later with a jar and twisted off the lid. "Vegemite, wanna try?"

The smell was horrible as it filled the small space, and I held back a gag. "No thanks."

"Yer loss."

I cocked an eyebrow as I washed my spoon and tucked it back into the drawer. "Make yourself at home. I need to get ready for work."

"I don't need much. I brought me laptop as I need to check in with me mum."

I scratched out the Wi-Fi password on the notepad hanging on the fridge, and for good measure, added my cell. "In case you need anything while I'm out." Stepping out of the kitchen, I walked past the door and slapped my head across my forehead. "Will you need to go out? I don't have an extra key."

"Nah. I'll veg out in front of the tube."

Sounded fun enough. I wished I could do the same.

When I finished getting into my green polo and a pair of pants, I closed my bedroom door. I wasn't sure if I could trust this stranger to not rifle through my private stuff. Remembering an old trick, I found an unused toothpick and propped it up against my door. If it was flat upon my return, then I'd know he snooped. It sucked not trusting people, but trust wasn't freely given away, despite what Father Bobby preached.

Robin was outside, foot up against the crumbling brick exterior and smoking a cigarette, when I pulled into a parking stall near the rear of the restaurant.

"Hey," I said, nodding in his direction.

He blew out a puff of smoke and tossed the butt into the snow, stomping on it for good measure. "How's it going?"

I plastered on a smile. "It's going."

"Meghan's on a war path today. Watch out."

"Thanks for the tip." Not that it was unusual. Meghan was always in a bad mood. "She really needs to get some, eh?"

He laughed. "She needs more than that, I suspect." A small spray bottle appeared in his hands and he spritzed himself over.

"What are you doing?"

"It rids me of the smoke smell. I hate that smell."

"So why do you smoke then?"

"Ah, a good question with no good answer." He stepped

over to where I stood. "How's your man?"

I hadn't spoke to James since that night, nor had I seen him. It had been nine days. He flew home yesterday, but with Ana's flight delay and setting up Ollie in our apartment, I hadn't yet had the chance to stalk him out at the library and at least say hi. Instead of answering, I shrugged.

"That good?"

"I don't know what to do."

"You like him?"

"Yeah, I do, at least I think I do. I don't know, maybe I just like the idea of him."

Thinking about dating while pregnant should be outlawed. Too many emotions and possibilities to mull over when there was no clear path.

"The idea of him?" He nudged me towards the back door, where he knocked on it.

The door opened, and Audrina's face poked out. "Get in here you two. It's freezing out there."

"It's not too bad."

The sun was shining which made the cool temperatures tolerable. Besides, it felt nice against my flushed cheeks. They started heating while I was driving back from the airport and weren't going away. I followed Robin to the locker area.

"So, what's up with the idea of this guy?"

Here I'd hoped he'd forgotten. "I don't know. It's complicated."

"I doubt it."

Without thinking it through, I asked, "What would you do if one of your many conquests came up to you and told you she was pregnant?"

His face paled, and he braced himself against the wall of lockers. "Why? Who showed up?"

"No one, I was just curious." If I told James, and I was one of his many conquests, was he likely to react the same?

"You're sure no one talked to you?"

I patted him reassuringly on the shoulder. "Robin, do I know any of the girls you've been with?"

"I don't know. You all talk." He closed his locker and secured the lock.

Well, that was true, but I didn't know who he'd ever been with. I wasn't keeping tabs, and he never mentioned any names.

"It was just a figure of speech. I was curious what you would do but seeing your reaction answered it."

"A figure of speech is something like an anaphoric sentence or something ironic. Asking me what I'd do if a girl I banged announced her pregnancy is hardly a figure of speech."

For a moment, I forgot Robin was working on a degree in language and literacy. While I rolled my eyes, I tucked my jacket into my locker and locked it up, securing my apron around my body. "Forget I said anything."

"Wait a hot minute... Joy, are you pregnant?"

Keeping my back to him, I leaned my head against the cool metal. I needed it to seep into my skin and reduce the flaming situation firing across my cheeks and forehead.

"Is this guy you're having issues with, is he the dad?"

I gave him a slow nod.

"Does this guy know?"

I shook my head, my bangs twisting against the locker door. "That's part of the problem."

"Oh, wow."

Righting myself and swallowing down the nagging morsel of shame, I stared.

"Shit. You're in quite the predicament. You're pregnant, you like him, but he doesn't know?"

My teeth scrapped across my lips. "See how it's complicated?"

"Yep, I do now." He tightened his own apron. "You plan on telling him?"

"That's the thing, I don't know. Right now, I'm just wanting to know more about him."

"And what, tell him years down the road?"

My shoulders lifted in a slo-mo shrug. "Maybe? I don't know. I don't want to be responsible for screwing up his life."

"Too late for that." He stepped back.

My face contorted into an array of messed up features, a swirl of anger and disgust and Robin's face blurred.

He came closer and put his hand on my shoulder. "Sorry, I didn't mean that how it came out."

My breath caught, and a lump formed in my throat. "It's okay, you were being honest." I wiped my eyes and checked my fingers afterwards. No mascara ran.

"No, it's not okay."

A cook waltzed passed us and into the bathroom, breaking up the attempt at friendship bonding.

Robin's eyes roved up to the clock in the back. "I don't want to end this conversation, but we need to start our shift. Can we go out after work? I think we need to discuss this more in-depth. I sense you need a male perspective on this."

I replaced my growing disappointment with my life with a question. "What about Celeste?"

The two of them had been quite flirty with each other, and I highly suspected a little thing brewing between the two of them.

"She gets serious way too quickly, and I'm just wanting a little fun. It'd never work."

We walked side by side to the serving station.

"So, coffee afterwards?"

I had never associated with my co-workers outside the four walls of Westside. It was a dangerous combination of mixing work and personal, but hey, he'd already touched my shoulder and accidentally caused me to cry, so I felt the line had already been breached.

"Sure, why not?" What else could I possibly lose?

Chapter Twelve

Robin and I took our places at the table in the back of the restaurant. I left my jacket over my shoulders, mainly to hide the fact I was wearing my pukey green polo uniform.

Robin removed his coat and wrapped it around the back of the chair, not caring in the least that he still wore his work shirt in a different restaurant. A competitor no less, albeit not a great one. But the dive was close, and the blast of fresh air felt nice on my face.

All evening long, I couldn't shake away my flushed cheeks and a nagging feeling I was coming down with something. However, I also argued it could be a side effect of pregnancy, or because I was overwhelmed with getting my life in order.

The waitress stared at Robin's name tag pinned below the black Westside embroidered logo and looked me over as well. "Ah, you two work there?"

Robin chuckled. "Nope. Just found these shirts at Goodwill and thought it would be fun to wear them out. I'll have a Coke please. What do you want, Joy?"

"A peppermint tea with lemon, please."

The waitress glared at Robin, deservedly so. "I'll be back with your drinks."

"You didn't need to insult her," I said, whispering.

"It doesn't take a genius to figure that out. Her comment was a little dumb, especially since the answer was obvious." He raised an eyebrow. "Back to you, Miss Joy."

I sighed. A text rolled in from Ana. "Sorry, I just need to respond to this."

Hey, how's Ollie?

I typed back. *I haven't gone home yet.*

Robin stretched out on the chair, his long legs knocking against mine.

"It's my roommate."

Ana responded. *He's been pretty quiet.*

Time change?

Probably. Text me when you get home, I need to know how my man is.

Will do.

I looked over at Robin and in a light laugh said, "Where would we be without our smart phones?"

"Invested in real conversations." He rolled his eyes, and a bored expression covered his face.

"I'm sorry." I tossed my phone onto the table, embarrassed. "It's just my roommate got home today from six months away in Australia, and her fiancé came with her and it's messy."

"You seem to have a knack for messy situations."

I readjusted the coat over my shoulders as a cool draft floated over my neck. "Only recently."

Robin leaned in closer. "What's up with that?"

"I don't know."

"I want a better answer than that. I think you do know."

Wow, he cut right through into the heart of the whole

debacle. I've worked with Robin for a couple of years, but I never expected this of him.

"When are you going to tell him?"

A gust of exhaled air sailed from my lips, and my gaze stayed focused on the table. "I don't know if I will."

"For real?" His tone was clipped and angry. "Why the hell not?"

"Like you said, once he knows, I'll be responsible for ruining his life." I pulled my jacket up more, trying to hide underneath it.

"Last time I checked, Joy, it takes two to tango. He's just as much a part of this as you are."

"And you'd be so compliant as to just naturally accept it if it were you? Stick with the cards you've drawn. I highly doubt it. You'd want a reshuffle." I stared at him point blank.

Robin was a player, and we all knew it. We just didn't know names but there were enough notches on his bedpost that it was never cold for long.

"You don't know me. And you don't know this guy."

I shrugged. "It's typical behaviour."

"That's bullshit. Just because one–"

Miss Insulted slammed our drinks on the table, glaring at Robin. "What would you like to order?"

"I'm fine with this." He gestured to the large drink.

The hard drop on the tabletop caused his Coke to foam, spilling part of the contents over the side.

"There's a minimum five-dollar charge per person in the evenings after eight."

Well, that certainly explains the lack of customers.

I wasn't hungry, but I wasn't going to accept a five-dollar charge for a cup of tea either.

"Split a club house with me?" It had been a while since I'd

last ate, but I wasn't famished enough to eat the entire order.

He nodded. "Sure."

"Anything else?" The waitress growled but never removed her eyes from Robin.

I answered before he could say something to further irritate her. "We're good with that, thanks."

Miss Insulted huffed away, and Robin wiped up the mess with a napkin, pushing it to the side when it was soaked.

"Wow, if Meghan ever caught her talking to customers like that, she'd be fired on the spot."

I couldn't agree more. "How do we convince Meghan to work here? I dislike that she's on evenings. I suspected things would get better, but they've gone so far downhill."

It was go-go-go with her. You were expected to be busy every single moment, and if it was quiet, you did extra cleaning.

"Sounds like you're looking for another job?"

"With what time? I'm due July first. Any other job I get right now, I'd have to work my required hours to obtain maternity leave and it would be three months until any employer would cover my health care premiums. I'm sort of screwed."

"You were screwed – that's what got you into this pickle in the first place." He laughed at his own joke and leaned back in his chair. "But seriously, you need to tell this guy. This mystery guy. He deserves to know."

I took a sip of my tea. Nothing fancy, just a peppermint tea bag soaking in mildly hot water. It wasn't great, but it would do. "I do plan on telling him at some point in time, I'm just not sure how or when. Before or after the baby comes."

"Sooner is better than later."

"Why?"

"How far along are you?"

A quick calculation. "Fourteen weeks, give or take. I should

119

know better, but I don't."

What kind of mother would I be if I couldn't even figure out how old my baby was? Sheesh.

"So sooner is better, see? Because he'll have more time to adjust to the news. If you were to tell him today, he'd have four or five months to accept that he's going to be a father before it actually happens."

"Do you think it would take that long?" That's less than half a year, surely more than enough time to wrap his head around it.

"He's not going to accept it overnight. Did you?"

I leaned back in my seat and sometimes I still wasn't sure if I had truly accepted it. "No."

"See? And you've had weeks with this."

Touché. I've actually had less time than that, but it's neither here nor there. I understood the point he was trying to make. I just didn't agree with it.

"But I carry it with me all day. It's on my mind constantly. Every thought about the future relies on it. Would a guy be the same way?"

Robin leaned closer to the table and pushed his drink off to the side. "If he's a decent fellow and respects you like he should, then yes. It should be on his mind all the time."

"What if he hates me?"

"I highly doubt that's even possible." His brows arched high enough to hide under the fringe of hair covering his forehead. "You're Joy – the bringer of happiness. Hey, now that we're not in Westside, what's your real name?"

Robin came on board where the nicknames were standard and like him, I didn't know his real name either. He was always Robin, the skinny guy who ate like a bird.

"You first." I tipped my head.

"Garrett."

120

"What, really?" I looked at him with his true name – he did sort of look like he could pull a Garrett off. Tall, lanky. I rolled the name over and over on my tongue. "Yeah, I can see it. It's a good name."

"Consider it for your baby, if it's a boy."

"Oh geez... I'm in charge of picking a name that will suit him or her. How can I choose if I don't know what they will be like as they grow?"

He chuckled. "You're overthinking this. I think a person grows into their name more than the name grows on them. Take my brother for example. What do you think of when you hear the name Evan?"

Hmm... I mulled it over while my stomach flipped, a wave of nausea crashing into me. "I think of a jerky dude who asserts his power over people."

Robin quietly laughed. "Do you know my brother?"

"Pretty far off?"

"Pretty bang on. He's a high-ranking police officer."

"What?"

"You just proved my point. You grow into a name."

"Well, I have some hard decisions to..." I scanned the empty restaurant, coming to a full freeze by the front door.

James and a lovely lady were following behind Miss Insulted to a booth not far from us. He folded his coat and set it beside him, sitting only when his lady friend did so first.

"What's up? Joy?" Robin waved a hand in front of my face, snapping me out of the long, blink-less stare.

But I couldn't look away. James hadn't noticed me and if he did, he didn't make a big deal out of it, or any deal really. Nothing he did indicated he'd spotted me. My heart sunk a little.

Robin cranked himself around and turned back to get in my face. "Who's that?"

My voice chilled and the words felt breathy and lost. "Just a guy I know."

Finally, my gaze focused on Robin, hoping to ground myself. My body remembered the sweet kiss on the park bench a couple weeks ago, and it ramped up the speed of my heart. The subsequent race of my pulse threatened to drown out all Robin's chatter.

"That Shia LeBeouf guy, that's him? That's the guy who knocked you up?"

Another wave of nausea rolled into me and the butterflies soaring in my gut took a wicked nosedive. "Such harsh words."

"But that's him, right?" He craned himself to get another look and then gave me a once over. "Not bad looking. Your baby will probably be cute."

I snorted, lightly, but still unladylike. "Probably?"

"Fine. Mostly cute." He smirked. "Here's your chance. Go tell him."

"He's on a date. I can't ruin that."

"You claim you're going to ruin his life, so what's the harm in ruining his date. Besides, no one brings a date here." He waved his hands around. "This place is a dump."

"We're on a date."

"A coffee date. Not a date-date."

"There's a difference?" I was just kidding with him.

As nice a guy as Robin is, he wasn't my type. At all.

"Completely. I'm not expecting a kiss at the end of this." He gave me a wink that should've had more of an affect on me.

"You expect only a kiss at the end of your dates? I thought it was something more."

"Well, there's that too. Go talk to him." He prodded my foot with his boot.

I slowly inched my gaze back over to the booth and tugged

122

my jacket over my shoulders a little more.

James was smiling at his date but wasn't making eye contact as he gazed over her head. Looking around, he connected with me. Very slowly, his focus shifted to Robin. He gave me a small nod and resumed conversation with the lady who shared his table.

My stomach did another flip, and the feeling went out of my legs as a violent quake shook through me. A feeling of doom flooded over me, and I wasn't sure why. But I felt instantly frozen.

"You okay?"

I shook my head and braced it against my hand. "I feel ill."

The waitress appeared with our food and set it in front of me. The smell of the over ripe tomatoes slipping out from between the overly toasted bread was too much.

"Excuse me." I rose and beelined for the bathroom, making it just in time.

With the toe of my shoe, I pushed the lever and flushed. I cleaned up and scrubbed my hands, giving myself a solid once over. The bags under my eyes had grown since this morning. I pushed them in, hoping to reduce them. All it did was leave me with red marks. Dang. My cheeks were a heated pink, a stark contrast to the ghost white surrounding them.

Paper towel clutched in my hand, I exited the washroom and made my way back to the table, eyeing James as I sat down.

"You okay?" James mouthed.

I shook my head and focused back on Robin, who had dutifully eaten his half of the sandwich and most of the fries. I pushed the plate toward him. "Finish it off."

"You really should eat."

"I don't think my stomach can handle it." I wrapped my hands around the lukewarm mug of tea, pulling all the remaining heat into my chilled fingers.

He took his eyes off the food and stared at me. "You look terrible."

"Thanks."

"No, I mean it. You're as white as a ghost."

"I think I should go home." I stood again and balanced myself as a dizzy spell rained down on me causing me to white-knuckle grip the edge of the table. Catching the attention of our waitress, I flagged her down. "Check please."

She reached into her pocket and ripped off a piece of paper. "They'll get you up front."

I patted Robin on the shoulder and squeezed it a bit when a stomach cramp overcame me. Sweat beaded on my forehead and a wave of doom flooded my insides once more. There was no way I was making it home.

"I got this," I said and pressed a twenty, along with the bill, into his hand and raced back to the bathroom.

When I came out with a completely wrung out stomach, Robin was there, holding my jacket. As I slipped it over my arms, I looked toward the table James was at, but it was deserted.

"Zip it up, it's cold out there, and whatever you have, it doesn't need to get worse."

I wasn't sure how it could be worse. I've never thrown up in a public bathroom before, and I did it twice in one visit. Embarrassment wasn't a big enough word. Leaning against Robin, thankful for his support, I stepped one dizzying footstep in front of another, wondering how I was going to drive home.

Parked outside the restaurant, right in front of the entryway was a red car. Exhaust billowed out the back end in the cool temperatures, which did the opposite of feeling nice on my cheeks. It chilled me to the bone, and I started shivering.

Robin opened the passenger door.

"Thanks," I said, leaning against the door.

My eyes wandered over to the driver's side, surprised to see James there. In a flash, I spun my head around, which didn't help with the dizziness. I stumbled over to the bush and emptied my stomach for the third time.

Robin ran his hands over my back and leaned in, whispering. "He offered to drive you home. How could I say no? Here's your chance."

He passed me a napkin, and I wiped my mouth.

A plastic bag appeared out of his pocket and with a snap, it bellowed open. "For the ride home."

My gaze flipped between James and Robin.

If I refused, I still had to walk down the street to where my car—and Robin's—were parked and possibly catch a ride home with him. Considering how my world was spinning, it would be an unpleasant walk at best. If I said yes, I'd be riding in a pretty fancy looking car, one that didn't need the smell of puke in it.

Robin waved the bag and wiggled his brows. "Your options are limited."

I snatched it out of his hand and with his help, lowered myself into James's car.

Chapter Thirteen

The split in my eyes widened as they opened to a dimly lit space. It didn't take more than a heartbeat to know I was in my bedroom; the pillows smelled familiar and the lemon-yellow comforter I've had since I was a teen was tucked around me. A slight twist of my head and a warm yet damp cloth fell off my forehead and landed beside my head.

Beside me was the outline and form of another body. Was it Ana? Did she leave her parents already?

The weight of several blankets on me was not enough to keep me warm as I shivered with my movements.

"Hey," the sleepy voice beside me said. Most definitely not Ana.

I turned my head, grateful a wave a dizziness didn't greet me even as its second cousin adrenaline did. My heart rate sped, and my extremities tingled as panic flooded my system. Moving fast was not in the cards for me; I was weak, and my body felt as if it weighed a thousand pounds.

James laid beside me, and as he sat up, he tossed off the

blanket covering him. He was on top of the comforter. If I wasn't so ill, I'd find the gesture sweet. He was still dressed in the same clothes I remembered him wearing last night.

"Hey," I said back, my throat raw and pained.

"How are you feeling?"

"Cold." I shuddered again, and he came over to my side of the bed and readjusted the blankets around me. I stole a peek under the covers. My Westside uniform was no longer on, but I was dressed in an old t-shirt with my bra still on. "What happened to my shirt?" My throat was raw and dry.

James fumbled over his words. "You were pretty sick last night and got some… ah… residue on it. It was pretty easy to convince you to change."

Oh geez, I must've looked like a nasty disaster. Vague memories of a stomach clenching car ride, and a hasty visit to my own bathroom floated into my head. I recalled begging to sleep beside the toilet as I dry heaved every few minutes.

"You have the flu."

Where would I have picked that up? I was so diligent with hand washing and sanitising. However, whatever I had, it had hit me pretty darn quick. I've never been so flattened by an illness.

My thoughts wandered to the little bean growing inside me, and my hands protectively covered my stomach. Would this flu be detrimental to his or her development? I needed to ask someone, but who? That pregnancy book would have the answers.

Oh my god, no.

Immediately my eyes wandered over to my nightstand where the book had been. Relief washed over me as I remembered tucking the book, and two others like it, into the drawer before I left for work.

I went to move but lacked the energy.

James sat by my knees and in a soothing motion, rubbed

127

them through the multiple layers of blankets. "What do you need? I can get it."

"Answers."

The sweetest laugh greeted my ears. "Twelve. Red. 384,400 kilometres."

"I don't want the distance to the moon—"

"You knew that?" His tone indicated great surprise.

"Yeah." It was a question from late-night Jeopardy. For some reason I remembered the answer. I tried to push myself up, but my spaghetti arms failed.

"Let me help you." Gently, he assisted me into a reclined position and fluffed up the two pillows, tucking them behind my back. A vanilla scented empty ice cream pail moved to my other side. "You haven't puked since I convinced you to get into bed, so I think you're safe there." He picked up the fallen cloth and waved it around. Folded, it rested against my forehead and the coolness felt heavenly. The back of his hand touched my cheek. "You're still very hot."

Normally, I'd take that as a compliment, but not today. Would a fever cook my bean?

"A drink?" He presented a bottle of water with a straw in it.

I had no idea where he'd found straws, but the lukewarm water soothed my scratchy throat. "Thanks."

"So, what answers do you require?"

The deep breath expanded my lungs, and a bolt of pain ran through me. My stomach and chest muscles ached. "How did I get here? Where's Ollie?"

"I didn't know you had a male roommate." It almost sounded like he was tsking me, but it ended as quickly as it started. "He's still in his room."

"Ana?"

He lifted my phone off the nightstand. "She keeps texting

128

and calling. I highly suggest you call her back before she breaks in."

"She lives here too."

My eyes scanned the multiple messages. Poor girl was freaking out. I sent a quick text that I was alive *barely* with the flu, and all was well with Ollie. I'd call her, but my throat hurt too much to have a lengthy conversation. I needed a spoonful of honey. Desperately. There was none in the apartment, but Chang's should have some. Overpriced for sure, but he'd have it in stock.

"Can you go to the store downstairs and get some honey please?" I tapped my throat. "My wallet's in my purse."

"I'll get it." He rose and stood over me. "What about Gravol? Or some over the counter stuff?"

"No," I said, my voice pitched in fear. What would those drugs do to my bean? I took a deep breath. "No, thank you. I prefer herbal, natural remedies."

He hung by the door and thrust his hand into a pocket.

"My keys for the elevator…" But I didn't remember where I left them. All I remembered was the many, many times I dry heaved.

"They're on the table. I'll be right back." He left the door open a crack as he exited.

Ana's face appeared on my phone, she was facetiming in.

Sure she'd seen me worse, I answered.

"Jo-Jo." Her semi-Australian accent was music to my ears. "You look like shit."

I waved. "It's the flu."

"Mom's got it too. Been ill since we got home."

Great, I shared it with them.

"Ollie still there?"

"Far's I know."

"I'm coming home soon."

"Things better now with your parents?"

"Much. Dad still thinks I'm a child, so what can I say?" She smiled and glanced around. "But he's not angry anymore. Wants to go out for dinner with Ollie and smooth everything out, man to man, dad to son-in-law."

A complete 180. Wish my own father had been so accommodating. He talked to me at Christmas, but it was forced and not the normal, easy going way he normally spoke.

"I'm happy for you," I said, the weakness overcoming me. My eyes flickered shut. "Later."

I blinked long enough for her to mutter something before sleep pulled me under again.

When I woke up, chatter and giggles greeted my ears. Ana was home, her infectious laughter echoed off the hall walls. Her blonde head poked into my room.

"Hey, sleepy head." She removed the cool cloth and kissed my forehead. "Ooh, still hot." The bed bounced as she climbed onto it. "So, about James?"

James was still here? What time was it? I twisted my head slowly and looked at my clock. It was nearly noon.

"Yeah, I ran into him last night and he brought me home."

Ana flapped the cloth through the air and after re-folding it, placed it back across my forehead. "And he stayed all night?"

"Yes, because the flu is a major turn on. Every guy wants to bed someone that sick."

"I think it's sweet." She smiled. "He's watching the tube with Ollie for a spell." She flipped the cloth over and replaced it back on my head. "Does he know about the baby?"

Her gaze did what everyone's did when that word was mentioned, it travelled straight to my stomach.

"No."

"You need to tell him."

I wasn't in the mood for this discussion right now. My priority was to get better, make sure the bean was okay and move on from there. "I will. I can't like this though."

She stretched out beside me and clasped her hands behind her head. "It's adorable the way he's taking care of you. I think he'd make a great father. Are you going to give him that chance?"

With great effort, I raised my brow back at her. "On?"

"You. Life. A relationship. Try it out. He seems pretty attentive. Maybe the baby news won't be as scary as you think."

I shrugged and pushed myself up a bit. The air around me still felt cold, so I pulled the mountain of blankets over me. "Let me get to know him first, and we'll see how it goes."

She shook her head, disappointment colouring her features. "That's really sad, ya know."

My own life was changing, no point in changing his too. The little bit of energy I had slowly leaked out of me like air from a balloon. My head dropped against the headboard and I closed my eyes. "Take my ticket for tomorrow night's party. Go with Ollie."

I'll just have to make do with YouTube videos of Colby Sacks.

Her voice perked and I heard the smile in it. "Are you sure?"

"I'm in no shape to go and won't be much better tomorrow."

"What'll you do?"

"Sleep," I said, feeling a wave of drowsiness wash over me. "Send James home too. I'm not good for company right now."

"Don't I get to be the judge of that?" His soothing voice came from the foot of my bed.

A pulse of fear awakened me, and I opened my eyes to see him staring. How much had he heard before he came in? Did he hear us talking about him and the baby? As I scanned his face, the lack of anger or disappoint implied he hadn't heard a thing.

"I got the honey." He wielded the container and a spoon around. "The last one."

"Thanks."

"I would've been faster, but some brat was having a meltdown because his mother wasn't buying him a chocolate bar." He walked over to the bed and sat down, shaking his head. "Seriously, some kids are a pain in the ass."

Ana patted my leg and rose. "On that note, I'm going to go hang with Ollie and tell him the good news."

James's face lit up. "What good news?"

Oh, whew, he hadn't heard much.

I snuggled down into the blankets. "I just gave him my ticket to Urban DC's party."

"That was nice of you." He filled a spoon with honey, and I opened my mouth, letting the sweetness sit on the back of my throat. "Supposed to be a helluva party."

Yep, and I was missing out on it. Biggest party of the year and I was stuck in bed with a fever and sore stomach. Happy New Year's Eve to me. "Don't have the energy to go."

"So, what are you going to do?"

"Sleep," I said, attempting a smirk as I closed my eyes. My energy reserves were being depleted and the flashing warning signs were going off. I didn't want to fall asleep mid-conversation, but it was going to happen.

"You're not going to watch the ball drop in New York?"

If I had the energy to laugh, I would've. "I don't anticipate being up that late."

"Too bad."

I cracked my eyes open enough to see him wink.

"I was hoping you'd be my first kiss of the New Year."

That thought gave me a fluttering of life, and I pushed myself up a little. "Really? You don't have anything better to do than hang out with a sick person on New Year's Eve?"

His hand found my leg and he rubbed it. The motion was soothing, and I melted into my pillows as he continued. "Is it a sad state of affairs that I don't? All I really need to do is take my dog for a run and check on the cat."

"You have a cat and a dog? Living together?"

A giant smirk spread from cheek to cheek. "My dog, Samson, is a beautiful Sheltie who enjoys longs walks in the park and fancies himself a pretty boy. My cat, Princess, lives up to her name and believes she is far superior to any other living being. But together," he squeezed the blanket pile. I think he was trying to hold my knee, but it was my ankle he touched. "Together, they really are the cutest. Princess will cuddle up to Samson, but only when she feels like it. And he takes it. You can see in his eyes how much he enjoys it."

"They sound cute together."

"They really are. You'll have to come and meet them. You're not allergic, are you?"

"But not today." My ten-pound eyelids closed off the world to me like room darkening curtains.

"Of course, not today." His smile came out with his words.

"Can you tell me a story?"

It sounded crazy to ask, but his voice was so soothing, he could tell me a story about war criminals and murderers, and I'd listen to every inflection, every pitch in the sounds flowing out of his beautiful mouth.

"A story eh?" The bed moved as he repositioned himself and got comfortable. "How about a fabulous story of boy meeting girl."

I mumbled. "Sounds great."

He tucked the blankets around me and spoke softly. "Once upon a time there was a noble knight, minding his own business as he finished a meeting of the round table." A soft chuckle rolled out of him. "As he left his knight friends behind, he stumbled upon an extravagant ball and lingered at the gate to watch. Suddenly, he saw the most stunning princess in all the lands. She was regal and elegant, and the knight was desperate to meet this beauty…"

Slumber pulled me under, and try as I did, I couldn't fight it even as much as I wanted to hear the rest of the story.

Chapter Fourteen

I started the new year off on the right foot, and then the left, but the day was nearly over. I'd spent it in my room, and not doing fun things either. It took a bit to get my bearings straight after being cooped up in bed for the previous two days.

Slowly, I padded my way into the living room, where Ana and Ollie were snuggled together on the couch.

"Hey," she said, pushing out of Ollie's embrace. She ran to walk beside me as if I'd fall.

I wasn't that weak. "I'm not even dizzy."

"So good to hear it." Still, she kept an arm around me as I guided my way to the sofa chair and Ollie wiggled in his seat. "What's on?"

"Reruns." A faint pink tinged her already rosy cheeks.

I stared at the tv. Indeed, it was reruns - of a show from the late 70s. No way were they watching that, Ana only liked reality shows, or had until her trip down under. The lowered volume indicated I had interrupted a make-out session.

"Sorry for... well, you know."

135

Ollie avoided eye contact with me. "All good, matey."

Ana squished herself into Ollie. "It's just nice to see you up and about."

"So much for throwing you a welcome home party. Everything went downhill." I had tinkered with the idea of having a few friends over to celebrate but the plans changed. Maybe in a week or two.

"Actually, it was nice." She snuggled her back into Ollie's chest and pulled a blanket over her lap. "Gave me time to adjust to the time and the cold. I miss the heat."

I laughed. Ana and I had that in common, the cold always got to us. The difference was she was moving to a place where a cold day was our warm spring day. "Have you settled on a date?"

"For our wedding?" Ana choked out.

"Well, that, and a moving date?"

"Not until the start of summer at least. We discussed it, and I want to be here when the baby is born." Her eyes fell to my stomach. "How's that going?"

I shrugged one shoulder. Late last night I managed to get some reading done about fevers and pregnancy. However, my fever broke as quickly as it came on, so I didn't worry too much about it.

"Since it's not an emergency and everything non-essential seems to be closed for the holidays, I'll just wait until my doctor's appointment next week. I'll find out then, but I assume nothing's changed. I've been eating, now that I can keep food down again, and drinking lots. I'm just waiting for my energy level to come up."

I'd been awake for a couple of hours this morning and made another call into work taking yet another day off. Being paid hourly and working for tips, my income took a hit with every day off. I needed to work and save my money for the future, but I couldn't give my illness to anyone else. I'd already shared it with Ana's mom.

"How's your mom doing, by the way?"

"Marginally better. Dad's sick too, so it's even worse for mom. She's trying to get herself better and she should be resting, but dad turned into a big baby and whimpers all the time." She rolled her eyes. "I've been told to stay away."

"Probably best that you do." I pulled a blanket off the back of the couch. "Where's James?"

"At work, I assume." Ana cracked a grin and looked back up into Ollie's face before focusing back on me. "He's so sweet."

My energy level was high enough to let a snort out. "You'd know better than I."

"How? Whenever he's been here, he's been in your room with you. He even brings himself food to eat so he's not eating from the meager food supply here."

"Yeah, sorry about that." I had meant to do a big shopping trip, but it failed to happen. I blamed the lack of hunger.

"S'all good. Ollie and I ran out and picked up a few things. Stopped by Chang's too."

"I'm sure he missed you."

"He sent me back with a small package for you." She pointed to the table.

I knew that bag. It was a bag of Swiss Cocoa Creams, the kind that only had three inside the small foil-wrapped bag—just enough for Day Ones; those nasty first days of my period. "Aw, that's sweet."

Maybe when I felt up to eating something decadent, I'd indulge. Until then, they could sit on the table.

"Anyways," Ana sang out, breaking my attention away from the bag. "Back to James."

I flipped my gaze between her and Ollie. "What do you want to know?"

"Are you dating?"

I tipped my head to the side. "No, why?"

"Because he's here often enough. He brought you home all sick and stuff."

It really should've been Robin as I was with him on a non-date. However, any guy that hung around as I puked my guts out, well that showed something. "Maybe."

"Maybe what? Girl, you need to stop holding yourself back and give in already."

But what would I be giving in to exactly? A short-lived romance with my baby's daddy? Why did that already spell disaster? There'd be no way I was intellectual enough for someone who was in the process of gaining a very advanced degree, where I only held an advanced high school diploma. Sure, there was a physical chemistry between us, but it didn't matter that he looked amazing and always smelled so good, and that our child would likely be gorgeous, there had to be more there. But I didn't know exactly what the *more* needed to be.

"Give it a shot, Jo-Jo. Nothing ventured, nothing gained. If it doesn't work out, then you're right where you were a few days ago. But if it does..." A sparkle formed in her eyes as she glanced from me back to Ollie. "You'll never know if you don't take the chance. Love is the greatest risk with the biggest payoff."

Watching Ana and Ollie make googly eyes at each other was awesome. I loved seeing her so completely happy. She didn't go to Australia looking for love. She went for a break from here after receiving her teaching degree, to search out adventure. Everything she wanted to do, and all the places she dreamed of visiting, she set out to see. And somewhere along the way, love found her.

How people fell in love was amazing. My parents, who had been together for thirty years, were still madly in love with each other. And they met on a blind date. Mr. and Mrs. Shapiro were also crazy in love. I didn't know how they met, but it had been twenty-five years at least. Jeremy and Narina had found true love by being in the right place at the wrong time. Narina had brought her car to the dealership for a fixing, but messed up her scheduled time, arriving an hour later. Had she arrived on time they may never have met. Even CeCe and Victor. Victor worked at a local radio station, in charge of promotions. CeCe won a prize and went to pick it up. Turns out she picked up a future husband along with her concert tickets. And my boss and former co-worker, Audrina, found love when she hired Chad to make some renovations on her house, and he fixed what was broken inside her.

Everyone I knew had a great love story, something incredible to share with people who asked how they met. My story would be how I had a drunken one-night stand and months later ran into the father. No great flicker of romance there. More like a roping in. Maybe I wasn't destined for a magical story.

Feeling a little shame and self-pity, I reached for the remote. "May I?"

Ana and Ollie nodded, and I flipped through the channels until I found something worth watching; a re-run of last season's *The Bachelor*.

Go Nick.

Secretly, I wanted the red rose.

My phone rang after I managed to eat a slice of toast topped with peanut butter and banana slices. I answered the unfamiliar number. "Hello?"

"Hey, you're awake."

I'd know that sultry voice anywhere. *James.* "Hey." A flutter settled in my core as a wave of euphoria blanketed me. "How'd you get my number?"

"Ana."

Naturally. The silly girl had aimed her Cupid's bow in my and James's direction.

"How are you feeling?"

"Better. I'm up and have been for a few hours. I've eaten too." My stomach rolled with the mention of food, but I hoped it was because it was digesting and not planning another revolt.

"That's super. Can I come by and hang out? Would be nice to visit with you while you're not sleeping."

How much sleeping had he watched? "Sure."

"Great. I'll be there in thirty minutes."

We hung up, and I pushed myself out of the chair I'd made my new temporary home. Zipping down the hall, I hopped into the shower for the world's quickest scrub down, taking off a couple days worth of sickies. It felt good to feel fresh, and I even applied a tinge of makeup just to cover up the pallor.

The towel wrapped around me fell to the floor as I brushed my teeth, and I took a long hard stare at my tummy. And it stared back at me. The tiniest little protrusion was just sneaking above my pelvis. It wasn't there a couple of days ago. The area between my hip bones was taunt and flat. I'd prided myself on that. But all the same, there it was.

I re-wrapped myself in the towel and left the bathroom. Every woman carried differently, depending on her frame and her genetics. Apparently, I was destined to be one of those who would be huge by time I was six months along and people would be asking when I was due, and I'd have to explain I still had another three months to go. I was going to be a house.

But I had nothing to go on. I had no idea how my mother carried me. Did she expand beyond her pelvis early? Was I an easy pregnancy? Was her labour with me hard and difficult? All I knew was that she was a teen mother. Young teen too.

I sighed and flopped down on my bed.

The buzzer rang.

"That's for you," Ana called out, her voice singing down the hall.

I buzzed James in and unlocked the door. At this point, it was unnecessary to change into jeans and a t-shirt. He'd seen me at my worst, so a clean nightshirt and clean panties were a huge improvement. Plus, they were comfortable, and I needed to be comfy.

A soft knock against the door, and I opened it.

James, ever the handsome one, stood there with a bag in one hand and the other behind his back. He passed me the heavy bag. "Supper, I figured you could stand to eat something."

"Thanks," I said, unable to keep the smile off my face.

"And this is for you." From behind his back, he produced a single rose, in the most beautiful shade of red. The head was closed, but the petals were close to blooming; the edges were on the cusp of curling outward.

"It's gorgeous, thanks."

"It doesn't even compare to you." He leaned in close and whispered in my ear. "I'm trying my best to take things slow, but damn woman, you are so beautiful you're making it hard."

With that, my cheeks tinged to match the rose. I waved him in, and set about finding a container to hold the flower in. Vases were in short supply in my apartment.

"Hey, matey," Ollie said.

Ana waltzed into the kitchen. "We're going to go out dancing and leave you alone." She arched her brows as she gave me a quick peck on the cheek.

"Have fun," I said, wiggling my fingers at her in a child-like wave.

"Don't wait up." She giggled. "Bye, James."

"Ana," he said to her back as she and Ollie closed the door behind them.

"When did you eat last?" James asked, lifting the bag.

"About an hour ago?" It was an educated guess. I hadn't really noticed the time when I dropped the toast into the toaster.

"For later then," he said and stuck the bag into the fridge.

"Did you eat?"

"Yeah, had a supper break around seven." A hint of aftershave wafted through the air, tantalising my thoughts.

Trying to ignore the feelings springing up inside me from the close proximity, I found a tall skinny water bottle and placed the rose inside to hold it up high and proud. "Thank you for the flower. It's really nice."

He leaned against the counter, his hands supporting him. "I'm so glad you're doing better."

"Me too. I may even be able to go back to work tomorrow. For a short shift."

James tucked a strand of my hair behind my ear. "Just don't push yourself too hard."

"Hard not to," I whispered. "So, do you want to watch a movie?"

"Whatever you want. I'm just happy you're on your feet again."

I looked down and wiggled my toes. "Indeed, I am on them once again."

He snickered. "You're funny."

"A total riot. You just wait until I'm 100% better. I'll have better comebacks." It was hard to breathe being so close to him. I pushed past him, hoping he'd follow. He didn't disappoint.

I curled up on the couch and pulled a blanket over me. "Anything special you'd like to watch?"

"Whatever. I'd even watch a chick flick for you. Because

you're sick." He sent a quick wink in my direction.

I let a small giggle escape. "No chick flicks tonight. I'd prefer something gritty, with drama and science."

"May I?" He reached for the remote. His fingers touched mine, sending a wave of electricity up my arm.

His touch rendered me speechless, and all I could do was nod.

He flipped through the multiple choices on Netflix. "Remember that book suggestion?"

"Yeah." It had been a very interesting read, high on the science, higher on the drama, and just darn exciting to read.

"They made it into a movie, but the book is so much better."

I played along. Ana and I watched the movie in the theatre the weekend it came out, but he was so cute the way he subtly suggested it. "Always are."

"But the movie's pretty great."

The Martian flickered onto the screen.

"Want to?"

I shifted a little to get closer. Heat rolled off him, and I was very cold and needed to stoke my internal fire. "Sure, why not?"

Not quite the same on the small screen as it was on the giant Imax screen.

The idea of re-watching the movie made me drowsy, and sitting next to James, so warm and snuggly, I could cuddle and nap in complete comfort. But James' proximity, his breath against my neck, sent prickles up and down my spine. I knew I'd see another successful rescue from Mars with James' alluring presence this close by. He wrapped his arm around my shoulder and adjusted the blanket, tucking it around my body. It was out of this world.

Chapter Fifteen

The screen flicked off.

"What did you think?" James asked.

I readjusted the blanket as I'd been sitting on the edge of my seat for the latter part of the movie. "It was amazing."

The movie was probably one of the best movies I'd watched in a long time, however, maybe it was because I'd been snuggled up to James for the length of it. There was something nice about being able to lounge around in my jammies with him. He was easy to be with, and everything between us felt natural. I'd never experienced before.

I stood up and stretched. "Bathroom break."

"Good idea. Time to refill drinks." He rose and made his way into the kitchen as I prattled by.

Upon my return to the living room, James had placed a couple bowls of soup, two buttered buns and two mugs of tea on the coffee table, which he'd pulled away from the couch. The lights were low and classical music played in the background.

"A carpet picnic," he said.

144

I took a seat on the floor, on one side of the table, and James took the other. "I can't say I've ever had one of these before."

"Are you referring to the store-bought food?" He laughed.

"No, just having a picnic in my own living room. It's so…" I couldn't find the right word. *Magical? Romantic?*

"If I had candles, I would've lit them."

"I do." I pushed myself up and dug through the drawer under the tv. All I'd found were four tealights.

"That'll do." James retrieved a lighter from his pocket, set the candles aglow, and turned off the kitchen light.

I stared at the red lighter wondering if he carried it because he was a smoker, which would be odd as I've never smelled even a hint of cigarette smoke. The thought disgusted me.

However, my curiosity waned as my living room, even with the tiny candles, was bathed in the soft, romantic flicker of candlelight dancing across the walls.

He sat beside me, inching closer and lifting his spoon. "Mmm… perfect."

As I gazed upon him, I couldn't agree more. Watching the spoon slide into his mouth and his lips seal around it. Oh my gawd, it lit me up.

"Eat," he prodded, and pushed my bowl closer.

But I wasn't hungry, at least not for food. Maybe it was instinct or something else, but I was looking at James with fresh eyes. Eyes hungry for him to feed my soul, to fill me. Perhaps Ana was right. It was time to give him a chance. But I needed clarity on a few things first.

"I wanted to ask…" I pushed my bangs off my face and fallen pieces from my haphazard knot over my shoulder. "The other night, when you were at Reddy's with that woman…, who was she?"

"You're not jealous, are you?"

145

"No," I fired off instantly. "I feel bad you ditched her to drive me home."

"She was staying at the hotel."

"Oh?" Was she another notch for his bed post?

He took a quick drink and set his mug down. "She's my sister."

I'm the world's biggest idiot. Why did my mind instantly go there? What was wrong with me? He's been nothing but kind, and here I was, thinking the worst.

"She flew home with me, and since her flight out the next morning was early as she currently lives in Europe, she didn't want to chance waking me up."

"But you weren't even there."

"Originally, that was the plan." That dark eyebrow of his rose and a sweet little smirk crossed his face.

"So, you're okay with plans changing?"

A quizzical look crossed his face. "Sometimes, yes."

"Good to know." I had a few spoons full of soup. "Thank you, by the way, for taking care of me that night."

"No problem. Your friend seemed to know me. He addressed me by name."

"He what?" I choked on a swallow of chicken noodle. Coughing a bit, I managed to clear my throat and breath a little deeper.

"You okay?"

I nodded and took a sharp inhale of air and coughed again. Clutching my tummy, I caught my breath. "I'm fine. You were saying?"

"Oh yeah, your friend. Nice guy."

Was he being sarcastic? "Why what did he say?"

"After your second run to the washroom, he asked how well I knew you, to which I replied a little bit. After a weird giggle, he launched into a quick story of how your car was back at your work and so was his, and would I mind giving you a ride?"

"And you took it upon yourself to give me a ride to my apartment?"

A grimace forced the removal of his smile. "Once you threw up into the bag, I thought it best I did. You were in no shape to operate a motor vehicle. And once we got here, well, I couldn't just leave you, even though you begged me to let you sleep on the bathroom floor." His smile returned, although I didn't understand why. It couldn't have been a pleasant memory in the least.

"Well, James, you are a very sweet man." I cleared my throat of residual soup.

"I'm trying my best to respect your boundaries."

What boundaries? I didn't remember a hard and fast outline, just that we should take it slow.

Oh. That. I took a bite of bun, and a smear of butter touched my cheek.

James extended his hand, and his finger gently wiped it off.

"Thanks," I whispered, worried anything louder would ruin this moment.

He inched even closer. "I want to kiss you, but after the last time... I'm afraid you'd shoot me down. Maybe it's better if you finish eating."

"I'm not even hungry, so feel free to..."

As if I were a delicate rose, his right hand cupped my cheek, the heat from his palm warming it on contact. I closed my eyes, and lips as soft as velvet tickled against mine. A low, instinctive groan rumbled inside me. His other hand touched and held my other cheek, and he pressed with more urgency.

A throaty sound emitted from him. "Oh, Josephine."

Never in my life had my name been pronounced with such lust and sexiness.

I threaded my hands through his thick, dark hair, pulling him as close as I could in the physical sense. His tongue danced with mine and his hands moved through my hair, finding the messy up-do I'd been sporting, and untangling it with ease.

"You're much prettier with it down," he said, pushing it off my shoulders.

I scooted into his lap, straddling him, and hooked my ankles together. My firm but tiny and oh so achy breasts pressed into his chest, his rapid heartbeat pounding fervently against them. I inhaled his scent around his neck, kissing his fleshy earlobes while my fingers tangled into his hair.

His hands wrapped around me, sliding down my back and pulling my bottom close enough I felt *it* strong like an ox as it pushed against the fabric of his pants. His low, raw groans caused heat to pool in my panties and a flush of sexual excitement to ripple over me.

"Are you cold?" he asked, his voice barely whisper loud.

I pulled back to look him in the eyes, and I shook my head. Words escaped me, so I pressed my lips to his.

He lifted me and lowered me onto his hips, the bulge firm as it pressed against my thigh. "I could kiss you all night long."

"Aren't you afraid to catch my illness?"

"Too late now." He brushed my hair. "Gawd, you are so beautiful."

"As are you."

The glow from the candlelight bathed his features, turning his golden skin into one there was no colour for. Like a cross between milky coffee and wet sand mixed together with caramels. It was heavenly. It was James. And it was perfect.

His hands slowly caressed from my neck down to the small of my back, and he pulled the edge of my nightshirt up and over my shoulder. The cool air a contrast to his hands, his fingers slid down my electrified skin. They waltzed over the top of the cotton panties, touching and intensifying the sensations on my bare back.

I thought I'd explode right there, and I worried James may have too as he shuddered. I pulled my shoulders in and covered my breasts with my arms as his warm, tender fingers searched out the delicate and highly sensitive skin.

"Is it too fast?" His eyes pleaded.

I knew if I said no, he'd stop, but I had no intention of stopping. I had a fire burning inside me and there was only way one to put it out. I simply shook my head.

My night shirt pulled up and over my head, covering my breasts with the fabric. Slowly, I slipped each arm out, making sure to not expose myself. I had no bra on, and with my nightshirt crumpled on the floor beside me, the only article of clothing I wore were the flimsy panties I was soaking.

"You don't need to be shy with me." His soft words whispered into my ears, the syllables tickling me.

I wrapped my arms around him, flattening my breasts with the pressure, and kissed the side of his neck, licking my way up to his ear again. I took the fleshy part of his lobe and pulled it into my mouth, flicking it with the tip of my tongue and nibbling on it.

"You're going to undo my last vestiges of restraint, woman."

That was my plan. While I deftly worked his left ear lobe, my other hand found his right and massaged.

He groaned in my ear and bucked underneath me. His lips found mine and firm hands pulled me closer still.

"I want you," he breathed out, his hand moving down my back and under my behind. Expertly, he pulled the elastic on my panties aside, and slipped his hand under. "I think you want me too."

The mere touch of his fingers against the warmest part of me roared my fire to life. My head tipped back, the ends of my hairs skimming across the small of my back. "Oh, James," I panted as he dipped a finger inside of me.

Extracting his finger, he placed it in his mouth and sucked. "Just like I remembered."

Heat and lust filled his eyes, and he kissed me once again. With his hands firmly on my hips, he rubbed against me, touching me in all the right ways. I didn't think it was possible to feel so close to going over the edge like this.

"Not yet," he whispered.

His hands caressed along the length of my arms and found my hands, bringing them to my sides, exposing my breasts to the air as he did. My nipples peaked as his eyes greedily took me in.

"Good Lord, woman, you are perfection."

Gentle fingers slowly circled and fingered my tender and achy breasts as his head lowered. The heat from his mouth was the most amazing sensation I'd felt yet, and I knew we were far from finished. His tongue flicked while his mouth sucked almost as if everything I'd performed on his lobes he was replaying on my nipples. No wonder he groaned. I groaned too, heat and dampness flooding between my legs.

Naked from the waist up, I'd never felt more beautiful and more alive. He treated me like a sensual flower, gently coaxing me open. And I gave him free rein to do so, relishing the feel of his fingers on my sizzling skin. But I needed him. Needed to feel him inside me.

I unbuttoned his shirt, my fingers working quickly to free his chest from the fabric and to take him in, in all his glory. He did not disappoint as I pushed his shirt off his taut arms and stared at perfection. I wanted to lick his nipples and run my hands over his chest, taking in every inch. Instead, my hands unbuckled his belt, struggling with the fastener.

"Allow me," he said, the moment of passion temporarily

put on pause while he crawled out from under me and unzipped. He rose on his knees, and I practically ripped his pants and underwear off him. "Easy there. I still need to wear those home."

My hands fought to move slowly, and I savoured the feel of his tight behind as I pushed his green underwear over two perfectly sculpted cheeks. "Oh my gawd," I whispered, cupping them.

His hands stroked my breasts before circling their way lower to my core. His hand slipped between the fabric and my skin, over the most feminine part of me, and back into the deepest part.

"James," I breathed, trying to undress him while intense sensations swam around me, heating me up and threatening to split me in half.

His mouth found mine again, and our tongues danced. One arm of his pulled me close, and the other worked me into a frenzy. It was hard to stay on my knees as my legs felt like spaghetti. I wrapped a free arm around him while my other worked at pushing his underwear off to free the beast.

The crest of the wave slammed into me.

"James," I panted, feeling the wave push me higher and higher. I gripped him tighter and buried my mouth into his neck, sucking and nibbling to help relieve the building pressure.

His fingers were everywhere, inside and outside, rubbing and stroking and pushing and touching. His manliness pressed into my leg as my body turned to give him better access.

The wave pushed me to the stratosphere and all around me, the edges darkened.

His magical hand moved, tugging my panties aside, and the most male part of him touched against my highly-charged and sensitive skin. I gripped tighter, digging my nails into his muscular shoulder blades as my legs gave out beneath me.

He cradled me and rolled onto his back, holding me close as *it* moved and pulsed between my legs, creating the most earth-shattering orgasm I've ever had.

Unable to properly breathe, I stuttered out, "Your turn."

He fumbled beside me, rooting through his pocket. A moment later, a long moment later, he was sheathed and ready to enter me. Still on his back, I straddled his hips, my panties still on, but exposing me. It was a dirty type of fun feeling. I had full control as I rose and slid over top, sliding down the length of him until he was fully enveloped, and we had become one. Hands cupped my breasts, and I braced myself on his shoulders, his dark brown eyes staring up at me making me feel as beautiful as he claimed.

"Damn, Josephine."

I tipped my head forward, my loose hair acting like a curtain to cover myself.

"No, back. I want it to tickle my legs." He brushed the sides of his hands up and over my shoulder.

I closed my eyes and stretched out my neck as my hair fell backwards. I moved my hands to brace myself against his firm thighs and his hands trailed down my chest and over the tiny swell of my belly, touching the fire between my legs. I was desperate for air once again as his two thumbs expertly rubbed my nub, while I rocked up and down his shaft. The pressure was so intense, I found myself riding another giant crest of orgasm, and I pumped harder in response.

"James... don't... stop..." I said with each bounce until he did.

He squeezed my hips and bucked hard; once, twice, three times. He shuddered between my thighs. If that last thrust hadn't felt so good, I'd have worried he'd torn me in half.

"Let me finish you off," he said breathless.

I shook my head. "I can't hold myself up anymore."

He curled and pushed me onto my back, moving his head between my breasts. Each nipple got a flick, and kisses trailed down my belly, until he reached my core.

It was nearly instant. The heat of his tongue lapped against me, sinking deep into places no man had dared kissed before. My thighs pressed against his cheeks as another orgasm rocked my world. "Oh, James…"

A sense of satisfaction filled my soul. I pulled him up to face me and kissed him fiercely, tasting me on his lips. It was sweet and different.

"How was that?" He breathed out and propped himself up on an arm.

"Ah-mazing. And for you?"

"Out of this world." He rolled onto his back, the tiny space between the tv stand and the coffee table suddenly filled with our two bodies.

I snuggled into him and he pulled me close, my nearly naked body, sweaty and sexy, stretched out along the length of him. I breathed him in, trying to slow down the rapid pounding of my heart. "Was that… like how it was… that night of the wedding?" I searched his eyes for the truth.

"No," he whispered. "Tonight, was even better."

I woke to the smell of bacon cooking in my apartment.

When did we get that?

My feet hit the carpet as my tummy growled. The greasy smell was heavenly, and I followed my nose into the kitchen.

James pulled out a baking sheet and set it on the stove top. He flipped over the pieces of bacon and peppered them up.

"Smells good," I said.

He jumped a little. "Good morning."

"What are you doing?"

"Making breakfast. I know my cooking skills are bad, but I

thought that was obvious." He winked and smiled, resuming his flip and pepper.

"I gathered you were cooking, but why?"

"Just because." He reloaded the pan into the oven. "Everyone should have someone make them breakfast at least once."

"That's sweet."

He seemed pretty comfortable in my kitchen and knew where everything was stored. Guess he had made himself at home during my illness. "How do you like them?" A carton of eggs shook in his hand. "I don't know you well enough yet to assume completely."

I stared, my head tipping to the left.

"Oh, you don't know that rule? Maybe it's a guy thing."

My back touched the wall. "What rule?"

"That you can tell a lot by a woman based on if she keeps eggs in her fridge and most importantly, how she likes her eggs."

Surprise coloured my expression, and I crossed my arms over my chest. "This should be good."

"You see, if a lady keeps eggs in her fridge, it means that she wants her date to stay overnight."

"Or that she just likes eggs." Because I certainly had not gone shopping in recent days to get them. They were just always there.

He put his hand up. "Or... it could mean that it's an invitation to get to know her better by finding out how she likes her eggs, which is highly indicative of her personality."

"Been reading a lot of *For Dummies* books, have you?" It was the most bizarre thing I've ever heard of, and I'd heard lots.

"No, but I'll prove it's correct."

"How?"

He stared at the carton of eggs. "Based on what I know of

you, I'd say you are a single egg eater, if done the right way."

"And that would be?"

As if I were a final test, he studied me. "If you ate scrambled eggs, you'd have two eggs. But... if you had an egg sunny-side up, it would just be one." A hopeful look jumped onto his face.

I nodded, not wanting to let him think he was maybe onto to something. It was a bit of a stretch, but still. "So, am I a crazy scrambled kind of person, or one who looks at the sunny-side of things?"

He pointed a finger in my direction. "That's what I can't figure out." The distance between us became unbearably constricting. "I think you are mostly sunny-side up, but something in here," he touched my chest beneath my collar bone, "is a little scrambled."

I swallowed and stepped back.

"I'm right, aren't I? The egg theory is never wrong." A Grand Canyon sized grin split his face in half as he cracked a couple of eggs into the frying pan. "So, what has you unable to sort out your thoughts?"

He knows.

~Chapter Sixteen

I smiled at James and took my place at the table. Wanting to rid the air of the elephant hanging in the room, I asked, "Where are Ana and Ollie?"

"She left you a note." He pointed at the centrepiece on the table.

A note? Refocusing my gaze from the hot man making my breakfast, to the bowl of fruit I spotted the folded piece of paper and read it. "She went job hunting?" It was barely nine am. "What day is it?"

"It's Tuesday."

"Tuesday?"

"Yeah, Tuesday January the second."

My hand clamped to my forehead. Holy smokes. It had been four days since I was last at work. And I needed to pay bills and check my balance in the bank account and set leftover money aside for the baby. My credit card payment will be late if I didn't get my act together and stop shirking my responsibilities.

I stared at the man making himself at home in my kitchen.

He'd blended in so seamlessly, with so little effort on his part despite my reservations. It was like he'd always been there, but he hadn't been. Unless you counted his growing seed within my belly, then maybe. *Maybe I should tell him the news before things get serious?*

I cleared my throat and covertly placed my hand atop my belly. "Does the egg theory work on men?"

He laughed; a sweet yet deep throaty laugh. "Nope. We invented it."

"So what kind of theory exists for women to uncover the hidden truths about a man?"

"Thought that was called women's intuition?"

"I don't have much of that." My gaze faltered.

It was true. I second guessed everything, and my first thoughts were typically incorrect. Any of my previous boyfriends would attest to that I was sure.

He put a plate of scrambled eggs with three slices of bacon and two slices of toast in front of me. "I'm sure your intuition is high enough. You've let me into your home, and maybe into your heart."

"The heart part I guard pretty well."

"Touché."

"But I'm still interested in knowing all about you. To figure things out."

"Like whether or not we should be a couple?"

My heart did a double beat. I hadn't thought about us being a couple, not really anyway. I wasn't sure what was going on between us, and what would become of us, but I really did enjoy his company. But our relationship status was a question mark at best. I shrugged to his question with a smug look on my face.

"I don't want to risk anything that's not fully ready to be explored. There's still so much about you I don't know."

He gave me a cynical look. "Tell you what," he sat beside me with his own plate of food. "You ask me any question you want, as long…" He waved a fork in my direction. "As long as I get to ask you the same question. And you only get ten questions."

"Oooh. This could be tricky." And lots of fun.

"Exactly. By your questions, I may find a way to sneak into your heart."

I stabbed a forkful of scrambled eggs and took a bite. They were spicy, with pepper sprinkled in them, but it was a delightful flavour.

What question could I ask, that he would ask in return, which wouldn't give away anything too personal and yet, let me know lots about him?

I stabbed another forkful. "Favourite colour."

"Seriously? You're using up one of your questions for that?"

I nodded and nibbled on my toast. "Colour?"

"Green. You?"

Hmm. I could see him as a green. Fresh and natural like. "Mine's yellow."

"Doesn't surprise me." With the edge of his fork, he cut off the white of the egg and slipped it onto his toast. Gross.

"How often do you talk to your parents?" I wondered how in touch he was with them. A man who kept in close contact was a good man, I suspected. But then again, I had been wrong before.

"Every two days at least." He answered without hesitation. "You?"

"Not as frequently as mom would like, but it's hard."

Dad and I were still having disagreements on my future plans, on the baby and whether or not I'd ever introduce the father to my father. Ha-ha. Not likely. Dad would chew him up. It was enough he was mad at me. Besides, I still needed to find the courage

158

to tell James the big news.

"My dad's retired and home more often, so I don't phone home as much. We're disagreeing on many different things these days."

"Like what?"

"Are you going to use that as one of your questions?" I raised my eyebrow and took another forkful of food. "Since it's not a question I think you can answer, best to skip it for now."

Besides, one of my questions was going to be what he thought of kids, so depending on how he'd answer, I wasn't in the mood to talk about how Dad and I thought the whole situation should be resolved. He wanted me to be married before my child was born.

James broke the yolk, and yellow goo spread over his plate. I watched in horror as he mopped it up with the soft part of his toast.

I pushed my plate away.

A curious expression filled his face. "Thought you liked a sunny-side up egg?"

"I did. But the yolk was always cooked." And raw egg was a huge no-go in pregnancy.

He laughed. "That's over hard."

"Whatever." I never ordered eggs in a restaurant, so I supposed it didn't matter. I cooked them at home, and always punctured the yolk while still in the pan.

The remainder of his egg disappeared. Deciding I was still hungry, I pulled my plate back and nibbled on the toast. For some reason, it was very tasty, even though it appeared like regular bread.

"Back to the questions. You have eight left."

"Alright, eight." I tried to figure out the most important question to ask. "Hmm... okay. Got one. Previous lovers. How many?" It was important to note how much of a player he was. Somewhere I'd heard the golden rule was whatever the answer was, multiple it by three for a lady, and divide by three for a guy.

His eye narrowed as he thought about it. It took a bit for the answer to roll out his mouth and I was worried the number was in fact higher than I expected. "Including you? Thirteen."

Thirteen divided by three was four and a bit. That seemed low. Unbelievably low. James was supremely good-looking. That number had to have been higher.

"Really?"

"How much of a hound dog do you think I am?" His face pulled back like I'd slapped him, however it disappeared just as quickly. After a brief pause, he asked, "Your number?"

Well, there hadn't truly been that many as most of my relationships were long term. There was Noah in high school, until graduation. Then a fling with Jed for a couple of months. Alex followed after, and we were quite serious until his career took him across country and I stayed here. Gerald was a hot Italian guy rebound guy from down the hall, and surprisingly that relationship lasted for eight months until I called it quits. I suffered through a really nasty dry spell for a year until Crystal's wedding, and then there was Jagger.

"Umm… Five." I tapped out on my fingers with each name. "Six, including you."

"So, fifteen?"

"What? No."

"Rule of Three."

"I swear to God it was only five." Beyond horrified to think it had even been that many.

"I'm just kidding." He winked but it did nothing to put me at ease. "I got one for you. What was the best part of those previous relationships?"

My eyes widened and my lips pursed together in deep thought. "I'd have to say…" What? What's the best answer? Each guy had a unique personality which made them better than the guy before. "Hmmm…." I thought long and hard. "I guess it would be that we started out as friends."

"Are you still in touch?"

"Is that one of your questions?"

"Yes," he said, and pushed his empty plate to the side.

I slowly chewed an end of the bacon strip. "No, I'm not."

Breakups never ended well. Names were called, things were thrown, precious trinkets given to the other broken. Yeah, friendship didn't exist after that.

"Interesting." He stroked his chin in a long downward pull.

"Not nearly as interesting as your answer."

"Yes. I am still good friends with two of them."

That bothered me, but I didn't fully understand why. Could it be that he would move beyond the friendzone with them once again, if his needs weren't being met? Was he comfortable with that? How close were they? Had he shared with those two girls about me? I shuddered at the thought.

"You're quiet. Does it bother you?"

"Yeah, a little."

He wrapped his warm hand around mine. "They're both in relationships with other guys if it makes you feel any better."

It didn't, and I retracted my hand to grab another bit of bacon. I was running out of questions. "Did you ever think about marrying any of them?"

In a heartbeat, his demeanour changed, and his focus moved away from me as he shifted uncomfortably in his seat. Clearly, he had.

"When?"

"A year ago."

I swallowed and asked the question I wouldn't think I'd have answered if asked. "What happened?"

"I proposed. She said no. She didn't see us having much of a future together. Figured it would be more fun if she started dating her prof. Sylvia married in October."

The pieces were clicking into place. "Thanksgiving weekend?"

"Yes." He hung his head. "I'm not proud about it, but I needed to go to her wedding, on the sly. I needed to see if it was really true love."

My heart ached imagining him looking on as his first love married another. I couldn't even begin to think how that would feel.

"Turns out it was a shotgun wedding."

I softly closed my eyes. "Oh dear."

"Yeah. Heard from mutual friends. Nice, eh?" He shook his head and appeared like he was on the verge of tears.

I covered his hand with my own. "I'm so sorry. For it all."

"Thanks." He gazed into my eyes. "I didn't mean to crash your friend's wedding. But I needed an outlet, and dancing with everyone seemed like a good plan."

Blood pulsed in my veins like a pounding river. "Are you more upset that she left, or more upset that she left and started a new future so soon after your breakup?"

"You mean the children part?"

I nodded.

"That really surprised me, but only because she and I were on the same page with having kids. I don't know what changed her mind though."

"You don't want children?" I heard the recoil in my own voice.

"There's no shame in not wanting to procreate."

I covered my tracks as well as I could. "You're right. Not everyone wants kids."

"Nope. Some do, and power to them. I, however, am not

that person. I want to travel and see the world, and be free to take off on a moment's notice and not be tied to a child's schedule. My sister says I'm completely selfish, but I don't want to be responsible for another human and I don't want to add to the over population of Earth."

I nodded as my heart fractured, piece by piece, piling up in the space where my full heart used to be. My composure was held together by a very thin string, and I worried I wouldn't make it through the rest of the day. Bile rose in the back of my throat, and I swallowed it down.

Guess this thing brewing between us would be short-lived, like a fling. "Fair enough. The Earth is very populated."

Didn't matter that I was adding to it, purely by accident, but the truth laid itself bare on the table. My future with James was on borrowed time. Very borrowed. Once he knew the secret, it was over. Completely and forever. The future had sliced open my heart.

# # #

"It's been three weeks and you haven't told him yet? What's a matter with you?" Ana said, her voice pitching high enough for the neighbours to hear.

"Settle down."

I dropped the stack of brown construction paper cut-outs on the table. It was Saturday and I'd been roped into helping Ana cut out teddy bear masks for her temporary teaching position. She'd accepted a maternity leave position until the end of June and was trying to sweeten up the grade one students she was responsible for with a teddy bear picnic on Monday.

Ana's scissors clipped at a rapid pace as she cut around the outside part of the mask. "You need to tell him. I'm sure he can see it anyways. How are you getting away with that?" Her eyes settled on my midsection.

I shrugged. "I'm finally putting some weight on?"

That was the truth. My eating had picked up, which seemed to please everyone from my parents to Ollie to Ana and James.

"But we also keep the lights low. More romantic that way."

Every time we did the deed—because I needed to make sure I got enough of him that when we split, I'll have enough to last the rest of my life—we only used candles. It made my skin look healthier, not the pale shade of permanent winter. I kept a nice stock of candles on the ready and kept Chang's in business as it made him happy I was buying from him again.

"When do you plan on telling him? The first time he feels the baby kick?" Her perfect little eyebrow rose with her snooty tone.

I was going to have to cut him loose soon, despite the fun I was having. He wasn't interested in children, ever, and my belly wasn't as flat as it was. The weight gain wouldn't defend me much longer. The secret was going to reveal itself before I could say anything.

"This is only a temporary thing." Maybe after Valentine's Day I'd let go? I did a quick count on my fingers. Probably not. I'd for sure be pregnant looking as I'd be about twenty weeks. No, like it or not, I was going to have to break my heart and set him free.

"For the record, I think you're nuts for not having told him. He's going to feel so betrayed."

I crashed the scissors onto the table as rage boiled in me faster than ever before. "You know, maybe if everyone would stop telling me how betrayed he's going to be and how I'm going to ruin his life, maybe it would be easier to tell him."

I stood abruptly, and my chair pushed back with too much force, falling to the carpet. Righting it, I stormed to my room, tears streaming down my face. For effect, I slammed my door and threw myself onto my bed.

James desired a child-free future; he'd made that much clear. It was stupid to not have said anything yet, but we were having such a good time with each other, I didn't want that to go away. In my head it made the most sense to make what was going on between us a fling, a temporary situation, but a wonderful one all the same. In due time, he'll learn the truth, but until then... We're having fun. There's been no talk of commitments or futures or of even calling each other boyfriend and girlfriend. He could even be dating someone else for all I cared. Okay, I'd care. I knew I was falling for him. He was the jam to my peanut butter; we just went well together.

Ana knocked on my door. "Can I come in?"

"No. Go away."

The door creaked open, and she walked across the room. "I'm sorry."

"For what? Telling the truth?" I propped myself up and stared.

"No, for bringing it up. You must know what you're doing. I just don't understand, is all."

"I've said it since the beginning. Once he knows the truth, he's going to take off. He's not interested in having children. He told me as much, and I've seen how he reacts to them."

We were out for dinner at a trendy restaurant when a couple allowed their toddler to roam the place. He was so disgusted by the situation, it nearly ruined our night. Yeah, I wasn't pleased when the toddler waddled up to our table, but I didn't recoil when he tried climbing onto the chair beside James. But when the parents arrived laughing and saying how cute their son was and how he just loved visiting new people? Well, James wasn't the sweetest guy and told the parents that we weren't at a nice place to be harassed by children and they should be more respectful of other patrons as not everyone wanted a visit with their delightful child.

As much as I agreed that a higher end place wasn't a McDonald's, I was also embarrassed. Clearly, it wasn't that he didn't want children, he didn't *like* children.

So, it was important to savour this limited time together.

Sympathy crossing her face and she squeezed my hand. "Do you really believe that?" She tapped my chest, just above my heart. "In here?"

I wiped away my tear. "I have to." I shrugged. "This is my journey, and I can't make him a part of it if he doesn't want to be here. I'm prepared to go it on my own."

"Yeah, I know you think that."

"Believe it, because I refuse to be a single mother on welfare. I can, and will, make this work. For me and the baby. James doesn't need to be involved."

Ana's voice lowered. "He maybe doesn't need to be, but he should. And by keeping it from him, you are denying him a chance to accept it and let him make his own decision on how involved or not he wants to be."

Tears fell fast and furious. "I'm protecting my heart."

"Too late for that," she said, opening her arms.

I crawled towards her and hugged her tight, not wanting to let go.

"Maybe I should consider staying here for a while after the baby's born."

"As much as I don't want you to move to the other side of the planet, you need to go and be happy. Your happiness isn't here." I pulled out of the hug. "It's there. You haven't been you since you've come home."

"Well, living with Ollie isn't all it's cracked up to be."

"What?" I smeared my mascara-stained tears across the top of my hand when I wiped it over my eyes.

"He's got nothing to do here. It's driving me crazy." Her

fingers spread far apart as she raised her hands into the air. "He can't get a job, and he follows me around like a lost puppy."

"But the apartment's never been cleaner, and we always have food now, plus he's a pretty decent cook." It was an unexpected perk to Ollie staying with us. But really, what else was the guy going to do?

"He's going home at the end of the month." Ana hung her head. "And I'm looking forward to the break. Does that make me a bad fiancée?"

I rubbed her shoulder. "No. I think it's great you understand your boundaries. How did he take the news?"

She smiled. "I think he was relieved. He'll come back for a visit in March and again in June, if I'm not moving there right away."

"Please don't stay here on my account."

I didn't know how I'd feel if I was the sole reason she put off her move. I wasn't worth anybody rearranging their life for. I was just me. Ana could get a teaching job in Perth, she'd have all the heat and sun she could handle. She could find her happily ever after there.

"You could come with me." Her eyes sparkled at the thought.

"As much as I love the heat and would love to swim in the ocean, I couldn't. My family's here. CeCe's getting married…" I quickly flicked my eyes over to my clock. "Oh, dang it, I'm going to be late. I forgot CeCe and I were going to go wedding dress shopping today. She wants to narrow down a few choices before taking mom." I scurried off the bed and hopped over to the bathroom to freshen up. "Leggings and a long sweater should be fine, right?" I didn't have time to change.

Ana followed me. "Are you picking her up?"

"No, thank goodness. I'm meeting her because she's getting

167

picked up by Narina." I stopped as I bolted past the mirror.

Standing sideways, I took in my full form. Even with the sweater on and sucking in my stomach, there was noticeable bump. I gulped. "Ana?" Terror waved through me. I looked pregnant and it seemed to happen overnight.

Ana wrapped her arm around me and rested her head on my shoulder as we both stared; a sad smile forming on her face. "Times up. He needs to know."

~Chapter Seventeen

ecelia, Narina, and I hung out in the dress shop, the cheapest dress shop I was sure CeCe could find. Hidden in the basement of a tailor shop, there were no chairs for us to sit on, and worse, there was only one tiny dressing room and it couldn't hold a dress, let alone the bride getting into it. All the dresses hung haphazardly on hangers with no rhyme or reason for sizing and not in nice dress bags either. There was concrete as far as the eye could see, aside from the white variations of wedding dresses and the lighting was horrible; a weird blueish glow cast an unhealthy colour over everyone. It was like being stuck in the first *Twilight* movie.

"I don't know what kind of dress I want. Should I go all out foo-foo girlie? Or wear something simple?" CeCe asked, touching dress after dress, having yet to pull anything off and admire it.

Narina piped up, after looking at a few of the price tags. "Go with elegant, you can never go wrong." She winked in my direction. Clearly, she'd heard CeCe's complaints about the cost of everything. And calling something elegant didn't stamp a price on it as fast as foo-foo girlie did. That just sounded princess like.

"I want something like Crystal wore, but I'm not finding anything similar."

I clamped my mouth shut. Crystal was a size two, if she were even that, where CeCe was a little more voluptuous size twelve. They'd never be able to pull off the same dress, if CeCe could even afford it. Crystal's dress alone cost more than the wedding budget my sister had prepared.

"Crystal was very princess," Narina added, rummaging through the racks. She pulled out a couple. "What about these?"

CeCe took one look at each and tossed her head back. "No. No, thank you. I don't want beige."

It was more of a light cream colour than beige, but she hung them up anyways. "White and elegant," Narina mumbled as I stifled a laugh understanding suddenly why the wedding dress shopping process took months.

We flipped through racks and racks of dresses, checking out the entire stock.

"I don't think there's anything here," I said, trying to hide my displeasure.

I was hoping for CeCe's sake, we'd find at least a couple for her to try on. But the utter disorganised mess, and the lack of a salesperson to assist us, was driving me crazy. We'd been in the basement warehouse of a wholesaler for over an hour. I bought the Jeep in less time.

"Why don't we go to Donalda's Bridal." Narina folded her arms across her chest.

She'd given up her search a while back and had devoted her attention to the world wide web hunting for a dress shop catering to brides on a budget.

"They're so expensive," CeCe whined.

"You haven't even checked it out." I raised my eyebrow.

"But I know that place, I've driven past. The storefront looks expensive."

I sighed and tossed my head back a bit. A dull cramp ran across my midsection and I froze. Taking a couple of deep breaths and counting to ten, the pain disappeared, although the speed of my heart increased.

"You okay?" CeCe said, walking over.

I was probably as pale as I was suddenly cold. "Yeah. I just need to sit down." I grabbed my purse. "Since there's no place to sit down here, I'm going to head out to the Jeep. Give me a few minutes and I'll come back."

The entrance was on the floor above us, which felt like a million miles away.

"Yeah, not this one either." CeCe hung up the wedding dress she held in her hands. "I'll come with you. I give up here."

"Thank goodness," said Narina.

The three of us headed up a long, rickety flight of stairs and waved goodbye to the tailor who spoke minimal English. I bundled inside my jacket and stepped out into the wintery air. Maybe leggings weren't a good choice, as my legs froze instantly in the breeze. It was a long, chilly walk back to my vehicle.

I climbed into the driver's seat and caught my breath, rubbing my ungloved hands together hoping to bring some warmth to them. Narina and CeCe climbed into Narina's little boxy car parked ahead of me. The mysterious cramp fired up again, spreading right across my pelvis. I gripped the steering wheel until it passed, counting 'til I reached eight. Thankfully it didn't last as long as the one in the store. My breath fogged my windows since I still hadn't started running the Jeep. A quick crank and the vehicle rumpled to life, and warm air blasted across my cheeks.

My cell chimed with an incoming text.

CeCes willing to try Donaldas. Meet you there in 15?

I typed back an affirmative and drove off after plugging the address into Google maps.

As it turned out, the bridal store happened to be blocks away from James's apartment. He claimed he lived in the better part of the hood, but I knew better. Everything within a seven-block radius of the bridal shop was rough; filled with gangs and drugs and crime. It was one of the reasons I didn't stay over at his place and he walked me to my vehicle every visit. It wasn't the type of neighbourhood you'd feel safe walking the streets late at night.

I parked the Jeep in front of the store and pried my tightened grip off the steering wheel. The weird pain happened twice; once while driving past the ski hill and the other four minutes ago. Thankfully, I breathed through it and kept my focus on the road, but it was intense.

The doors stayed locked, and I scanned the streets around me.

Donalda's Bridal was an independent store, and not part of a nation-wide chain. The exterior was brick and stucco, an odd combination, but the window display held the most beautiful wedding dress imaginable. The kind every little girl dreamed of wearing. A sweeping skirt, a fitted bodice and sparkles everywhere. If I got married and could pick any dress in the world, it would be that one.

An adorable man out walking his dog approached the right side of my vehicle. Surprise, surprise. It was James.

I rolled the passenger window down and smiled. "Hey."

Even dressed in multiple layers with big mittens and a warm-looking toque, he was cover-model handsome.

"Hey, Josephine." The way he said my name warmed me to the core; no need for the heat to be running on full. "What are you doing over here?"

"My sister's wedding dress shopping in there. Or will be

shortly." I hopped out of the Jeep and paused.

Jeepers creepers. Another dull cramp made an appearance.

Maybe I'd done too much today? I didn't think I had. I shook my head and closed the door, pulling my jacket down. Thankfully all the layers I wore kept my secret safe… for now.

"Hey, Samson." I lowered myself to the Sheltie's height and gave him a rub behind the ears. "Who's a good boy?" I said in a silly voice that always rolled out of me when I was around dogs.

Samson responded to my question by giving me a lick.

James cleared his throat. "You going to be here long?"

"I have no idea."

"You work tonight, right?"

"At four." I rose up slowly and stared into James's dark eyes, fighting to keep the rolling pain from reaching my face.

He scrutinised me. "You okay?"

Guess I failed. "Yeah, I think I'm just tired or worked out too hard in dance class."

Zumba had moved to Fridays since the start of the new year. Not an ideal day, but still manageable.

He leaned forward and gave me a kiss, breaking away when a vehicle pulled up behind my jeep. "Your entourage?" He tightened the rein on Samson's leash.

Dang. I hadn't meant for James to meet my family this way. This wasn't part of the plan. I hadn't thought to introduce him at any point. To anyone.

CeCe was the first to run up to me, and asked in a cutesy voice, "Who's this?"

"Cecelia, this is James."

"James, hi." She shook his hand and a huge grin stretched from ear to ear. "He's the–"

"Boyfriend, yes." I scrunched my face, hoping he didn't see. I didn't want to lay an official title on him just yet, but it was better than spilling the beans as this was definitely not the place to announce he was the father of my baby.

"Boyfriend, eh?" he said comically.

I leaned closer to him. "Sorry. I figured calling you my friend seemed weird and wrong."

"I'm not complaining." A twinkle appeared in his dark browns as he smiled at me. "We hadn't really discussed it before, but I like it."

Narina joined us.

"James, this is my brother's girlfriend, Narina."

"Pleasure to meet you." James extended his hand, and she gave it a quick shake, giving him the once over and a silent yet questioning gaze.

Instead of allowing her focus to linger between us, she squatted down and gave Samson a rub behind his ears. "Cute dog."

The dog whimpered and wagged his tail.

"Samson, sit." James gave a gentle tug on the leash.

Three of us surrounded the Sheltie, but CeCe held back, keeping a small distance between her and the dog. She was more of a cat person.

Another cramp crossed over my pelvis and I shuddered, briefly closing my eyes to the pain. One-two-three... I resumed counting when I hit ten. After it passed, I shook violently as I opened my eyes and tried to cover. "Sheesh, it's cold."

I needed to sit down, but not here. There needed to be a touch of distance from James as nothing could slip out if he wasn't around. My eyes lingered on the door and an involuntary shiver ripped through my body.

"You lovely ladies should get inside and shop where it's warm." He put his free hand on my back.

Yes, yes. Let's go.

"Nice to have met you.." CeCe waved and walked away.

"See you around. Bye Samson." Narina followed CeCe into the bridal shop, leaving James and I to ourselves.

I blinked away the intensity. Whatever was going on, it was close to bringing me to tears. I needed to catch my breath.

"After you're done dress shopping, did you want to go for dinner? There's this great new place I've been eager to try."

Samson pushed himself against my leg.

"Hey, boy, easy there," James said, his voice lowering to a whisper.

Jeez, Louise. Another wave gripped my pelvis, and I braced one hand against my Jeep and cradled the other around my belly. My legs weakened beneath me.

"Josephine?"

"CeCe," I called out, my voice cracking. Something wasn't right. I needed to get to the emergency room.

From a distance, the bells above the Donalda's Bridal jingled and James spoke loud enough to hear over the thundering rush of my pounding heartbeat. "Cecelia, you're needed outside. Pronto."

An instinct to curl into James washed over me but I couldn't breathe, let alone move.

CeCe appeared by my side. "Jo, what's wrong?"

Visions from a bad episode of Grey's Anatomy appeared like an unwelcome guest.

"Something's not right." I fought to hold back the pain-filled tears dying to escape. The intensity had ramped up and even breathing through it took effort.

Narina's voice plucked at me in my world of darkness. "What's going on?"

"Is it the baby?" Cecelia's tiny hands touched my bump.

"Baby?" James said, stepping back, reining Samson closer to him.

175

Oh, crap on a cracker.

I winced and bit back the pain lancing itself over my pelvis and through my heart. There wasn't a word to describe the expression on James' face. It was as if a hurricane of emotions blew over him. Confusion and curiosity followed by hurt and pain, but it was the look of betrayal that caused me to tighten my grip on my belly and slam my eyes shut.

"You're pregnant?" His voice broke. There was no bandage for the cut I'd just created.

CeCe whispered, "Oops."

Squeezing my tummy and holding my breath, I hopped into my Jeep and carefully stretched myself out, as sitting felt worse. "Can you drive?" The keys rattled in my hand.

Narina took my dangling keys. "I got it. Ces, hop in."

My forehead rested against the window. There was so much I wanted to say to the man on the sidewalk, his face as pale as a ghost. But first I needed to make sure my bean was okay.

"I'm sorry," I whispered, my breath fogging up the glass and blotting James out of my view.

With that shattered look forever imprinted on my heart, I knew I'd just ruined any chance of a future with him.

~Chapter Eighteen

"Well, aren't I the boy who cried wolf," I told the on-call doctor.

She unhooked the monitors and tugged my hospital gown down. "It happens to the best of us."

"Really?" I pushed myself up on the thin and narrow bed and scooted back.

When the true labour started, I hoped I wouldn't have to deliver on this. An ice-cold floor would be marginally more comfortable.

She sketched down some notes. "You're a little over eighteen weeks along and you could have an irritable uterus, so if you experience this again, I'd have your regular OB look into it. But I think you're just experiencing Braxton-Hicks contractions. Some women feel them, and some don't."

"Can't wait for labour," I deadpanned. If false contractions hurt like this, the real thing was going to do me in. Finally, I understood why most women screamed for pain relief.

The doctor turned and faced me. "You'll be fine. It's all in what you make of it. If you think it's going to be the worst pain imaginable, then it will be. If you believe that it's a day's worth of work with a pretty amazing reward at the end of it, then you're going to be fine."

I sighed and threw my legs over the side of the bed. "Everything's okay?"

"Everything's fine. You're a little dehydrated, which could account for the pain being so noticeable. I advise you to go home, rest and drink lots. Otherwise, we can hook you up to a saline drip."

"I'm good with drinking at home." The clock beyond the curtain showed I still had time to get to work. "It's okay if I work tonight? It's only four or five hours."

I was still playing catch up with my hours and income.

"I'll leave that up to you." Her tone said otherwise.

"What about…" I leaned a little closer to her. "Sex?"

She laughed gently. "You're fine. The cervix is closed up nice and tight."

"Could that have brought on these… what were they called? Braxton?"

"Braxton-Hicks could be brought on by any orgasms as the hormone released during them makes your muscles contract."

The room got really hot as the doctor spoke, tendrils of heat spread over my cheeks and neck.

"The prostaglandins in his semen could also cause contractions."

I felt as if I were nine years old and having the talk with my mother. I wanted to be any place other than where I was. I'd only asked if it were okay to have sex, I didn't want the nitty-gritty details.

Despite my embarrassment, she carried on. "As a general rule, the nipples are super sensitive, and when stimulated, they can also cause the uterine muscles to contract."

My arms instinctively covered my chest. "So, I shouldn't do it anymore?"

There maybe wasn't much chance of it now that James knew, but I could hope. Very strongly hope.

"You should, if you're comfortable. If you feel any contractions, just relax and have a glass of water." She patted me on the shoulder. "Everything looks good and normal. Aside from some minor dehydration, you're good to go."

"Okay," I said. Utter foolishness and naiveté blanketed me.

Was every first-time pregnancy like this? I pulled on my leggings and sweater, grabbed the remainder of my personal effects and walked out from the curtained area to the desk where the nurses buzzed around.

"Where's the waiting room?"

"End of the hall," the nurse closest to me said.

I walked past a curtain which clearly had a lady in labour behind it. Her moans were deep and demonic, and she was begging for drugs. Suddenly I was very afraid I'd never survive labour. My feet stumbled beneath me as I raced beyond the curtain and over to the waiting room.

CeCe and Narina stopped talking the second they spotted me and jumped to greet me.

"Everything okay?" CeCe asked, placing her hand on my belly.

I nodded. "Everything's fine. I need to drink more water." I pinched my lips together.

"You'd better call home." Narina placed her arm around my shoulders. "CeCe called your mom and she's probably called half the city by now."

She rolled her eyes. Narina understood my mother all too well, as mom tended to overreact. It was either because she loved the attention or, and it seemed more logical, she was worried and if

179

she shared her fears, bad news would be easier to handle. I honestly didn't understand her need to share any of my news with family, when I hadn't yet shared it with anyone outside our little family. James included.

Eating crow pie wasn't a favourite past time of mine, but one I was all too familiar with. I needed to explain everything to James. He was too important to me to lose this way.

I pulled out my phone.

James, I'm so sorry. Please call me. Please text back. I need to talk to you.

"Oh, Jo-Jo." My best friend stood by my parking stall and wrapped me in a hug the moment my feet touched the snow-covered asphalt. "Are you okay?"

"It's definitely lessening." I grabbed my purse and checked my phone. No response. Typing frantically, I sent James another text.

Please. I can't do this over message. I need to talk to you in person. There's so much I have to tell you. My thumb pressed the send button, and I waited for the word 'delivered' to appear. I couldn't tell if he read my messages but at least I knew he got them. However, the dull ache deep in my pelvis was nothing compared to the large rift forming in my heart.

Ana led me over to the back door entrance and into the building.

# # #

Pants I'd worn just two days ago, suddenly were very snug. It was amazing how uncomfortably tight the waistband was. How was I going to work feeling like that? I unbuttoned and unzipped my pants. Sweet relief. Sifting through my closet, my skirt was the only other article of black clothing I owned, and black bottoms were a requirement. What to do?

I glanced around my room and spotted a hair-tie.

Yes, that should work!

I looped the elastic through the buttonhole and back over to the button. It kept the pants mostly closed, and my apron would cover the rest. It was more comfortable than doing them up. Guess it was time to purchase maternity clothes, or something with a stretch band waist. The horror.

I walked into the main entrance of Westside as if I were concealing something. My apron tied through the belt loops, but it still felt strange knowing my pants were essentially undone. However, that fear dissipated as the spicy smell of cooking steak churned up my insides and turned me into a raging, hungry momma. Since I'd arrived early, there was time for a quick bite.

"Hey, Trigger," I sweetly asked our chef. "Could you whip me up a half bowl of steak and rice, with the rempa seasoning?"

He nodded.

I avoided everyone and took to the back to tuck my things away and check on my makeshift pant buttoner. My jacket was draped over my shoulders as I'd planned on eating in the dining room and didn't want to sit out there in my tacky green polo. Plus, it was frowned upon to be in full uniform, dining, during open hours.

My bowl was assembled when I got out to the front, so I took it and a clean fork and headed over to the staff table. The first forkful of steak and rice hit my mouth when Audrina walked over.

"Hey, Joy, how's it going?" She slipped herself into the seat across from me.

I swallowed down the savoury food. "Great. Best food I've had all day."

"Really?" She gave me a quizzical look.

Sure, Westside was popular, but not typically with the staff. When you're around the smells and spice all day, it got to you. I hadn't eaten much today aside from breakfast, so anything would've tasted good. I dug in and had another forkful, feeling my waist expand as I did. I ran my hand over the makeshift pant holder, feeling for the bulge from the ponytail holder; it was still intact.

"Since you're here," I said, wiping my mouth, "there's something I should tell you."

I took a deep breath and stared at my bowl. I've worked with Audrina for the past six and a half years, but we weren't friends. Our relationship was strictly professional. Employee to boss, now that she was my boss. She used to work on the floor with the rest of us servers.

I was stalling. I looked to Audrina, her face calm and patient, waiting on whatever I needed to tell her.

She scooted into the booth and placed her hands on top of the table.

A band of sweat broke over the nape of my neck and I wiped it away.

"Everything okay?"

I pulled my top lip in and rolled it between my teeth. "Yes." My hand tapped against my fork, and a force from deep within propelled me to speak. "I'm pregnant." My eyes roved up to search her face.

Thankfully it was still calm, although her eyes were deep in thought. "Congratulations."

"Thanks." It felt good to tell someone while I wasn't under duress.

"How far along are you?"

That was the hard part and I braced myself. "Eighteen weeks."

Her eyes widened. "Eighteen weeks, really? Wow."

There it was, and to be honest, I expected nothing less. Her smile faded, and a frown replaced it. I was sure most employees mentioned something at twelve weeks, not at the almost halfway point. Working until I was thirty-seven weeks was doable, maybe even longer, but still, it didn't give them much time.

"I'm keeping all my appointments to early morning, so it won't affect my work schedule. Provided I can keep myself healthy, I shouldn't need to skip out on any shifts and should be able to continue working well into June."

"What's your due date?"

"July first."

She nodded, likely running numbers and such or whatever it was managers did when faced with this news.

"I'm sorry," I said, tipping my head down and taking another bite.

"Oh my goodness, why would you be sorry?"

"Because this will mess everything up."

"Joy," she wrapped her hand around my free one. "We'll manage. We have lots of time to train a replacement."

I shook my head. "Just please, not another Jacob."

We both laughed.

Jacob had been a temporary employee we hired back over the summer. He seemed to work out fine, until Audrina suspected him of stealing, and I caught him.

"Yeah, no more Jacobs. Maybe more Celestes, or Robins."

As if they heard their names, the two-thirds of the evening trio, walked onto the floor, dressed in Westside's finest garb.

I pulled at my own green polo, which had become more constricting over the past few days.

"Will you need a new top?"

My head tipped down. There were no grease stains on it. I was fantastic at getting those out. "No," I said, shaking my head.

183

"I mean a size up, to have room for expansion."

Oh dear. I didn't actually want to move up a size. I've been perfectly happy being a size small. "Don't these stretch?"

She gave me a sympathetic grin. "Not really."

Well, I still had a little more room. If my breasts fit nicely under it and my tummy wasn't pushed out as far, I was good. "I'm okay for now."

I needed a change in topic. Either that, or Audrina needed to leave. And since she was nicely settled into the booth, that wasn't about to happen.

"Good." She shifted in her seat and glanced toward the door.

I followed her gaze. Meghan stood at the till, running another report. She gave a nod and a welcoming smile to an incoming couple as Robin escorted them to a booth.

"The reason I came over was I need to schedule an employee performance review with you."

I sighed. Great timing for me to have announced my pregnancy. I should've waited. Darn it. I put my fork down. "Sure," I said, trying to convey confidence. "When?"

"I know the timing sucks, but we'll be undergoing some major changes soon. How about tomorrow before you start? Meghan needs to be there with me."

I gave her a slow nod. "Absolutely."

"Great. Can you come in an hour early? We're giving out yours and Robin's tomorrow, so we'll need you to alternate on the floor."

"Won't be a problem."

Audrina pushed herself out of the booth. "You'll be fine."

In all my years at Westside, I'd never had a poor review, in fact, they were always glowing. But for some reason, a nagging sensation grew in the pit of my stomach. Would tomorrow's be as sparkly, especially now that the baby news was out?

"Hey, Audrina?"

She turned around and stepped back to the table.

"Don't say anything to Meghan about the baby."

"She'll need to know."

"I know," I nodded repeatedly. "I just don't want it to taint the review. I'll tell her afterwards."

"Fair enough." She click-clacked her way over the tiles, disappearing behind the till.

I resumed eating, despite the food sitting like a dead weight in my gut.

Chapter Nineteen

The lead weight of undigested food remained all evening as I made sure to make each table feel supreme so as not to taint any negative reviews for tomorrow's review.

The worst though was the radio silence from James. There could be any number of excuses why he wasn't responding to me and most of them were legit. He was at work, or he'd left his phone at home or, the truest of all, he wanted nothing more to do with me.

I drove home with a heavy feeling in my heart. Like a zombie, I took the elevator up and stumbled down the hall.

Following people's advice, even well intended advice, was not my strong suit. Everyone told me to tell him sooner rather than later, and I'd ignored it all, especially after he said he never wanted kids and then I witnessed him around the little darlings. What was I supposed to do with that information? Obviously, my game plan changed at that point and yes, it probably was a bit manipulative, but I wanted a sweet fling, something wonderful to remember him by. He wasn't a bad guy, in fact, quite the opposite, and I'd found myself falling for him, despite knowing it wasn't for a long term.

My key found its way into the lock, and I twisted the knob. The chain on the door prevented me from opening it fully.

"Just a minute," Ana yelled.

I closed the door and waited for what felt like an eternity.

"Sorry," she said as the chain slid off and the door creaked open. Our throw blanket from the back of the couch was wrapped around her body.

Ollie sat on the couch, red-faced even from this distance and made no effort to get up. Likely covering himself up with stray articles of clothing. I hoped there was at least a towel underneath him or I may need to toss the couch. Gross.

"I'm going to my room," I said, hanging my coat in the closet. There was no desire to sit with them, especially after breaking up their fun.

Ana grabbed my arm while keeping a tight hold of the blanket. "How're ya feeling?" Genuine concern on her face.

"Heart broken." Tears fell from my eyes, and I dropped my bag on the floor.

"I'm sorry that's how he found out." She wrapped me in a one-armed hug. "He just needs time to adjust."

"Yeah, maybe." But I knew better. He just needed to forget about me and move on with his life. "I ruined his life. He never wanted kids."

"Maybe he'll change his mind because it's you."

I laughed. "Yeah right." I broke free from the hug. All I wanted right now was to have a pity party, group of one. "I'll talk to you later."

Staggering down the hall, I grabbed a fresh set of clothes from my dresser and headed to the bathroom. A hot steamy shower to rinse away the yuckiness of the hospital visit was in order.

Steam filled the hallway as I walked out towards my bedroom.

Ana approached, a mug of tea in her hands. "Figured you could use something to drink."

"Thanks." I took the mug and inhaled. Chamomile, with a hint of lemon. My favourite.

"Why don't you come out and sit with us? I don't think you should be alone."

I tightened the belt of my fuzzy bathrobe. "Actually, I'm okay. I'm rather tired and will drink the tea and read a book. I plan on being asleep in half an hour."

"You sure?" She gave me a questioning look; the one that suggested I was avoiding something.

"Positive. Thanks for the tea." I closed my bedroom door behind me, giving her and Ollie private time.

My phone buzzed from my nightstand and I raced over, tea sloshing over the sides of the mug as I did. Picking it up, I was disappointed to see it wasn't from James. It was from my mother. One hospital visit, and her check-ins were hourly.

I must've slept soundly, sleeping through a middle of the night text, and I had turned the volume louder so I wouldn't miss it. It was from James.

Is it mine?

Nothing more, nothing less, and yet those three words had so much weight to them.

I texted back—yes—and waited, heart pounding hard enough to give me a headache. The phone flipped over and over in my hands, wondering if he was reading it and formulating a response. Or had he already read it and decided that was enough information for him? Evil thoughts about how much he could possibly hate me swirled in my brain. The disappointment pressed on my shoulders and a pinch of pain crawled across my neck.

Five minutes passed.

Ten minutes.

Twenty minutes.

He was either sleeping or he didn't need anything further from me.

My tummy roared with hunger, and my headache flared. Tiptoeing down the hall, I wandered into the kitchen and prepared myself a healthy breakfast, complete with a glass of milk. I wasn't a milk drinker but understood that the calcium was important. Otherwise, the growing baby pulled it from my bones. As an added bonus, the ER doctor said it counted toward my daily fluid intake; there was no need for a repeat of yesterday.

Brushing sleep from her eyes, Ana padded down the hall. "Morning," she grumbled and fiddled with the coffee pot.

"Didn't get much sleep last night?"

She shot me a look. Ana wasn't a morning person, not even on her very best days. "I was busy."

I laughed. "That explains the noise." Not that I had heard anything, not even my own cell phone.

"He goes home in two days. I got to get in as much as I can, so I don't go through withdrawal while he's gone."

"I'm sure that'll happen anyways."

"Probably." A small smile smeared on her face. The coffee pot beeped, and she poured herself a mug full and lifted it up in my direction. "Want one?"

I shook my head. My phone buzzed and excitedly I reach for it. It was my mother. Again.

"Hello, mom." I braced myself for a long-winded conversation and arched a brow at Ana.

"Oh darling. Are you home?"

"Yep." I shovelled in a slice of apple, coated in cinnamon and rolled oats. It was sort of like an apple crisp, except not heated.

And definitely not as sweet. And really, not as tasty as I'd hoped.

"How are you feeling?"

"Hungry." Like I could eat all the time, a stark contrast to a few weeks ago.

"Watch your caloric intake, you don't want them to have to alter your bridesmaid gown."

"They're going to have to anyways. I'm going to be as big as a house." I rolled my eyes and looked over at Ana.

She leaned against the counter snickering. Her mom and my mom could've been sisters for the way they talked to their daughters.

"Anyways..." she said, ignoring my self-depreciating comment. "I just wanted to see how you were doing. You didn't respond to my texts last night."

"Well, I was working, and I was tired when I got home. But I assure you, I'm fine."

"Good, your father and I were worried." She sighed. "Just a second..."

"Josephine," my dad's voice filled the phone line.

"Hey."

"How's my girl?"

"I'm okay."

He sighed, and I imagined his broad chest expanding with the inhale. "You gave me quite the scare when Cecelia called to tell us you were in labour and delivery."

"I wasn't in labour and delivery. I was in pre-assessment. There's a big difference." But leave it to CeCe to make it more dramatic than it was. Probably had them all convinced I was in labour and about to give birth.

"But... everything's alright? You're okay? Your baby... is it okay?" There was more concern coming out of him in those few words than I'd heard in him since the day he found out I was having

190

a baby out of wedlock. "I'm headed to church in an hour to meet with Father Bobby and I wanted to know if I should say prayers of gratitude, or if I should pray for healing."

Tears welled, and my vision blurred. Maybe the little scare had softened him. Regardless, all I wanted to do was bury my face into his chest and have him wrap his fatherly arms around me and kiss me on the top of my head.

"Prayers for thankfulness, Daddy." I swallowed back the solid lump forming. "Both of us are just fine. Baby's measuring just like he or she should." I rubbed my tummy and etched a small smile on my face in Ana's direction.

She returned it with a beaming one of her own.

"Praise God and Jesus and the Holy Mother," my father said, sounding as if he were choking back tears of his own. "I'm happy you're both going to be okay." Another gust of air released from him. "Are you coming for afternoon lunch? We're eating at one, at the usual place. I'd love it if you came."

"Yes, I'll be there." I raised my eyebrow as Ana turned her head in my direction and made eye contact. Was the standoff with my father over?

The phone call over, I tossed it to the side, relaying the brief conversation to Ana.

She leaned against the countertop, mug firmly wrapped in her hands. "Maybe all those lit candles at church worked. He got an answer to his prayers."

"I don't think so." Her coffee smelled so good, and I desperately wanted one. It shouldn't hurt, should it? I grabbed a mug from the cupboards.

"Sure. Someone above put into his heart a morsel of fear. Thinking about mortality does wonders for some."

"It wasn't my mortality, Ana. Death wasn't even on the line. For me or the baby."

191

"Still." She shrugged. "Whatever it was, maybe he's making amends, and I say, let him."

I nodded in agreement and had a sip of the dark, steaming liquid. It tasted exactly like I'd hoped. But it wasn't what I wanted. I rummaged through the fridge, pushing aside jars and plastic containers, still hungry. The apple crisp concoction did nothing to take the hunger pangs away. The leftover pizza looked appealing however.

"This still good?" I asked Ana, pulling out the box.

"Should be. It's from the other night."

I heated it in the microwave, my mouth practically drooling as the cheese melted. The little bit of grease coating the pepperoni bubbled. From the table, my phone buzzed again. "Probably mom again. I didn't talk with her much." The vibration from the text rattled in my hand as I flipped over to read the display.

James.

My breath caught in my throat, and I flashed the phone at Ana, the single line of text highlighted in green.

We need to talk.

Chapter Twenty

*a*na rushed over to me and stared at the display. "Whatcha waiting for? Reply."

A nervous energy washed over me, and my hands trembled as I typed.

When?

I willed an answer to come quickly as I didn't know how much more waiting I could handle.

Thankfully, James seemed to be on the same wave-length.

Thai Palace on Roper. Does an hour work?

"Type back yes." Ana nearly screamed at me. "Honest to God, girl, I don't know why you're taking so long to respond."

"What do you think he wants?"

"To meet. To apologise. To tell you he has deep feelings, and he wants to move forward."

"I'm not buying it."

She leaned over my shoulder, her voice oozing with excitement. "Maybe he just wants answers. Whatever he wants, it's a start."

193

I typed back an affirmative. Nothing further pinged.

"Let's go get you dressed." She pushed me down the hall.

"Seriously, Ana, I can handle this myself."

"Amuse me." She stood in front of my closet. "What to wear?" She tapped her finger against her chin. "What about a dress?"

I checked the weather. "It's minus twelve outside."

"So, you wear a sweater and leggings." She retrieved my favourite sweater, a black knee-length cardigan type. There was no dress in my closet it paired well with, however maybe leggings and a nice shirt. But Ana was into fashion about as much as I was, which wasn't much at all.

Properly fitting clothes were in short supply. My work pants were more than snug, my jeans too tight in the thigh and waist. All I had at my disposal were forgiving leggings and yoga pants. The black leggings hit my bed, along with the cardigan. But picking out a shirt was more daunting.

Ana held up a few, including a yellow shirt.

"I'm not going as a bumblebee." I reached behind her and pulled out a grey tank top. It was a longer length and covered my hips. "This will be fine."

She coughed jokingly. "If you say so."

I quickly changed into my outfit noting for the first time how snug my leggings had become since the last time I wore them. A sideways glance in the mirror was all I needed. In the tank and leggings, it was clear I was pregnant. There was absolutely no way to conceal it.

"Aw, look atcha. Look at my baby." She cupped her hands around my belly and stared at my reflection in the mirror. "You're so beautiful."

I rested my head on her shoulder. "Thanks."

"Whatcha going to do with your hair? We want to make

194

you irresistible to him."

"What I wear and how I look are not going to change anything with him. I've ruined his life."

"He was an equal partner in that, and yet somehow you always seem to forget that." She actually wagged a finger at me.

"Well..."

"Well, nothing. I think you should go there and dazzle him with your brilliance."

"My brilliance? Ana, I'm a waitress."

She cocked my head so I stared directly at myself in the mirror. "You're a bright star amongst the heavens. You're as beautiful inside as on the outside. You're charming and a loyal friend with the biggest heart. You're the most amazing person I've ever met, and if James can't see that, well, that's his loss. Because you're brilliant, and I love you with all my heart, and I wantcha to be happy."

I wanted that too, but I wasn't sure how to go and achieve it. I had no idea of where I even needed to look. All I knew was I had fallen hard for James, real hard. And I couldn't help but wonder, if it hadn't been for the surprise pregnancy, would I have attempted to seek him out? Would I have run into him at the library anyways, and would we have started a romantic journey without an outside— or inside—force to bring us together? So many what ifs, and too many of them unanswerable.

"Can I braid your hair?" she asked lovingly, diverting my attention from the mirror as she ran her fingers through my thick hair.

"Sure, but nothing tight." I preferred a looser braid, so the stray strands would fall out and give it a softer, more romantic look. Maybe I did need to make myself more feminine and less life ruiner.

Just before the hour mark had passed, I sat in the corner of

Thai Palace hoping the heart I wore on my sleeve was under wraps. I didn't want to give away my emotions.

James walked in at the top of the hour, looking crisp and clean and pulled together. Handsome as always, he sauntered over. "Hey," he said coolly.

"Hey," I whispered back taking in his fine form. His beautiful smile, the kind that lit up his eyes, was notably missing.

"Did you order?"

I shook my head.

"Let me go order, and I'll be right back." He hung his thick coat on the back of the chair and stepped over to the cafeteria-style counter to place his order. A tray with two bowls of soup, two buns and two coffees sat on the table. "Figured you could use a bite to eat. It's a spicy Thai chicken and rice."

It didn't matter if I'd eaten an hour ago, the soup smelled yummy. After carefully wiping the silver-tone cutlery on the disposable napkin, I dug in my spoon and lifted it to my lips.

"First things, first." He took a quick sip of his coffee and searched deep into my eyes. "You're okay?"

Not at all where I expected the conversation to start, but it was sweet. A soft smile came to my lips. "Yeah."

He inhaled sharply but dropped his gaze to the food in front of him. "And the baby? All good?"

"Yes."

"For sure it's mine, right?"

"Yes." I met his gaze head on. It was all out in the open, no sense running from it anymore. My left hand sat atop my protruding belly.

He stiffened and released a long breath. "How far along? A few weeks?"

I gulped.

James was a smart guy, just clearly not observant. Had he

really not noticed the swell of my midsection? *I* couldn't stop staring at it. His innocent question led me to believe he assumed I was recently pregnant.

I twirled my spoon through the thick soup, the tendrils of orange cheese swirling around in a weird pattern. "Eighteen."

"Eighteen!" The wooden chair scraped across the concrete floor and his voice pitched enough to draw attention to us.

I pulled myself into my jacket and kept my eyes down.

With a quick readjustment, he scooted back closer to the table, and inched himself in my direction. "How can you be eighteen weeks along?"

Incredible. For someone so smart, he sure was acting dumb. My focus flickered back to him. "Thanksgiving weekend."

Questions and uncertainty rained down over his face. "Thanksgiving?"

"Yeah, the weekend your ex got married, and you crashed my cousin's wedding." I couldn't help the nastiness in my voice from slipping out.

His face morphed into pain and sadness. "Right." He nodded. "That was a long time ago."

It had seemed like it, and yet, it felt like that weekend was only a couple weeks back. Not knowing how to respond to his comment, I simply shrugged.

"So, you're halfway through the pregnancy. When were you planning on telling me?" His tone was so full of crushing hurt, it made me ache.

I needed something in my mouth so I wouldn't speak, and a spoonful of soup was the best option. It lingered and I tasted all the flavours; it was heavy on the ginger and very low on the spicy, sadly. It was rather disappointing. Ollie made a better soup.

He rubbed the back of his neck and tapped his finger against the bun.

"Truth is…" I swallowed back the rising bile and morsel of fear climbing up my throat. "I wasn't sure if I ever would."

"What?" All the hurt and betrayal I expected him to have raged in his brown eyes and stretched out across his face. His shoulders hung, and he braced his forearms on the table for support.

"I mean I was going to, but when you said you never wanted children and, well, that… well, I kiboshed telling you after that point." But fate intervened to make sure he found out anyways.

"Unbelievable." His voice broke and his eyes widened, a haunted look settled into them. His clasped his hands over his head and brought his elbows in tightly. "So, you've known about this for like what? Sixteen weeks?"

"Actually no. I've only known since early December."

His hand covered his mouth and gripped his lips. A breath squeaked through the edges of his fingers. "Still. You understand that I'm running through a laundry list of emotions. Hurt, surprise, anger and betrayal, to name a few."

I nodded, not expecting anything less. "Completely."

For a moment, his eyes squeezed shut, and he inhaled a few shaky breaths. "Before you found out I wasn't interested in children, what prevented you from saying anything?"

"You wouldn't understand." I took another spoonful of soup. Despite the tension and anger in the air, the spicy Thai was warm and comforting, and I needed that.

"Try me. I need to make sure I have all the facts laid out in front of me."

I gave him a slow nod. "Well, at first, once I realised I was pregnant, I had a bit of shock to deal with."

A snort of ironic laughter emitted from him. "Welcome to my world."

"Well…" I hummed and hawed over what precisely to share. "Then it was a matter of tracking you down. All I had to go with is your first name."

"No, I left you my phone number after the wedding."

"I left it behind. I'm sure I told you this." My eyes closed softly as I recalled our meeting at the library. It had to have come up.

When I opened my eyes, he had shifted nearer. His hand was close to mine, almost as if he wanted to touch me but couldn't bring himself to do it. "You probably did but I don't remember why."

"Embarrassment," I whispered. "I don't do one-night stands. Ever. And after you left, I figured I'd never see you again."

"So, we're back to you finding out, and still not telling me."

"Yeah," I sighed. "About that."

The gorgeous man sitting across from me was neither seething with anger nor thrilled with my avoidance. Instead, he displayed a deep curious nature mixed with the utmost disappointment.

"That look. The one on your face right now, that's why I didn't tell you."

"Because of a look? You are incredulous."

I hated him using big words; it made me feel small and inept. "It's more than that. My parents said I had ruined my life, and my friends said if I told you, I would be ruining yours as well. My own ruined life was enough, I had no desire to place any of that on you."

He ran his fingers through his dark hair, the strands in the middle stood straight up but it gave me something to focus on. "Once you knew, did you try to find me?"

"Of course." My gaze ran all over his face while my hands twisted together. "I went to the photographer's studio as Crystal thought you were the assistant."

"You know I wasn't." His hand twitched and inched a touch

closer. It took everything in me to not grab it and hold on, but I needed him to make the move first.

"I know that now, but I didn't back then. Crystal didn't recognise you, and after ruling out the assistant thing, she figured you were someone's plus one. And then I took any name on her RSVP cards that had James or a Jay and searched through Facebook to find a match." I hated being on the defensive. "So yes, I did seek you out once I found out. But only because I wanted to know more about you. Not for any other reason than when my child asked about his father, I'd be able to explain what I knew. I never had any information on my parents. I know nothing about my heritage, and I don't want that for my child. Our child."

"It's a boy?" His eyes opened wide, and he leaned closer to me.

"What?" I shrugged, wondering where he picked that up from. "I have no idea."

"But you said *his father*."

I rolled my eyes. "I meant it as a figure of speech. It's easier to say he than he or she."

He gave me a slow nod, almost like he was unsure if I could be trusted or not. At this point in our relationship, I wasn't sure if I was. "So mainly, you were getting intel on me."

"Essentially."

He pulled his hand back and gripped it around the bun, tearing off a chunk between his teeth. Slowly, while maintaining a solid lock on me, he chewed. He gulped down a few more spoonfuls of soup and tore off a bite of bun.

The air between us was as thick as the spicy chicken soup I continued to swirl around, and on every fourth lap, I'd take a taste. I waited patiently for him to speak, and while doing so, managed to eat most of my soup. He had done the same.

He cleared his throat. "If I'm following correctly, you were only interested in getting info about me. There was nothing more? All those times we did it…, it meant nothing to you?"

Oh geez. "The reverse, actually. And that became the problem. Because it did mean something. I couldn't stop myself from feeling what I did." My heart ached at the thought.

He raised a brow and an angry chuckle tumbled out of his tightly restrained lips. "And what would that be? Raging fear? Betrayal? Anguish? Confusion?"

All things he was no doubt feeling right now.

"There was fear. Don't get me wrong. I figured once you knew, you were going to leave me, and I wouldn't have blamed you. It was selfish really, because I knew we weren't going to be able to continue much longer before it was clearly evident."

His eyes fell to my stomach, hidden by the table. Like he was using x-ray vision, I felt the penetrating glare. "You betrayed me. You betrayed *us*. Your selfish act ruined anything that could've happened between us. *Anything*."

My heart ached hearing him speak so harshly, but I deserved it. I had held it back from him, and everyone told me it was a ginormous mistake. "I know."

However, he hadn't left, which I took as a sign. Maybe even a good one. He wanted to discuss this and hadn't given up on the conversation, or on me. Yet.

Still the air between us was punctuated by orders being placed and bells dinging and the idle chit-chat from customers and staff. Somewhere in the back, I made out the chatter on a radio.

Surrounded by so much, I felt desperately alone.

"At what point were you going to break up with me?"

The question flew at me so fast, I was blindsided by it, and I muddled around for the right answer. The honest answer. We weren't ever really classified as a boyfriend-girlfriend pairing, it only was said the day he found out.

"I figured you'd break up with me, when you found out."
Or Valentine's Day as a fallback, although I hadn't set a hard and
fast date. Just sometime before I was really noticeably pregnant.

"That's soon."

"I didn't expect things to happen."

"What things?" His brow furrowed.

I looked long and hard in his eyes, searching for a crack I
could explore. Nothing presented. "I didn't think I'd find myself
feeling what I feel."

"Really? Sure it wasn't a form of back-stabbing betrayal?"
A hint of scepticism laced his comment.

Like a sucker-punch to the gut, I was breathless. I'd been
honest and hoped it would at least soften the hardened expression
on his face. And as with everything else in my life, I was wrong.

"That's not it." I stared at my hands. The truth was painful,
and even more because it was loaded with emotion. I swallowed and
searched his face. "I found myself falling for you."

"You have a sick definition of love."

"Probably." I shrugged, but there was nothing else to do. I
wasn't going to cry. I wasn't going to plead my case to him
anymore.

"Here I'd thought I was falling for you too."

What, really?

"Thought I'd found someone to hang out, who made me
feel good, who I wanted to spend time with. Instead, I found a
fraudster of the highest order, who was doing nothing more than
fulfilling some selfish, immature notion of love."

"Hey," I said, my voice rising with my anger. "You think I
planned all this? You act like I tricked you into getting me pregnant.
Truth is, I'm terrified. I don't know what to do. I'm so confused and
scared and worried I'm going to screw up my child's life.
Everything in my life has or will change. I worry about what I'll eat,

and if I'm eating enough or too much. If I'm getting the right nutrients. I'm scared I'm not going to be able to give it everything it deserves. And I'm wholly afraid of doing it on my own. But I won't screw up anyone else's life. Mine and the baby's are more than enough. I have to do what's best for my child and that is *not* a selfish or immature notion of love."

"But you'll deny it a father?"

"I'm giving you an out. This doesn't need to be your problem, and I'm not asking for it to be your problem. I am willing to handle it all, and now that you know, you can be as involved, or not, as you want."

James pushed back on his chair and snorted like an angry bull. "Thanks for nothing." He stood and tucked in his chair, grabbing his jacket from the back. "Goodbye, Josephine."

He may have stomped out the door in anger, pushing the glass door with so much force it hit the wall, but it was my heart that took all the damage.

~Chapter Twenty-One

obin was smoking by the picnic table by the parking lot as I pulled into an available stall. He wasn't in uniform yet; his jacket flapped gently in the breeze, the trails of smoke blowing away from him.

"Good afternoon, Joy," he called out, extinguishing his cigarette.

"Hey." My heart as heavy as the thud of the door I closed and locked.

"Ready for the evals?" He walked the thirty feet from the table to my car. "Hey are you okay?"

I shivered and pulled my hands into my sleeves. "I'm having a craptastic day."

He placed a comforting hand on my shoulder and gave it a little squeeze. "Anything you want to talk about it?"

"James found out about the pregnancy, and once I explained everything to him, he walked out of my life." A cold, damp ache settled over me.

"James found out? You mean you hadn't told him yet?"

I shook my head. All afternoon long I'd replayed the past few weeks over and over in my head. Different scenarios surfaced but the outcome was all the same. I'd unwittingly ruined his life and telling him earlier wouldn't have changed that. If anything, I'd given him a few extra months of believing his life could be exactly what he'd planned.

"I'm sorry. I know you were hoping for a different outcome."

"I really was." I had always expected him to leave, but really—secretly—hoped he'd stay, if for no other reason than for his child. But it wasn't enough to keep him. Tears I'd kept a tight rein on all afternoon, pushed against their threshold.

Robin wrapped me in a hug. "I'm going to tell you everything will be okay, although you might not believe me right now. As your friend, I'm here to help you, you just have to tell me how."

"I just need to get through this eval."

He pulled out of the friendly embrace. "Would a joke help?"

I twisted my head up to see his face. Such sincerity on it. Inside, I kicked myself for not making friends with him sooner. He was really a nice guy. "Not likely but try me."

His arm hung around my shoulders, and he led me to the warmth of the main entrance. "Did you hear about the new restaurant on the moon?"

I narrowed my eyes and shook my head.

"Good atmosphere but no food." He stopped and clapped a hand to his forehead. "Wait I screwed that up. I meant, good food no atmosphere."

It worked. Not the punch line because he royally screwed it up, but his delivery was hilarious. I'd never seen Robin look so floundered before.

"Ah, she smiles." He opened the door. "After you."

I walked in ahead of him, scanning the restaurant for Meghan and Audrina. They were nowhere to be found and sweet relief blanketed me. I had time to run to the back and freshen up.

After reapplying my mascara and dabbing dusting powder across my shiny nose, I redid my hair into a messy bun and ventured out into the kitchen. I plastered on my best smile, the whole fake it until you make it attitude I was known for. At least until recently. Maybe they'll re-nickname me Sully or something. It was a bad joke, but it made me smile.

Saying hello to the staff, I waltzed by and headed to the front.

Meghan and Audrina stood by the till, yakking with Robin.

He looked in my direction and whispered, "All good?"

I nodded as I approached and stood by him.

"Which of you would like to go first?" Audrina asked.

I glanced to Robin, who remained tight-lipped. "I'll go." I had nothing to fear; the evaluation was either going to go well, or not, although there was no reason why it should go south.

"Excellent. Right this way." Audrina led the way over to the booth, an inkling of a smile on her face.

"Robin, you're to help out as needed on the floor."

Both of us scanned the restaurant. One couple sat at a booth on the opposite corner from where the staff booth was located, and there was no one at the door.

I winked at Robin. "Try not to run your feet off, don't want to wear yourself out before the end of the night."

"I'll try my damnedest. But it's sooo busy." He mocked a whine.

Meghan released a no-nonsense sigh and click-clacked her way over the ceramic tiles to the staff booth.

"Good luck," Robin whispered.

I leaned in close. "I'll break her down for you."

He laughed and patted me on the shoulder.

I made my way over to the table as Meghan stared at my expanding girth. It was almost embarrassing.

"Meghan, are you ready?" Audrina said, taking the folder from her.

"Ah, yes." They opened it up and I slid into the booth.

No surprise to anyone at the table, myself included, my performance factors were outstanding. But we knew that, as I could do the job in my sleep. We all could.

Meghan gave me a copy of my review. "Everything seems in order." She closed one folder and took another from Audrina. "Moving forward, Audrina and I have discussed this at length, and we would like to offer you a shift manager's role."

Audrina winked at me and lifted the folder just enough to withdraw a stapled set of sheets.

Meghan didn't look up as she searched the papers. "The position would start on March first, and would become a full-time position by May first, with your benefits package effective your first day as full-time shift manager."

"Would it be part-time until then?" I was slightly confused about how it would all work. As exciting as it would be to get a manager's role, complete with manager's pay and benefits, I knew I couldn't do part-time until May.

"Yes. You'd be a manager during the week, and a server on the weekends. You wouldn't have to sacrifice your weekend tips and could slowly get into the new position during the week when it's less busy." Meghan slid the sheets Audrina held and pushed them in front of me.

It outlined the manager's pay, perks, and benefits. There

were two numbers at the bottom. "What does this mean?"

"This number is your gross earnings, based on your three weekly shifts. You'll receive two cheques which I know is weird. One will be your managerial earnings and the other is your waitress pay." She rambled on about shift lengths and some other stuff, but I stopped paying attention.

Shock held me firmly as I couldn't believe I was being offered a job. A move up. Something better than waitressing, more consistent.

"Days or evenings?" The right answer could make or break my decision.

"Days," Audrina answered, and I shot my focus over to her, desperate to hear an explanation. "I finished up my accounting course and will be moving to Chad's business starting May first."

Chad ran a very successful construction business and was hiring additional help for upcoming projects. Never thought Audrina would be one of the new hires.

"So, what do you say?" Meghan said in a voice that sounded like I should be thanking her for this.

And I wanted to because it was an incredible offer. It would make maternity prep a little easier financially. "I think..."

I stared at the numbers. It was everything I hoped to earn, and mentally I felt ready to move into something challenging and move up the limited corporate ladder but... the timing sucked.

I pushed the offer back towards Meghan. "I think you should offer this to Robin. He deserves it more than I, and I know he'll be able to offer you the consistency you're looking for."

Meghan looked at Audrina and back to me. "Are you serious?"

Audrina leaned in a little closer, the set of sheets coming back in my direction. "I *really* think you should think about this."

"I'm flattered, honestly, and this would solve my financial

woes, but I can't. I'm pregnant and due Canada Day."

Meghan gasped, and covered her mouth.

"I couldn't expect you to train me, only for me to take time off and you have to spend time to train someone else for my leave. That's not fair to you or the company."

Unless I took a shorter leave. Could that work? Would I be able to put my young child into daycare and have someone else with my child for a better part of the day? It would be hard enough to do when the baby's a year old. Gosh, I hadn't thought far enough into the future. I needed more time to think about what would happen after the twelve-month leave. But right now, this wasn't fair to anyone. I pushed the dream away.

"I'm sorry, really sorry, but I have to turn down this amazing offer." My hands linked together on top of the table. Twisting them, it kept me from bolting out the door. It pained me to refuse the deal, but it wouldn't work. A few months ago, sure. A year from now, that was a strong possibility. Just not now. Dang it.

"Could you give us a few minutes?" Audrina asked me and whispered to Meghan.

"Sure." I scooted out of the booth and gazed upon my two managers. I did a quick turn and walked over to the till, giving the floor a solid once over. Only one other table had come in.

Robin sauntered over to me. "How'd it go?"

"Fine." I smiled. "Surprisingly well."

He playfully punched me on the shoulder. "As if it wouldn't. You feeling better about things now that this is out of the way?"

"Meh." They were what they were. I'd still be doing my waitressing job, saving to prepare for mine and James's baby. James had removed himself from any further relationship. My life was set. This was it. The quicker I accepted the dealt cards, the easier it would be.

A couple walked into the entrance, hand in hand.

"I got this. Your eval is next." Smiling, I waltzed over to the couple, introduced myself, and took them to their seats.

Meghan called Robin over for his evaluation, and I worked the floor with Cat, one of the daytime servers who walked like her namesake; she was silent and sneaky.

When the restaurant was this quiet, we were still required to keep busy, so I focused my energy on cleaning the server station, wiping and dusting and restocking. It was menial work, but gave me a chance to think, which wasn't what I wanted to do, I'd rather be busy serving customers and keeping them happy. Abandoning the station, I walked back out to the floor, did a walk-by of each table, and headed over to visit with Cat.

"How'd the eval go? You pass?" she asked. Cat was still in high school and only worked on Sundays, one of my normal days off. I guess she didn't know I'd been working here since she was still in elementary school.

"I did." I re-stocked the napkins, and fiddled with the cutlery in the bin, my eyes flickering over to the staff table to see how things were going. No one was smiling. Mind you, I was only seeing Audrina and Meghan's face, one of which never smiled.

"Aces," Cat said and danced over to check on her tables.

Pretending to scrub the railing around the wait station, I watched the staff table with great interest, hoping something exciting would happen. It didn't. Exhaling a long sigh, I made my way back to the kitchen on the hunt for anything to occupy my mind.

"Only if you're sure," I overheard Meghan say as I walked out of the server station.

Laps in the dining room were the only thing I could do.

"Joy, can we see you a minute?"

My body pulsed with anxiety as I stepped over to the table.

210

"Please join us again," Meghan said and pointed to the seat beside Robin.

Robin slid over until his shoulder was against the wall. A smugness peppered his face.

"We were discussing options for management, and your little dilemma has caused us to rethink a few things," Meghan said, disdain ebbing from her.

My heart did a beautiful imitation of a belly flop in my stomach. "Okay," I breathed out.

Please don't fire me. Please don't fire me. There was no reason why they would, but they both looked so serious. The only amused one was Robin. *What did he know?*

"We," Audrina said, pointing between her and Meghan, "think it would work out if you both became part-time managers."

Robin's smirk widened.

"How would that work?" My eyes flicked back and forth between my two bosses.

"From March first until May first, you would each work two manager shifts, and three serving shifts a week. You're both our strongest servers, so we'd keep you on the floor for the Friday and Saturday nights, plus a shift each during the week, in addition to your two shifts for management training. Every couple of weeks one of you would manage a weeknight in tandem with me. As of May first, you," Meghan addressed me, "would become full-time. Robin will stay part-time until you start your maternity leave in mid-June." She passed me a hastily sketched calendar, outlining which of us would manage which nights. On paper it was perfectly clear.

Audrina nodded. "It makes the most sense and is a win-win for all us. We have plenty of time to hire front-end staff, but we don't want to lose you."

"I wasn't going anywhere." My next ten to fifteen years belonged to Westside, as I hadn't planned on leaving. I couldn't.

"You deserve this promotion, Joy, and so does Robin. It's been long overdue." Audrina smiled and with everything laid out in front of me, it was very hard to say no.

I choked back tears. It felt insanely good to be wanted, and to have someone fight for me and try to make things work. It's a sad state of affairs that it was my employer and not James.

Blinking away the fuzzies, my head twisted in Robin's direction. "What do you think? I often thought you were more management material than I was."

"If it means you'll be taking one of your serving shifts when I'm on a manager training night, I'm all for it. I'd love to boss you around." He snickered and gave me a playful nudge.

"I take it back. You're not ready at all." But I laughed just the same. "Seriously though?"

"It's not a bad deal." He grabbed a stack of papers. "It works out well for us both, and you'll be sticking around with more confidence for your future."

"It does help that out."

He tapped his long finger against the list of perks, pointing to a couple of items that were too good to pass up. "I'm in," he said, "if you are."

"And if I'm not?"

"I'm still taking it. But it would be more fun to advance with you and not ahead of you. You've been here longer than me."

I continued to stare at the list. A little bit of financial security would be nice. The tips were always flexible, but the higher—much higher—steady hourly wage for a manager's position, plus the additional benefits, well, I'd be foolish to turn it down. Again. Especially with Robin on board to cover my maternity leave. I wouldn't be putting anybody out and may have helped Robin a bit.

I looked at him, and my heart lightened. "Let's do it."

Chapter Twenty-Two

couple days later, I sat curled up in my living room, contemplating my life, when my little baby gave me what I could no longer ignore as gas or intestinal discomfort. It was most definitely a kick.

"Hey, baby," I whispered, although I was sure my voice echoed inside my body and it had to have been louder than the whisper spilling out of me.

It booted me once again.

My hands covered it protectively. "Mommy screwed up. Big time. But I'm going to make it right. I'm just not sure how."

"Tell him you love him," Ollie said, walking into the living room. His rucksack slung high over his shoulder.

"I did already." I rose to give him a hug. After being here for over a month, Ollie was heading back home to Perth. "I'm going to miss you."

"Nah, you'll be good." He winked. "Take care of my Ana for me, she's kinda a wreck."

"Promise."

Ana shuffled out of her room wiping her face. Shifting about in one of Ollie's giant sweaters, she joined us.

"Time to go?" Her voice cracked. As much as she had said she was looking forward to the break, it was clear the time and distance between them would be long and painful. She wiped her face with the edge of his sleeve.

"Are you going to be able to drive?" I asked.

"Yeah, I'll be fine." She gave me a slow nod.

Hopefully concentrating on the drive would soothe her a little, even if she was taking her fiancé to the airport. Slowly, she rolled the jacket up and over her shoulders and the keys jingled as she retrieved them from the bowl by the door.

I gave Ollie another hug. "See you in seven weeks?"

He was supposed to come back for a week at spring break. It wouldn't give them much time, but it would be better than waiting until the end of June. That was still a long time off.

Ollie returned the embrace and whispered in my ear, "Invite him to the baby appointments. If you want him to be as involved as possible, gotta start there." He winked and strode over to Ana.

I waved goodbye and curled back up on the couch. With the touch of my thumb, I opened the messaging app on my phone. The seven texts I'd sent to James went unanswered, even though they all had said *read* and included the time. I flipped over to my social media pages and read the unanswered messages there.

My calendar app opened, and I looked at the upcoming baby appointments. Ultrasounds, blood work, doctor's visits. The next month had three appointments alone. And the frequency of the appointments would only increase the closer I got to July. I added his email to my account and edited the baby appointments in the calendar to sync to his, if he accepted. This way, if he wanted to, there was a list, and he could pick and choose which he attended.

I was leaving the ball in his court.

A pad of paper and a pen lay on the table, so I picked them up and began to write.

Dear James,

Isn't it terrible to start a letter like that, sort of like a Dear John thing, except I'm not breaking up with you, since that has already happened. I'm sorry. I know this whole thing is not like how either of us planned. There's supposed to be a logical order to these things. You meet, you date, you fall in love, get married and have a baby. Somehow, we've reshuffled the standing order and started at the end of the line. Well not the end of the line, but ... ugh! I hope you know what I mean.

Maybe for us, this is the way it was meant to be. For us to get pregnant, then re-meet and fall in love. Maybe one day, when we're really old and watching our grandchildren play in the front yard, we can look back on this and say that it was set up perfectly for us. Because we're different. So different. Our upbringings, our lifestyles, our careers, and yet here is this unifying being bringing together the light and the dark (and I'm in the dark in this scenario, just so you know). And really, when you look at it this way, it is perfect.

I'm in love with you, and the baby knows it too. Every time I think of you my heart races a little bit more and the baby responds by wiggling and moving. I even felt it kick me today and I wished you could've been there to feel it.

I want you in my life. I want you to be a part of your baby's life, he or she needs that, but I also know I can't force it upon you. It took me a long time to accept the fact my life was heading in a radically different direction than I planned, and I will give you all the time you need to accept it too.

My next appointment is next week – I've added you to my baby appointments. The ultrasound is the big one, and I'm not sure if I should find out what I'm carrying. Would you want to know?

XOXO
Josephine

I dug around for an envelope, and after folding the letter, tucked it inside and held it close to my chest. Should I really give it to him? So much of my heart was poured into the letter, did I want to seem so weak and vulnerable? Would he see me as desperate, or would he understand and be receptive to what I'd said? Not likely. I pulled it from the envelope. The paper scratched against my palm as I crumpled it up, ready to toss it into the recycle bin.

"Dang it." I spread it open across the table, flattening it out with the side of my hand.

Maybe it was best to give it to him. Nothing ventured, nothing gained. All I had to figure out was how to give it to him. Did I mail it, or drop it off in person or stick it on the windshield of his car? I wasn't sure. Using my neatest penmanship, I wrote his name on the envelope.

The letter was super personal and mailing it or tucking under a wiper blade would be a stark contrast to it. It was best to give it to him in person, even if it would be the hardest thing to do.

The library wasn't far, and it was a gorgeous day out, so I slipped on my jacket and messy bun hat and stepped outside. The sun shone down, taking off the chill. It's true what they said about living here, *even when it's very cold, if the sun is shining it's tolerable.*

With all the thoughts swimming in my head, the walk was fast and easy. It surprised me how soon I was striding up the last sidewalk to the library and walking through the sliding doors.

A blast of heat hit me as soon as I stepped into the main entrance, and immediately I searched for James. The library was packed with moms, babies, and some of the fanciest strollers I've ever seen. Did I need something that high tech or not?

Pretending to browse at the stack of books, I gazed intently at the four-wheeled Porsche model of baby carriages. It had a cup

216

holder and a huge storage area underneath the baby bucket. The baby was buckled in with enough harnesses to send it safely into orbit. How did they learn to do that? Was there a class?

"Excuse me," I asked in my sweetest voice.

The lady bouncing a tiny baby in a black holder wrapped around her body a dozen times turned to me with a disgusted look on her face. "Yes?"

"This may seem weird, but I'm pregnant too and am curious about your stroller and about this contraption you're wearing to hold your baby."

"It's a Mobi Wrap." She gave me a solid once over and glared as she walked away. "I can't help you." Pushing the stroller, she joined a group of Starbucks toting moms, all with the same make and model of Porsche strollers, and the same baby carrier.

I sighed.

Another lady walked over to me, steering another less expensive brand of stroller. "I'm sorry," she said, putting a soother into her baby's mouth. "I couldn't help overhear. You were curious about strollers?"

"Yeah." I glanced over to the other group of moms. "I'm not sure even where to start to look for these things." It all felt so overwhelming. "Is there a class to take that explains what all you need to have a baby?"

She gave me a warm smile. "All you need is love. You could keep your baby in a laundry basket, and as long as it's fed, dry and warm, it's all good."

"A laundry basket?" Oh, good grief. I was really out of my element.

A sympathetic look crossed her face. "A good prenatal class will steer you in the right direction." She rifled through her bag and handed me a magazine. "It's local so it lists all Edmonton and area birthing classes and is filled with great information. You can find these free all over the city."

I held the golden ticket in my hands and gave it a quick flip. "Thank you."

"Check out the library's website as well. They have lots of meet and greet playgroups."

"Thank you again." I wanted to hug the woman but felt it may be awkward.

"Good luck," she said, pushing her stroller into the huge room.

There was so much to learn. I thought having the baby would be the hardest part, but apparently it was so much more. Mom groups and prenatal classes and parenting classes. It was enough to make my head spin. I braced myself against the bookshelves and leaned my head between my arms. How did I think I could do this alone?

"Can I help–"

As soon as the voice spoke, I lifted my head in recognition.

"What are you doing here?" he asked in a low tone, the smoky voice plucking at my heartstrings.

My rambled breath blew out of me, and I patted down my pockets, retrieving the enveloped and thrusting it into his hands. "I came to give you this."

"I don't want anything from you." He turned around and stepped over to another patron, ignoring my best *just-stay-and-let-me-plead-my-case* expression.

I marched behind him. "Fine, if you won't read the letter, I'll read it to you." My finger hooked underneath the flap and pulled it down, a slight ripping motion filling the space.

His hand settled over top of mine. He darted his eyes around, and his voice dropped an octave. "Please don't make a scene and embarrass yourself."

"I have no issues with that." I struck a pose matching my

earlier expression. If it was one thing I was good it, it was making a fool of myself.

A pleading voice rippled out of him. "If you claim you love me, you won't embarrass me. This is my place of work."

"Is that what I'm doing?"

"Yes."

Well, dang.

"I'm sorry, Josephine." He bridged the distance between us but not close enough to I could breathe him in. His finger tapped the envelope's edge. "No matter what you've written in there, I'm sorry to say, it won't replace the hurt and betrayal I feel in here." He placed his hand over his heart. "I have so much to think over and too many possibilities to consider. My thoughts are all jumbled and nothing makes sense anymore." His voice cracked and he stepped back, bumping into a low bookshelf. "I'm sorry, but you need to stop calling and texting."

"It's over?" It fell out a whisper, and my heart cracked with the omission. I'd held out a tiny morsel of hope, just enough to keep me going. "I know I screwed up, and I can't apologize enough but…"

I was just desperate enough to beg him to return. Glancing around, I took in the surroundings. It wasn't fair to him to do this at his work, and if he did it at mine, I'd be mortified.

He mouthed the words "I'm sorry" and turning slowly around, walked over to assist a customer.

The envelope still clutched in my hands, I gripped my arms around my fragile heart and tiptoed over to the front desk, leaving the letter behind with a staff member to pass on to him.

~Chapter Twenty-Three

The day of my ultrasound appointment arrived. Pacing in the waiting room, because a full bladder was not conducive to sitting for very long, I kept glancing at the doors every time it opened, foolishly hoping James would walk in. That he'd be interested enough in knowing about his child to come see him or her on the big screen.

I stopped in front of Ana, who took time off from work to join me. "You'd think they'd run these things on time. My bladder is going to burst."

As it was, we were fifteen minutes behind schedule. My focus left Ana and flittered to the door as a man walked in, his wife right behind him. It wasn't James. If he was going to show up, he would've done it by now. Dang.

"Josephine Monroe?"

I turned in the direction of the voice and walked over.

"I'm Elizabeth; your tech for your ultrasound. Did you have your last glass of water an hour ago?" She held open the door to a darkened room with a long cushiony bed illuminated by the flickering snow coming from the computer monitors.

I nodded, and my bladder stretched even more knowing it had to climb onto the bed without rupturing.

Closing the door, she pulled out a chair for Ana and directed me. "Hop up and pull your waist band down, and your shirt up to your breasts."

Crossing my legs at the ankle, as if it would help prevent me from peeing, I laid back on the bed. Warm goo dropped onto my belly and the tech moved the wand through it and over the lower portion of my pelvis, stopping abruptly.

"Okay. You can go relieve a little bit."

"What?"

She passed me a cup. "But only one cup's worth. Your bladder is too full."

I gave her an *are-you-serious* look. "Only that?"

There was a litre of fluid inside me raging to get out. I wasn't sure I'd be able to stop once I started.

She wiped my belly free of goo. "One cup. Or you'll have to wait."

I returned a few minutes later somewhat relieved. It felt good to release but holding the rest back was a new form of torture. Resuming my position on the bed, the warm goo smeared once again across my belly and the wand bounced back images onto the screen.

"Let me take the needed measurements, and I'll give you a show. You're twenty weeks and two days, is that correct?"

"Yes."

"Oh my goodness, is that the l'il bean?" Ana whispered beside me, squeezing my hand.

"Hey, bean," I said, running my finger over the imaged curve of its head.

The tech moved the wand back and forth over my pelvis,

sometimes pushing it hard into my belly, stopping and clicking every couple of seconds. Nothing on the screen made much sense to me, it was all grainy and the noises were like a weird static you'd get off a bad radio connection. I had no idea how they deciphered the images.

Before long, she finished. "All right, the necessary parts are done. Let's show you your baby." The wand moved over to my right hip. "You have an active little one in there."

"Tell me about it." I laughed.

Little athlete liked performing a high-intensity gymnastic routine, usually late at night when I was trying to sleep.

"Here's the head…" She pointed to the screen.

The head was recognisable, and huge, but it had the sweetest little slope of a nose.

"And here is the spine." She ran a finger the length of the monitor as the wand moved across my belly. A little hand appeared, almost like it was waving at me. "This here," she tapped on a faded rope, "is the umbilical cord."

"What about that dark spot in its chest?" Ana asked, a hint of apprehension in her voice.

"The heart. Want to listen?"

I nodded as she fiddled around with the knobs below her monitor. Suddenly the room filled with the sound of a rapid heartbeat like what you'd hear through a stethoscope, only scratchy. "It's so fast."

"One hundred fifty-two beats per minute. Normal."

A tear slipped out of my eye, and I looked over to Ana who had many tears falling from hers. I squeezed her hand.

"Do you want to know the sex?" The tech scrolled and clicked on her machine.

"No," I answered quickly.

"Yeah," Ana answered at the same time and whispered to

222

me. "Dontcha wanna know, to make it better for shopping and decorating and baby names?"

I shook my head. "There are so few true surprises in life. I think I'll wait until its birthday to find out."

"Really? The pregnancy itself was a big surprise." She scrunched up her face when I raised an eyebrow. "What about James? Do you think he'd want to know?"

If he'd wanted to know, he would have shown up, or at least expressed some kind of interest, instead of telling me to stop contacting him.

"I can always put the sex onto a piece of paper, and you can check it out later if you change your mind."

Ana nudged me. "Do that. Then I can find out, and you won't have to know." A giggle escaped from her as she spoke.

"But if I know you know, I may want to know, or you may say something accidentally. Like at the airport." I gave my best stern expression, but it was hard.

My baby's heartbeat still floated through the air, its body moving as it stretched and pushed against my bladder. My very full bladder. I swore pee leaked out, and I needed a bathroom badly.

I turned to the tech. "Put it on a piece of paper. Twice, please. And I'll give one to the father."

Turning the screen away from us, she moved the wand over to my left hip and pushed in, wiggling it around. "Oh, there you are. You're hiding this from me," she whispered as she clicked. "All done." A slightly damp, but warm cloth draped over my belly. "You can go to the bathroom now."

I didn't even pull the waistband of my pants back up, just lowered my top, and dashed out of there like the place was on fire.

Sweet relief filled my body as I came back to the room.

The tech handed me two pictures and two envelopes baring the words *Baby's Sex.*

"I'll take those," Ana said, reaching for the envelopes.

"Oh no you don't. If I'm waiting, you're waiting."

"Damn," she said, smiling.

I had a sneaking suspicion she already knew and that's why she was so accepting of my refusal to let her have it.

"Okay, that's it. We're going out." I rose and stood beside the couch where Ana was slumped. It was the same thing every evening and weekend since Ollie'd left. She was under a blanket, in sweatpants and his sweater, watching terrible chick flicks and moaning about how much she missed him. It had been three weeks since he flew home. How was she going to make it to the end of March?

"Why?" She whined and pulled the blanket higher up.

"Because. This isn't good for anyone. You're depressed, I'm depressed, and we just need to get out."

"But we did. Last week. We were the only two single losers at Boston Pizza on Valentine's."

"Yes, but it was heart shaped pizza and the money went to a good cause. Besides, you know I love you."

"I love you too."

"That's why it's time to get up. You're not doing this today. We're going out, for a coffee, maybe grab a book to read, do some window shopping or something. But we're leaving, Ana. For a minimum of two hours."

"But we can stay here, in our jammies, and be miserable. We don't need to share this with the world."

"Get up! Are you like this at work?" I shuddered to think what she'd be like teaching a class full of energetic grade ones in this mood.

"Of course not." Her tone changed to an indignant one but at least it was something different than melancholy.

224

"Good." I smiled and reached for her hand, pulling her onto her feet. It wasn't too hard, she didn't fight me much. Maybe she knew it would be good for both of us to get out of the apartment for just a little bit. "Go get dressed." It was easier than I thought to push her towards her room. "You have fifteen minutes."

She stopped and spun around, glaring at me.

"Fine, thirty." I fired back, laughing as I went into my room and pulled out something comfortable to wear. Sheesh, I needed new weekend clothes as the last two outfits I'd purchased were for work. Lounging, relaxing pants were in short supply, as were properly covering tops. All my tops exposed my belly, and I wasn't thin enough to pull off that style. Leggings and a long sweater it was.

"Where are we going?" Ana begged, as I drove around.

I didn't really know precisely where we'd go. We just needed out. The thought had crossed my mind to hunt down a bridesmaid dress, but I wasn't feeling sexy enough to try on a bunch of dresses that would only emphasis the size of my still expanding waistline. However, I did need some new clothes and pulled into a parking lot full of big box stores, including some outlet stores.

"Let's go here." I pointed to the maternity store sitting fifty feet away from us.

"Fun," Ana said, and she jumped out of the Jeep.

We wandered around the store, and I pulled a few tops off to try on. I wasn't sure why, but I was impressed with the styles. I figured most would be frumpy-looking, or adorned with lace, or in some god-awful pattern. But most were anything but.

I came out of the change room in a purple top. It was beautiful on the hanger, but I loved how it drew attention to my bigger chest and hugged my belly.

225

"Wow," Ana said as her jaw dropped. "I like that one."

My profile stared back at me, and I rubbed my baby bump. It was much smaller than the lady who waddled past me, she had to have been carrying twins. A bump that size looked uncomfortable.

"This is a gorgeous shirt on you. The plum colour goes well with your complexion and blond hair," the saleslady said. She was older than my mom but impeccably dressed. "May I?"

I wasn't sure what she was about to do, but I agreed anyways.

She pinched some of the fabric near my waistband and gently stretched. "This material is very generous and will easily accommodate you until the end of your pregnancy and beyond. It washes nicely and doesn't stain easily. And it's on sale."

Turning slowly, I admired myself again and pulled out the fabric to imagine what my forty-week belly would look like verses the twenty-week one before me.

"Use this pillow." The saleslady handed me a fluffy white disk of padding.

Having no shame, I lifted my shirt and pushed it under, rearranging it so it didn't have bumps and weird dents. "Wow." I was huge, my additional belly far exceeded my boobs in the sticking out department. How big would I get? "Ana, what do you think?"

She stood beside me, head on my shoulder. "I think you're gorgeous."

I wrapped my hand around her waist and turned to the salesperson. "I'll take it. Do they have this in a jade green?"

In a week, I'd be starting my shifts as a manager. Maybe Meghan would let me wear this with a nice black sweater? I could hope.

"No green at all. But it does come in black and navy."

Well, there went that. "I'll take the black one and this one."

"Excellent, I'll go find one for you." She walked away.

"I still need some regular tops," I said to Ana.

"While you were changing, I found a couple. Over there."

Changing back into my regular clothes, Ana led me to a rack where I picked out three looser fitting tops and added them to my total. I also grabbed two pairs of leggings, one in a concrete grey and one in navy. Something different. Everything went on to my credit card.

"And it begins."

First the clothing, and soon I'll be out buying the basics – a crib, a car seat, and baby clothes. Figured I didn't need a change table, I could use my bed, and I didn't need a highchair yet, I could get that when the time came. And really, I didn't even need a crib for the first few weeks; my bed was big enough to co-sleep.

It had been a huge weight lifted off my chest when I started looking, like really looking, at all the baby stuff. Most of it wasn't a need, it was a want. And there was only one thing I wanted.

James.

But he hadn't responded to any texts, hadn't shown up to any appointments, and the one time he spotted me at the library, he didn't so much as say hi. The dull ache in my chest spread a bit. I missed the way he'd care for me, and the way he'd made me laugh, his wonderful smell, the way we could sit together and feel so comfortable we didn't need words. I missed him so much it hurt. But how could I want a man who didn't want children?

"Okay," Ana said, "it's coffee time. Time to get you out of your head." She grabbed the bag of clothes and pushed it into my hands. "Here you go." Hands on my shoulders, she guided me towards the entrance.

"What's good around here?" I shielded my eyes as we stepped out into the fresh air.

The sun shone down brightly, but it didn't pack enough warmth to melt any snow. The temperature hovered around the -

10C mark, however, it was tolerable. The worst of the winter was behind us.

"Let's put this bag into the Jeep and then grab a decaf maple latte."

"Ooh, that does sound yummy." I unlocked my vehicle and reaching into the back, I tossed the bag inside. A sharp pang raced across my midsection as I stretched out. Inhaling my breath, I breathed the pain away while standing up proper. "Definitely time to sit for a moment."

"You okay?"

I winked. "Just fine."

No point in getting her all excited. It could just disappear. The ones I'd gotten during work never lasted very long.

A few minutes later, we sat in an overcrowded coffee shop, trying to enjoy our special drinks. "This isn't working."

There were too many people, and twice I'd been elbowed in my back.

"Yeah, let's go." Ana pointed across the parking lot. "Let's go there."

The store holding her fancy was a buybuy Baby.

"I don't know."

"We need to start shopping. You're going to need a crib, and clothes, and a car seat, may as well look and when you find the one you like, watch for a sale." She pointed a finger at my purse. "And...if you open that envelope in there, you can find out what you're having, and we can pick up something appropriate to bring the l'il one home in."

She sounded like a child in a candy shop asking for the biggest piece of candy, and of course, I was the weak one for agreeing.

Coffees in hand, we walked the length of the parking lot and entered through the double doors of the baby store. The serenity of the few minutes of being in the fresh, peaceful air was gone in a heartbeat, replaced by the loud cries of children and the booming overhead voices announcing a flash sale on baby monitors.

The woman from the maternity shop who was much more pregnant than me, pushed me out of the way as she waddle-bolted over to whatever aisle the sale was happening in.

"Sheesh," I said and made my way over to the cribs, located at the far corner of the store. It wasn't as busy in this section.

"I grabbed this." Ana pushed a thick catalogue into my hands.

"From where?"

"Over there." She pointed and shrugged. "Look. It's got everything. Wall decorations, furniture, clothing, diaper genies and everything in between."

Another sharp pain.

Spotting a small grouping of rockers, I slumped down into one. The need to breathe was first and foremost, to calm the rising panic building. The little bean's constant kicking wasn't helping to sooth me much. I leaned back in the chair and found myself rocking it, gently back and forth. Each sway relaxing me.

I opened my eyes and looked at Ana, sitting on the matching ottoman. A deep breath filled my lungs and the sharpness of the cramp ebbed away. For a few minutes more, I allowed the gentle motion to wash away my anxiety. It seemed to work on the little bean too, as he or she stopped beating me up from the inside.

"I need this. Definitely." My hands ran the length of the armrests, the soft material caressing my fingertips. "It's coming home with us."

Confident the pain had gone away, I pushed myself out of the chair and hunted for the price tag, surprised to see it was cheaper than I expected. The item tag in my hand, I went to the cashier to pay for it, who called for a page to help us carry it out.

"Where's your truck?" he asked, loading a giant box onto a flat deck trailer.

"My Jeep's over there." I pointed across the parking lot, not that it made it easier. The teen had no idea what vehicle I drove.

"Does it have a large trunk?"

"It's modest."

He pushed the trailer through the mucky snow towards my vehicle. As we approached, I popped the trunk. His head flipped between the box and the empty space. "Yeah, I don't think that's going to fit."

A little grunt and he lifted the box, laying it on the lip of the bumper.

"What about in the backseat?" Ana suggested.

"We can try that," the teen said as his face changed in colour. The rocker must weigh a tonne.

In the distance, a red car captured my attention. Slowly, it circled the lot, and finally finding a free spot, pulled in. James exited the vehicle. He was across the dividers, and I had a perfect view as I stood behind my Jeep. Inhaling sharply, I stood motionless as he smoothed down the creases in his pants and buttoned up his peacoat. His focus was on his trunk as he opened it, shifted something off to the side and slammed it shut. In doing so, he turned just enough to spot me.

I held my breath, wondering if I could become invisible or if I stood still enough, would he not notice I was there? He didn't want me to contact him, but I wanted to yell out and say hi. I wanted to run to him and once more, beg for forgiveness. Instead, I stayed frozen to the ground. And he stayed his.

"It's not gonna fit," Ana yelled, the Jeep beside me shaking from side to side as Ana fought to get the box in it. "Damn thing won't fit."

The teen and Ana argued about removing the contents from

the box and putting it in a piece at a time back in the trunk. I tried to listen better, but my gaze wouldn't leave James. He stepped closer, but just. Four car spaces between us.

"Need help?" he asked over the distance.

Ana poked her head out through the trunk area, scowling at the teen employee. "Oh, James. Yes, please."

The employee backed away a foot or two but didn't go further, since he was still holding the back end of the box.

James kept his gaze locked on me as he approached and moved around me, as if stepping any closer than four feet would render him a puddled mess. It was happening to me.

"Ana," he said curtly. He waved her out of the way, and with a quick pull on a seat latch, folded down the backseat.

"Oh," Ana said, eyes wide. "That's how it works," she said to James as he started walking over to the passenger side. Another tug, and her seat folded flat.

"Now you have room." James assisted the employee and together they pushed the bulky box into the heart of the vehicle. He closed the trunk door and dusted off his hands.

Ana stood there dumbfounded. "Thanks. Didn't know the seats folded." She looked at me and shrugged.

I shook my head. I've never really checked as I never needed the additional space.

The teen scrambled out of the way, and without a further word, pushed the flat deck back into the store.

"This isn't the first big box I've moved before." His piercing stare burned a hole right through my chest. He gave his hands a quick rub. "Ana, I think you scared him with your yelling."

"Whatever." She rolled her eyes.

There was so much I wanted to say to James, but I couldn't speak, my tongue weighed a thousand pounds. Like an idiot, I just stared. And he looked good, so good.

His hair was a little longer, but it was brushed off to the side, and it suited him. A little overgrowth of stubble on his cheeks and chin led me to wonder if he was in the early stages of growing a beard. His eyes held mine, and they held so much curiosity in them it was hard to look away.

"You look great," he finally said, his eyes roving up and down my body. "Your pregnancy's having a positive effect on you."

"Thanks," I mumbled but I didn't think it was as coherent as I thought.

The distance between us diminished with each tiny movement.

"Even though I asked you not to text me, thank you for the updates about the appointments. Everything's going well I presume?"

The world around us drifted away, so it was just him and me. Our heartbeats shared the space. I breathed in his air and he breathed in mine. Nodding slowly, I tried to hide my stunned look. He'd said more in the past two minutes than he had in the last few weeks. I fought the urge to reach out, wrap my fingers through his, and see if he'd respond the same way.

"Give him the envelope," Ana said and tugged on my purse, drawing me out of the happy little two-person bubble I was in.

"I don't want another letter." James backed up, and a shadow of sadness crossed his face. "The last one was hard enough to read."

He read it.

And a million butterflies soared in my gut at the same time. "It's the ultrasound results."

My hands trembled, but not from the cold, and I pulled the ultrasound tech's scribbled envelope from the side pocket in my purse and gave it to him with the words *Baby's Sex* facing him.

"Do you know?" he asked, staring at the smudged ink.

I shook my head. "No, I'm going to wait."

"I see." The envelope smacked against his hands as his eyes searched mine.

"I may have withheld the news that I was pregnant, but I promise you, I haven't found out what our baby is." For effect, I crossed my heart. "I know I've said it before… I'm sorry. I really am."

"I never lied to you, ever. I never even *thought* about lying to you."

"I know, but it wasn't a lie."

"You withheld pertinent information from me."

"I only saw it as protecting you. Honestly. I didn't want your life to change any more than you did." I stepped closer and took in a deep breath as I reached for his hand. It felt so warm and perfect clasped in mine. "Can we try again?" My lip pouted out in a perfectly natural curl, my eyes begging him to say yes.

"If you were to keep something this major from me, what else would you keep?"

"Nothing, I swear." In an effort to prove I had nothing to hide, I let my brain run at full speed. "My dad's lighting every candle in every church to pray for my sins. The other day, I washed a load of whites and somehow missed a pair of red socks, and now I have Pepto-Bismol pink shirts."

"Oh, that's what happened," Ana's voice carried on a whisp of a breeze.

"At work, I let a customer have their drinks for free when the bill was too high."

"That's something you need to share with your boss, not with me."

"I'm not holding anything back from you, I swear. I've shared everything else since then."

"Not everything."

It was time to admit my deepest thoughts, maybe it would help convince him. "You're right." I hung my head and stepped closer. "I haven't been able to stop thinking about you since that first night, back in October. You're on my mind from the moment I wake up until I fall asleep. Every thought in between is somehow wrapped in you. Yes, I screwed up, big time. Yes, I'll regret it for the rest of my life. Yes, I love you even though I kept pushing you away. No matter what you say or do, I will always have a connection to you, and like it or not, you'll have one to me." My hands went to my belly, and tenderly rubbed it through the wintery layers of clothing.

I inhaled the cool air for courage to speak the rest of my thoughts. "Is it fear? Fear of not being enough for each other? Fear that we got thrown into this mess neither of us is ready for? Fear of our lives being changed forever?"

He stood speechless, his hand twitching. Did he want to reach out and hold me as much I wanted to be held? But he didn't make a move. His face remained blank but his eyes... They swirled with hope, then fear, then longing and finally hurt. It broke my heart.

"James, you need to understand, I love you."

He gasped and stepped back, allowing the cool air to swirl around us. "I can't do this." He broke eye contact with me and raked a hand through his hair. His voice cracked as much as my heart did. "I need more time to think."

If surprise was a drop of water, then I was the whole ocean. I couldn't believe he'd walked away. I just poured my heart out, and without looking back, he climbed into his car and drove away.

Ana wrapped an arm around me. "I'm so sorry. He looked like he was ready to forgive you."

I protectively placed my hands on my belly. "I thought I could convince him he was all I wanted."

"You have me convinced. Maybe a little more time is all he needs."

"I hoped he loved me too." My vision blurred as he drove out of sight. What was I going to do now?

~Chapter Twenty-Four

James

oday was a big day at work. We were launching what I'd hoped would be a great program – an information hour for expectant parents. Not so much a prenatal class, as those took up too many program hours, but a way for the community at large to help new parents on the life changing road that lay ahead. It was hosted by a nurse from the nearby Public Health Unit, and she'd planned on answering questions after a quick fifteen-minute slide presentation.

Intrigued by her notes I'd received via email, I made sure I was working that shift. I hadn't yet had the balls to share with any of my co-workers my own life changing news as I still wasn't sure what I wanted to do.

I really liked Josephine, she was different from the others in that she wore her heart on her sleeve. We connected so well together and right from the moment I asked her to dance, it felt as if she'd always been a part of my life and it was hard not to imagine her in my future. But a baby?

I had no experience with them. The majority of my interactions with kids were not positive. They were rude, inconsiderate little monsters with sticky fingers that destroyed toys and ruined books. I preferred the teenagers, especially the ones hanging out in the library. Those ones tended to be more on the nerdy side as they studied and prepped for exams or played in the gaming room. At least here they were safe and less likely to get into trouble. But kids and babies? That was a whole other ball game, and I wasn't prepared for that kind of upheaval in my life, although, to be fair, Josephine probably wasn't either.

I rolled my cart of books to the pickup shelves and starting with A, placed the holds into their spots while keeping my eyes trained on the front door. Would she be attending?

Pregnant couples of all ages walked in and followed the arrows into the program room. Boards inside the room were set up to highlight fitness programs, educational programs, apps, nutritional needs, and more for the expectant mother. I'd taken a quick tour of the set up prior to the doors opening but it all seemed very maternal focused, which I understood; the females were the ones to carry and provide for it. But I wondered how many dads were in my shoes, lost and confused about what to expect and how best to provide support and understanding?

A couple of ladies walked in and based on their level of PDA were more than just friends. But as they entered the program room, I saw her slink in behind them. Radiant and more beautiful than I'd ever seen her look before. Her hair, as light as the sunshine, was bone straight, the tiny hint of wave gone. Her swollen belly was nestled under a gorgeous shade of purple, and the colour looked amazing on her.

Before she had the chance to seek me out and pour her heart to me again the way she had many times before, I crouched down. From my vantage point I could see the sadness shadowed on her face and how the zip was missing from her smile when she greeted the person in front of her. What troubled her so much?

Hopefully nothing with the pregnancy.

She disappeared from sight and I righted myself, shelving the rest of the holds as fast as I've ever done and returning the cart to our back room. The presentation was to begin in five minutes, just enough time for me to do a quick walk around the library and then pop in and catch a few words from the nurse. Admittedly, I was more than curious, and I didn't know anyone pregnant, aside from Josephine, who I could talk with and inquire about things. Maybe the nurse would cover them?

I raced around the library, going from area to area to check on everyone and ended up chatting with the teens in the back over a complex math problem. Math was easy for me and it didn't take too long until I was able to point out where the mistake had occurred in their problem solving. Grateful for the guidance, they high-fived me. That was one of the reasons I loved my job. Libraries weren't just about books, it was so much more. I loved the connections I made, and getting people excited about things, in this case math.

I checked my watch.

The presentation part was over, as the lights flickered to life when I snuck in through the back doors. The participants had their backs to me aside from the nurse who aimed her remote at the smart board and closed out of the visual portion of the presentation. Damn it, that was the part I wanted to watch.

Hailey, one of our best Library Assistants, inched over to me and leaned in close. "Hey, would you be able to cover for me for a few minutes? I desperately need a bathroom break."

Wow, talk about perfect timing. Now there was a solid reason for me to be here.

"Of course," I whispered, my eyes scanning over the backs of heads hunting for Josephine. She'd likely be sitting alone, near the back. "Take your time."

There she was, sitting in the second row of chairs, the seats on either side of her empty.

Hailey rubbed my arm. "You're the best."

The nurse walked to the front of the room and addressed her audience. "What did you think? A lot of information, right?"

Heads nodded, and a quiet murmur filled the space.

"Does anyone have any questions, or anything they'd like more clarity on?"

One mom-to-be raised her hand. "It said on the slides prenatal classes can have a different focus, can you explain that more?"

"Great question." The nurse launched into details about having classes that cater to those having homebirths or having a hospital birth or having a scheduled surgical birth. Based on what type of birth they wanted, there was a class for that. However, she added as an aside, the public health centre offered an unbiased approach and covered it all in their prenatal classes.

Wonder which one Josephine is most interested in? The home birthing one sounds perfect for her.

"Anyone else have a question?"

A timid hand rose above her shoulders and she kept her head tucked down. "What about resources for single mothers?"

The hand fell out of view as soon as the words left her mouth.

Pain ripped through my heart hearing the hurt in her voice, and I braced my hands on the table behind me, leaning into it. I wanted to know this as well, so I knew the best way to support her. Obviously, there would be financial implications I'd need to address, and depending on her benefits, I could add the child under mine so that he or she was covered. I wasn't about to leave her high and dry. The child—my child—would be taken care of, even if it was from a distance. I owed her, and my baby, that much.

The nurse paused for a moment, and it seemed like she was finding a way to tactfully answer. "Let me get you some resources."

"I don't need food bank information, or that variety, as I'm financially stable. I'm concerned with how to find a parenting group strictly for single parents and a time management class, so I can figure out how to do this whole parenting thing alone. Mostly everyone in this group," she turned and scanned the crowd, her face falling as she took me in, "has a partner to help out in same way or form."

A cold shiver ran down my back from the cool, calculating way she looked at me. Not that I blamed her one bit. I hadn't been very receptive to her since finding out. There was still a lot of betrayal to deal with.

Hailey breezed on in and snuggled up with me. "Thanks. I was afraid I wasn't going to make it." Her hand found its way back to my forearm and her sugary voice gave me a headache. "You're a peach for helping a girl out."

But I didn't want to be in the room anymore and needed a breath of fresh air. Gently, I lifted her hand off me and walked out the door, back into the great hall and away from the program room. I made my way over to the teens and circled around the area, re-shelving books and directing readers to what they were searching for, but I couldn't get my mind off Josephine.

Forgiving someone for hurting me wasn't my strong suit. My mother often said I was like a teenage girl that way, and my sister agreed. But what did they know? I was confident Mom had never forgiven Dad for leaving us. He was the reason I swore I'd never have children, then I'd never have to worry about hurting anyone. What a jerk he was.

I was approaching the front desk when the need to see Josephine overwhelmed me. My feet, of their own volition, navigated me towards the windows allowing a quick peek in. A row of bookshelves four feet high and sticking out ten inches prevented people from peeking through the windows too long, as it was uncomfortable to peer over the top and into the program room. However, I was tall enough and had no problem keeping my eye on the woman who'd stolen my heart and then handed it back to me.

A sassy little blond stood beside me and gazed inside. "She's pretty awesome, ain't she?"

I turned my gaze to the bookshelf. "What do you want, Ana?"

She snorted. "The only thing I want is for her to be happy. And she ain't happy."

"I'm not getting into this with you. Goodbye." A turn on my heel and I started to put distance between us.

"Just a sec," Ana's cheeky voice called out behind me. "Who do you think you are?"

"I'm not that guy. I'm not the one she needs."

"Why don't you let her make that choice?" She crossed her arms over her chest and stared at me with defiance. "All she wanted from you was acceptance. A mistake happened, and she was willing to take the full blame and not put any of this on your shoulders. She never wanted any kind of obligation or pity from you, and still doesn't."

"Goodbye." I headed for the safety of the sorting room, knowing she'd be unable to follow me, and I could escape this lecture from someone who knew nothing about me.

"You're a freaking coward, did you know that?" Her voice was loud and crystal clear.

I stopped in my tracks and spun around, the anger boiling inside me threatened to explode, but I kept in under wraps.

"Man up." She pointed a finger at me, and a stern expression sharpened the daggers in her eyes. "Yes, it would've been better had you never found out because you broke her heart and each day it breaks more. It's painful listening to her cry herself to sleep every night, because she keeps thinking she's ruined your life, but your life isn't going to change. Because you're a coward. You're gonna stay on your precious little path to perfection and forget all about her like she was a bad dream."

I inhaled sharply and slammed my hands into the depths of my pockets. I may have ripped a seam with the thrust.

The last thing I was was a coward. I've done everything they told me I'd never accomplish, and you don't get that by running away. Just the opposite. This whole baby situation threw a giant kink in my life plans. There needed to be more time for me to sort through it all and figure out what the best thing to do was. That wasn't being a coward. I *was* trying to man up, as she so eloquently put it. I had plans. I just wasn't going to share them with Ana first.

"You wanna know something?" She stepped closer, and cautiously I did the same. "You broke her. And for the rest of my life I'll hate you for that." She did an abrupt 180 and hauled ass away from me.

I needed air. I needed to sit down. My world felt like it was crumbling underneath me. I grasped the nearby bookshelf and took a breath.

I broke her?

Slowly, I made my way to the back room and sat on one of the wooden locker room style benches. My head collapsed into my hands, and I shook with fear.

I needed to talk to someone. My best friend wouldn't understand, nor would anyone from my group of friends. I hadn't told anyone, but it was high time I did.

After announcing I was going on a break, I stepped outside into the garden area. It was a little chilly now that the sun had passed over, and the planters looked bleak as the flowers were only recently planted and hadn't yet filled the space. I lifted my phone and dialled the one person I should've talked to when the whole situation first surfaced – my mom.

~Chapter Twenty-Five

J pulled the Jeep in behind CeCe's car as she and Narina exited. Surveying the cars parked along the roadway, it looked like everyone important was here, Mom included. With a quick wave, they headed inside the bridal shop for CeCe's final dress fitting while I hung out in my vehicle, replying to a text from Ana.

It was interesting to me how CeCe returned to Donalda's Bridal shop a couple days after the scare, and within five minutes found *the dress*. The shop owner had only put it on display that morning. CeCe said it was all fate, because had I not had the scare, she wouldn't have had to come back to check things out and wouldn't have found her dream dress. A gentle punch on my shoulder and she told me to believe in destiny. As if.

An ache formed in my heart as I slid out and stood on the sidewalk, my gaze drifting down the street toward James' apartment.

"Josephine."

I was delusional thinking I could hear the melodic way he

called out my name. It carried on the wisps of the spring breeze.

"Josephine." He called out again.

Even though he wore a smile, it wasn't the kind to push up his eyes and bring out the sparkle. Deflated once more, I trained my focus onto the sweet little sheltie. I crouched down and gave Samson's head a gentle pat, who responded by licking the side of my face.

"Who's a good boy?" I hung out in the squat, unable to stand. "Help?" I asked James and stretched out my hand. He pulled me to a stand, and I shook out my legs. "Thank you."

His eyes fell on my tummy, which wasn't hard to miss. I was all belly these days. The little one, who remained sexless as I refused to open the envelope, kicked up a storm.

"Is he kicking?"

He knows.

"He?" I asked. Suddenly flashes of a blue tinted wall, and all things boy sprung into my head.

"Figure of speech, remember?" But his eyes didn't leave my belly, and movement from the gymnast pushed out the left side of my swollen midsection. "May I?"

It was kind of him to ask, so few ever did. Without hesitation, I reached for his trembling hand and placed it against the fabric on my left side. He deserved to feel his child.

"It likes to kick here." I covered his hand with my own and soon the little one gave a solid cartwheel complete with a head bounce straight into my bladder. I crossed my legs.

James face split in half and his mouth opened in surprise. "Wow. He, I mean, it, does that all day?"

I gave him a slow nod. "Most of the time, but not so much at work. I'm too busy."

His hand stayed firmly in place as my junior Olympian beat on me from the inside. Slowly, he trailed his gaze up to my eyes, and looked into the depths of mine. How I'd missed seeing that.

"How's work going?"

A flutter of activity strummed through my heart and out to the tips of my fingers. It sure felt good sharing space with him. "Good. I've been in management training for a month, alternating with Robin, and it's been an easier transition than I expected."

He was still so handsome, even with the shorter hair which looked recently cut. The sharp angle of his jaw had filled out slightly, softening his face, and he was close enough to breathe in the musky cologne intermingled with a touch of sweat. Pregnancy had heightened my sense of smell, and even though I could smell the lingering effects of a fast walk with Samson, it didn't offend me. In fact, I wanted to nuzzle my nose against his neck and inhale like it was the only thing keeping me alive. Too bad I still had feelings for someone who had none for me. Hormones were weird that way.

Instead, I cleared my throat. "As much as I'd like to stay and talk, I really need to go." I tipped my head toward the bridal shop. "I need to be in there, with my family."

"Oh yeah?" His head turned in the direction of the window.

I followed, laughing as three heads suddenly disappeared from view. "Yeah. They're waiting for me."

The cool spring air rushed between his hand and my belly as he lifted his hand away. "I'm sorry, I didn't mean to keep you." He shuffled backwards on his feet.

"It's okay," I whispered, not wanting to go. I inched closer to the door, but snails moved faster.

His Adam's Apple bobbed, and his hands thrust deep into the pockets of his jeans. "After you're done, would you like to come over for a drink?"

"I... I... It's ..." I wanted to, I really did, but now, I needed to protect my heart and it was clear with anytime around him, I didn't want to leave.

However, I owed it to myself to be strong and move past this.

"I'd like to discuss parental rights." There was an edge to his voice I'd never heard before.

My legs buckled underneath me, and I braced myself against my Jeep. All this time apart I'd prayed and hoped he'd come around and want a morsel of future with his child. Never in my wildest nightmares did I entertain a notion he'd want to take my baby away from me and discuss custody rights. Protectively my free hand crossed over my baby.

"I promise to be kind, Josephine." The lingering sweetness of my name on his lips no longer soothed me.

His *kindness* worried me. Radio silence from him since that afternoon in the parking lot, and nothing more than a glance when I spied him watching me in the library. He wasn't there to gain information on parenting, he'd probably cornered the nurse to inquire about lawyers and all that jazz. My heartrate sped to stratospheric levels, and I blinked away the edges of fog closing in. I wasn't going to lose my baby.

"Hey…" His hand rested against my back. "I just want to talk. Away from your friends and family." He glanced back to the window where three heads did a terrible job of retracting. "That's all. I swear. Just talk."

"Just talk?" A wisp of air inflated my lungs, and my gymnast kicked once again.

"That's it. Will you come to my place and talk with me? I think it's time we did." The sweetest half-smile filled his face, and there was a sincerity in his eyes that wasn't there moments ago.

I swallowed and forced myself to stand unaided on my wet spaghetti legs. "Sure." My head nodded slowly.

"Great," he said with more enthusiasm than I thought was acceptable given the fear racing through me. "See you in an hour?"

He tugged on Samson's leash.

"An hour."

It was the longest seventy minutes of my life. CeCe looked beyond radiant in her dress, which was elegant, but I was wracked with worry. What did James want? Was he going to take the baby away? It was so hard to focus. When Mom went to try on her Mother of the Bride dress, I couldn't handle the pacing anymore. I desperately needed to talk to James. I apologised to the group, and amazingly enough CeCe let me off the hook and told me to rest. Little did she know.

I climbed up three flights of stairs in James's apartment and breathlessly, knocked on the apartment door.

As he opened it, his face changed from expectant to concerned, and he reached out. "Are you okay?"

"Yeah," I said, trying to catch my breath. "That's a few more stairs than I'm used to."

The extra thirty-five pounds I'd packed on so far didn't help, and I still had twelve weeks ago. A shudder coursed through me wondering how much more weight I'd gain. I'd need a new postal code by the baby's birthday.

As if we'd been friends forever and I wasn't here to discuss—gulp—custody arrangements, he ushered me in. "How did the dress fitting go?"

I followed him over to the couch and spied two tall glasses of iced tea and suddenly, my mouth went dry as cotton. "May I?"

The ice in the glass clattered against the side as I raised it to my lips and allowed the sweetness to linger and fill my soul. However, I wasn't sure there was enough sugar to sweeten me up at this point.

James sat down first and patted the seat beside him. I sat

247

trying to swallow down the building tension but moved closer to the far end rather than snuggle up to him like I had in the past.

Princess stretched out under the patio window and sent a cattish glare in my direction. Cats totally deserved their nasty reputation, and Princess certainly lived up to hers. Samson, on the other hand, sat at my feet and rested his head on my lap.

I gave his soft head a rub.

"Everything went well?"

It was time to answer, I figured. "The fittings went well. She's going to be a beautiful bride."

"Good," he said, lifting his glass to his lips. The glass in his hand shook a little as he set it down, ice cubes banging around.

"You seem nervous," I said, feeling my own nerves firing rapidly. Of the two people in this room, the one who should be most nervous was me.

"I'll admit, I am a bit."

Maybe he's going to change his mind? Maybe he decided taking our baby away from me wouldn't be a smart idea, and he'd never win anyway? Don't custody battles usually favour the mother?

My hands twisted in my lap and my voice cracked. "Why?"

"Well, every time I see you, you get even more beautiful."

Heat flooded my cheeks lightning fast and descended across my chest. I gazed upon Samson who had snuggled up at my feet. "That's not true, I'm getting–"

A long piano-playing perfect finger covered my lips.

Oh, God. He touched me.

Somewhere deep in my core a new war battled; the one between wanting to jump into his arms and have him fill me in a way only he could, and the one that figured he was trying to get on my good side in order to make the custody agreement less painful.

"No, you are making a baby, and not just any baby… my

baby." His hands hovered over my belly and searched out an affirmative in my eyes. "May I again?"

If I was more compliant, would it make things easier? There was nothing more I wanted than us, to be together as a threesome, but that was a pipe dream. However, I twisted in my seat, giving him easier access to my belly, and lifted my shirt over my stretch-marked laden skin. The sugar from the iced tea was waking someone up; deep inside a kick or two happened.

"Here." As I pressed his cool hand against the front of my body, a warmth blanketed me.

An intimate moment shared between us. And he sought me out. My hand covered his for a long while and I watched with wonder while he experienced the kicks and rolls, something I'd become used to.

"It's real," he whispered in awe.

"Oh, it's real alright." It had taken me a long time to accept it wasn't some strange undiagnosed tumour. It was more than real; it was my future. I found myself encouraging him further. "If you talk to it, it may respond back."

He lowered himself closer to his baby. "Hey there, what are you up to?" He wiggled uncomfortably and looked at me.

"I know, it's weird, but just talk naturally to it. The more it hears you, the better it'll be at recognising you after it's born."

"I don't know what to say." He gazed up at me with a questioning look.

"It's okay." The baby was wiggling lots anyways, so the addition of a voice likely wasn't going to do much more at this point.

"That's so amazing," he said in a soft voice while his hand rested on my stomach, the heat from his palm etching a permanent mark on my exposed skin. "The whole pregnancy thing. How one cell from you and one from me can create this perfect little being, who is truly one of a kind. And you and your amazing body, it knows exactly how to grow this creature and keep it safe and protected." His eyes searched mine. "It's the most amazing thing ever."

"I have to agree." Because it was. The whole process was mind blowing when I actually sat down and thought it through. Ana and I'd had many late-night discussions about how incredible the human body was.

He lifted his hand and folded it with the other in his lap. His chin tucked in and his head lowered. "There's something I want to discuss with you."

A painful bulge formed in the back of my throat. *Here it comes.* Tears refused to stay at bay and instead blurred my view.

"What's wrong?"

"Please don't take my baby away, there has to be another way." Words choked in my mouth. "Please."

"What? I'd never…"

I pushed myself closer to the far side of his couch. "But you said you wanted to talk custody agreements."

A small smile tickled the edges of his lips and it turned up the corners. "Yes, I suppose I did, to a point."

How can he smile? What's he planning?

Tears streamed down my cheeks like sad, scared little rivers.

"Let me start again." He inhaled sharply. "This is coming out all wrong." He rose and paced in front of his flat screen. "Let me explain… A few weeks ago, I had an unpleasant run in with your friend, Ana."

"What? When?" My palm smeared my visible sadness across my cheeks.

"That day you were at the library for the informational class."

I nodded as I remembered. Ana had agreed to pick me up as it was supposed to rain later.

"She said some awful things that I didn't believe. After a lengthy talk with my mother, I realised they were all true."

What had Ana said? She never told me she said anything to him.

I continued to sit and stare, wondering if he was about to have what Ana lovingly referred to as a 'Jo moment', one of those moments where you pour your heart out to someone only to have them walk away. Although I wasn't sure I wanted to leave. I needed to hear the man out.

"Then as if that wasn't enough, a week ago I ran into your sister at the library. Actually, I think she ran into me." He shook his head. "It doesn't matter. The point is I recognised her and asked her how you were doing." The words stopped as he took a breath. "Is your sister a bit dramatic?"

My frazzled edges softened and a small laugh escaped as I recalled all the times CeCe had been overdramatic. "Just a touch."

"Well, she should win the Academy Award then."

"Why?" Instantly I pictured my sister dramatically re-enacting a story with grand gestures and high-pitched story telling. If she was expressive enough, I was sure she'd garnered an audience to watch and that probably made James cringe.

"She said you were quite depressed and had fallen into a bit of a slump."

"Oh." So not how I imagined that conversation going because a, it was true, and b, I thought I'd hid it from everyone. Guess I was wrong.

"Cecelia mentioned for the most part you stayed home, and only left to work. Nothing more, nothing less, aside from the occasional family brunch. She worried about you, and the baby, and me. Worried how two people who were so perfect for each other could fall apart as there was an obvious reason why the universe brought us together."

That sounded more like CeCe. She was all about destiny and things happening for the right reasons. I often thought it was a lot of mumbo-jumbo.

"I thought about that, about her words, and realised she was right, in very much the same way as Ana. I was a coward and destiny did bring us together, for whatever wild and weird and wonderful reason. And I can't stop thinking about you and it finally clicked why you didn't tell me you were carrying my child; our child."

I leaned closer, not wanting him to stop talking. Ever. He was on a roll.

"You really were worried about how it would affect me and my life, and I've got to tell you, it hit me like lightning."

"I'd told you that many times before."

"Maybe," he said with a smile, "maybe I just didn't hear you I guess." He stopped pacing and sat back down on the couch. "All the time I said I didn't want children, it wasn't because I couldn't afford them, or I thought they were too much work, there were a couple of reasons really. The first being my own father abandoned my mother when my sister was four and I was six."

I reached out to grasp his hand.

How awful. Mind you, from a certain point of view so had my mother. My birth mother.

"And I didn't ever want to become him. I talked with my mom for a long time that night and she told me she'd forgiven him. Of course, I was stunned because as a grown adult I hadn't yet done that. So, I asked her why. Do you know what she said?"

I didn't have the foggiest of ideas and in slow motion I shook my head and leaned in closer.

"She said she forgave him because despite his reasoning for

leaving, he gave her the two best gifts of her life – us. And it was hard to hate the man who gave her a piece of immortality."

Wow.

"Then it hit me like a 2x4 to the side of the head. Our baby was a gift, and I would be worse than the father I've held a grudge against my whole life if I didn't step up—man up, in Ana's words—and be grateful for the gift I've been given."

"But…"

"Yes, I know I said I never wanted children, but maybe my reasoning for that was wrong. Maybe it was because I couldn't imagine any one so perfect to be the mother of my child. That other woman, she wasn't the one, that's why it didn't work out and I needed to go to her wedding, not because I needed confirmation of her love for the other guy but because destiny knew that's where I'd meet you and truly fall in love for the first time."

The words were the sweetest I'd ever heard, and I started to laugh through my tears.

"How long exactly did you talk to CeCe?" It sounded so much like a fairy tale story she would've crafted.

"Can I show you something I've been working on?" There was a slight pitch to his voice.

"Sure?" I said, wondering what suddenly fired him up.

He stood and extended his palm toward me, which I slipped my hand into. I loved the way our hands fit perfectly together, like pieces of a puzzle.

Leading me gently down the hall, he stopped before his spare bedroom/office door. "You'll have to forgive the mess in here."

"Okay," I said with a nod knowing his 'mess' wasn't very messy at all.

The door slowly opened, and my eyes adjusted to the sunlit room decorated in hues of banana and chartreuse. A white crib sat along the interior wall, its sheets a pale shade of gold with tiny little teddy bears printed on it. Around the room hung pictures of said teddy bears, in the cutest poses; dancing, smiling, sitting. Against the wall that backed up to the kitchen was a dresser and changing table, fully stocked with diapers, wipes, and blankets.

"What do you think?"

"I'm... wow... it's beautiful."

The polite words fell out easily enough but deep inside I worried. A lot. There was a lot of effort put into this room to change it from his workspace into a room fit for a baby.

"Does this mean that you're wanting to share custody of our child?"

"God no."

I ran my hands over the bedding, something I hadn't yet purchased. Aside from a few gender-neutral clothes and the rocker, I hadn't bought anything. Nothing seemed perfect. But this room, it was everything perfect I would've picked.

"I'm wondering if you'd move in with me?"

"Where would I sleep?" His apartment was only a two bedroom; one was his bedroom, and the other for the baby.

"Josephine, my shared custody thoughts didn't only extend to having you here permanently, so I can help with the middle of the night feedings, and some of the diaper changes. I want to be here when he or she needs a snuggle, and I'd love it if you would occupy the lonely side of my bed. It's lost the smell of your conditioner and I desperately need it back." He sported the most genuine expression of hope I'd ever seen.

"You've only missed my smell?" But I was kidding.

He stepped closer and tried to wrap his arms around my waist. They didn't reach as his hands rested on my hips. "I've missed you. Your body. Your warmth. Your sunny disposition. You've already taken up residence in my heart, and I need you to take up residence in my home. You and our baby. I'm sorry it took so long to pull my head out of my own ass."

"I don't know…" But I did. I'd been praying for answers. "Hmm…" I stared into his face. "When?"

"Personally, I'd be good if you moved in tonight as I'd like to make up for lost time, but I know that's not a possibility. But soon. I want you here well before you go into labour." He broke our gaze and walked over to a cupboard. "I've been doing some reading."

One of the shelves was filled with pregnancy and labour books, as well as the first few months of infancy.

"Oh, and I'd love to join you and Ana in prenatal classes."

"Really?"

"Figured I put it in there, I should help you get it out. So, what do you say?"

Ever since the first time he crossed the ballroom floor and extended his hand for a dance, he's been all I've ever wanted.

"Yes. Yes, to it all." I held his cheeks in my hands and firmly plastered my lips against his. It had been too long, and I'd missed the way his lips meshed with mine, all hot and pepperminty. It seemed he'd missed it too as he kissed me back with a longing and rock-hard desire pressed into my hip.

That deep Grand Canyon wide smile appeared on his face, stretching from ear to ear. "I love you, Josephine. And our sweet baby–"

There was no way I was going to let him spill the beans on the baby's sex, and I quickly covered his sweet lips with mine again.

Maybe CeCe was right. It was destiny that brought us together.

Chapter Twenty-Six

My sister, the radiant bride in her beautiful white gown embedded with sparkles, giggled, and linked her hand through Victor's arm as they took their first walk down the aisle as a married couple.

I carefully stepped down the four steps from the gazebo to the grass, waddling and restraining a grunt with each movement. Today was my due date, and the little gymnast had stayed snugly inside. According to my doctor's appointment three days ago, he or she was in no hurry to arrive either.

The tailor had altered my dress as much as she could. It wasn't the giant basketball stretching out the fabric, as the lavender-coloured dress was loose and flowy, but it was everything north of the empire waist part. They never tell you in pregnancy books how much that area grows, and I was told to just wait. Breastfeeding would make the girls even bigger. As it was, it felt like the sweetheart neckline was a little too revealing.

Big boobs and swollen abdomen aside, I stumbled on my last step.

The best man, Victor's childhood friend Henry, grabbed my arm as I swooshed a little more to the right than expected. "You okay?"

"Yes," I said, heat rising in my cheeks, but I held on a little tighter, searching the crowd for James. He'd taken a bench near the middle on the bride's side. "I'm looking forward to getting out of the sun."

Indeed, after listening through the dual ceremony—a lovely mashup of both Catholic and Jewish services—I was ready to put my feet up. Or at least gulp down a litre of ice-cold water. Ooh, and maybe pour it over every square inch of my body.

We followed the procession to the edge of the garden and took our places along the fence in the shade, shaking hands and thanking people for coming out. More than a few people reached out and without asking, touched my very hot and very swollen bump.

Ana, who had joined the long line to shake hands with the bridal party, pushed away a handsy middle aged lady in front of her. "Ask her before touching."

"Ana."

"She ain't my family, and it's frickin' rude to touch without consent." She shrugged, the spaghetti strap on her shoulder slipping off. A moment of jealousy plagued me, sure in the knowledge that even my shoulders had gained weight.

"You look gorgeous, CeCe," Ana stated as she moved along.

"Thanks for coming."

I looked down the line to James, who was chatting with my mom. Mom was laughing, so that was a good sign. It surprised me how easily Mom had welcomed him. James made his way to my dad who pumped his hand with a little too much force. Dad was still adapting to the whole situation, but he was coming around. Slowly.

Finally, James said hello to the bridesmaids and groomsmen, where Jeremy tapped him on the back, like a brother would. It made me happy how they got along.

And after what felt like forever my handsome boyfriend stood in front of me.

"Hi, gorgeous." The sweetest kiss fell on my lips before he gave me a bottle of water.

"Thanks." I rolled the cool bottle over my chest before taking a sip. "I needed this."

With the program card, he fanned my face, and a little relief blew over me.

I nudged my sister. "Hey, CeCe, I need to sit down for a bit, okay?"

She craned her neck past James. "Sure, there's not many people left."

The family had all passed through the receiving line, as did close personal friends.

Linking arms with James, I started walking away.

"Just make sure you're ready for pictures in about fifteen minutes."

That gave me about ten minutes in the air-conditioned building a few steps away. Pulling open the door, it was like stepping into a refrigerator. Well, maybe not that cold, but after standing in the +30C sun for half an hour, the relatively cool hall was a blessing. It was also very dark compared to the blazing brightness outside. Also, a much-welcomed relief. I was sure I was going to have sunburn across my chest.

We joined Ana over at the bar, who already had a plastic cup filled with ice cubes. I stole one out and popped it into my mouth.

James produced a couple of baggies from his suit jacket. He went to the other side of the bar and filled them half full. "Place them under your arm pits. It should help to cool you down."

"I just need to sit." My ankles looked as wide as tree stumps. Darn heat and swelling.

Like magic, James pulled a chair from a nearby table and helped me on to it. I swear it groaned when I sat. I placed the ice bags into my pits and moaned with delight. Sweet lord, that was heavenly.

"Geez, Jo-Jo, keep the noise down."

I wasn't aware my moans were that loud.

"How's that feel?" James sat beside me.

I closed my eyes. The chill from my pits slowly made a path to my shoulders and over my chest.

James gentle touch rubbed through the layer of silk on my back.

"That's good." I pushed into it. My lower back developed a deep ache at the start of the ceremony. "It's sore there."

"Right there?"

"Very low. Like…" It dawned on me. It ached like it did the day my period started. Straightening up, I closed my legs together as tight as I could.

"You okay?"

I looked around the hall. We weren't alone by any stretch, but there was no one in the immediate vicinity. Still, I kept my voice low. "It's aching like I'm about to get my period."

"Do you think…" His eyes got a faraway look to them.

Ana's face lit up with joy. "Could it be today?"

I shrugged. "It could be a warning sign. These things start coming together days beforehand."

Although, if labour started tonight, I was pretty much given a free pass to leave. CeCe was totally on board even if she kept saying she hoped the baby would come before or after the wedding. Not on the actual day. However, labour took hours, sometimes even days. I was safe.

But first pictures.

The groomsman I was paired with, Henry, popped into the hall. "Mr. and Mrs. Grabenstein are ready to go. Are you?"

It took me a moment to get that Henry wasn't referring to Victor's parents, but to my sister and brother-in-law. I wasn't quite ready to go; I was enjoying the cool air around me too much. Regardless, and with a sadness of leaving the AC behind, I stood. After an hour of pictures out in a field, I'd be back in here. Grunting with the effort, I managed to push myself to stand and was greeted with the most intense belly tightening yet. It didn't hurt, but it was tight enough I could've bounced quarters off it.

Even James noticed, and his hand went straight to my belly. "Wow."

It was almost uncomfortable to walk with it so tight. "One thing at a time."

Just wait, baby.

"Okay," the photographer said after thirty minutes, "anyone not family can go cool off." He wasn't as good as Crystal's guy. This one was a little more abrupt and painfully slow. He set up some stools for the next round and in my opinion took way too long getting organised.

I leaned over to Jeremy. "Birth takes less time."

Jeremy shot a look at me and did a quick up and down over my body. "What?"

That was not what CeCe needed. "I'm not in labour," because I wasn't. "But I could probably give birth in less time."

Already I'd had to pee twice, but the second time was just because the break in the heat was so welcome and not a whole lot had changed in the minutes I was gone. Molasses moved faster than this guy.

"Okay, family." The photographer waved Jeremy and I over. "You stand there, and you," he said to me, "let's have you sitting right here."

Slowly, I lowered myself onto a stool I was sure would give out from under me. I'd never felt so unsteady before.

While I tried to make myself comfortable, a very noticeable contraction started, and my eyes widened at the intensity. I connected with James who hadn't removed his gaze from me. Trying to be discrete, and not take any attention away from my sister, I pointed at my belly.

James walked closer.

"Back, back," the photographer snapped at James. "Are you family? No. So stay there." He turned to face us. "Are we ready yet?" He adjusted a few knobs. "Okay, everyone smile."

After thirty painful minutes of posing and smiling, and enduring a couple of contractions, CeCe's side of the family was dismissed, and Victor's family was up.

I waddled to James as fast as I could.

"You had two contractions, and judging by the expressions on your face, they didn't last more than thirty seconds."

That was good. We were told it wasn't truly labour until they were lasting a minute and coming every five. There was still lots of time.

"It has to be the heat. I need to cool off." We beelined back into the building.

As soon as we were inside, I sat down. And the first chair I spotted was where I'd planned on sitting for at least the next half hour. It would take at least that long for the photographer to figure out how to pose the other family. Supper was an hour beyond that.

Ana brought me a glass of 7UP with a spritz of cranberry

261

juice, and James fanned me.

"Another one," I said, reaching for James hand and took a quick breath.

"What?" Ana pulled a chair closer and whispered, "Jo, are you in labour?"

"She's close," James answered for me. "But not quite."

"Okay, it's going away." I breathed out.

"That was longer. Forty-five seconds."

Ana's hands rubbed away the building tension in my shoulders. "I have everything in the car, just in case." Ana insisted I take my hospital bag everywhere I went.

"Well, it's going to have to wait." There was no way I was going to take away from my sister's wedding. She'd picked the date and everything before I announced I was pregnant. I could hold the little one in, and he or she could have their birthday on July second, not the first.

I leaned forward and rested my forehead on James's shoulder. It was going to be a long night of trying to act like everything was cool. Free pass or not, my place was here. I didn't want to take any spotlight away from my sister. She deserved her moment.

As wonderful as the steak supper smelled, I picked at my food, and to the questioning bridal party members I blamed the heat. James and Ana were sitting at a table to my left as I was at the head table in front of everyone. But we had a signal. Every time I tapped my drink, the contraction was starting, and when I tapped it twice it was going away. I don't know how often I touched the glass, but one thing was clear to me, like it or not, I was in labour. Just needed to get through the speeches and the first couple of dances.

The caterers cleared away the plates, and I used the time to stand and move around. Not that it helped. Every movement made the belly tighten and a wave of anxiety washed over me. I waddled away from the bridal party and over to James and Ana.

"I'm going to the bathroom."

"I'm going with you." She grabbed my hand, which I squeezed. "Another? James."

"Can you move?" he asked sweetly.

I could, I just didn't want to, but the contraction passed quickly as pressure built in my bladder. "If it head butts me again, I'm going to soak the floor."

"Let's go," Ana said, pulling me toward the bathroom.

Lifting the length of the dress and scrunching up what I could bundle, I wiggled down my underwear with one hand and barely made it onto the toilet. A contraction hit, and I banged on the side of the stall. "Ana!"

"It's okay," she said, her voice calm and breezy. Wish I matched that.

"Um… Ana." I had stopped peeing, but something was still flowing. "Ana." A small gush washed out of me. "Are we alone?"

"Yeah."

"My water just broke."

"Are you sure?"

"Yeah." I grunted as another contraction swept over me, rendering me speechless. The intensity was nothing like I'd endured before and it took all my effort to breathe and concentrate through it.

"Josephine?" What was James doing in the bathroom?

The contraction over, I opened the stall door and peered out.

"That was a rough one, eh?" He squatted down in front of me and rubbed my thighs.

Tears built up and I nodded. "Where's Ana?"

"Supplies." James stayed right in front of me, never taking

his gaze away, until my bestie came back with a small bag.

"Let's get you cleaned up and ready to go." Ana pulled out a giant, overnight-sized maxi pad.

"Speeches first."

"Really?" James cocked an eyebrow.

"Really." I could do this. I planned on doing this.

A few minutes later, and another contraction dealt with, the three of us left the bathroom to more than a few strange looks.

"She was overwhelmed," James told the strangers. "She's hot and very pregnant."

With that, a couple moved out of the way and a lady grabbed me a chair.

"I just need to get back to my seat, but thanks."

"There you are," CeCe's high-pitched voice called out. "We're about to get started."

She was flanked by her best friend, Annabelle, who had graciously taken over most of my Maid of Honour duties.

"Sorry, itty-bitty bladder syndrome." I hoped the inflexion in my voice was convincing enough.

CeCe laughed but Annabelle sent a questioning look my way after flipping her gaze between James and Ana.

Smiling and inhaling a sharp breath of air, I squeezed James' hand again. Good lord. It was going to be a long evening of speeches, wasn't it?

Somehow, I made it to my seat, and watched as James and Ana reluctantly took theirs. There would be no dancing, we'd agreed. After speeches, we were hospital bound.

Each speech I endured at least one contraction, or two through my mom's, and with each one there was a trickle of fluid. It was incredibly uncomfortable to sit there and act calm and interested in what the speaker was saying, when in truth, I wanted to scream out and close my eyes. Instead, with each agonising contraction I forced a smile and nodded my head, trying to hear what was being said. It was so difficult though.

A nudge from Henry. "Hey, you're up."

I cleared my throat and dug through my purse for the words I had selected. Almost done. I was just before the final speeches, which would be from the bride and groom. Locking gaze with James and then Ana, I pushed myself up, Henry gave me some assistance.

"Thanks."

The guests all stared in my direction and my mouth went dry. Didn't help that a contraction was building. I grabbed the glass in front of me and squeezed it tightly while I inched my way to the podium. Pain rippled up from between my legs to the top of my swollen belly, but I couldn't talk. I couldn't breathe. I just needed a moment and leaned hard against the podium, opening the folded paper with one hand. The other was in a death grip on my glass.

Henry rose and joined me. "Ladies and Gentlemen, it seems our Maid of Honour is speechless. That's a first."

The guests laughed, which I appreciated oddly enough. I could handle being the back end of a joke.

The contraction ebbed, just enough for me to breathe again. "CeCe and Victor," I started to say.

A gush of fluid raced out of me and I stepped back and looked down, expecting to see a puddle on the floor. There wasn't. Tears blurred my vision, and my arms shook.

Henry took the glass out of my hand and set it on the end of table. He tucked his head in close. "Are you really that nervous?"

"I'm in labour," I whispered. "But I don't want anyone to know."

It was a slow nod and he turned back toward the mic. "I'm going to help out our Maid of Honour." He wriggled the piece of paper free of my grip. "Okay, I'll try my best to sound like

265

Josephine." He cleared his throat. "My dearest sister–"

I shook my head. "I'm okay." I let my vision travel down the length of the table. "There's so much I want to say."

A sharp inhale as another contraction slammed into me and an intense pressure pounded in my bottom. My hand clenched onto the lip of the podium.

James jumped out of his chair, Ana at his heels.

Ana took the mic, which she wouldn't have needed, the crowd was pin-drop quiet. "Jo-Jo has so much to tell you, but she'll tell you later, kay? She's in heavy labour and we need to get her out of here."

The crowd gasped and CeCe's voice rose above. "The baby's coming. Help my sister."

Henry wrapped an arm around me while he spoke to James. "Go get your car, man, and I'll help her outside."

There was so much commotion, I wasn't sure who went where. All I knew was within a minute I was sitting in the front seat of James' car with my dress hiked up above my waist. Someone had the foresight to throw a tablecloth down first, so I wouldn't ruin the seat.

"Go," I growled.

Doors closed, and James took off in flash. "Nearest hospital is twenty minutes away." He shifted in fourth as he turned onto the highway and floored it.

"I'll direct you down the back roads," Ana said from the backseat.

"No, main roads only." Something was niggling at me that I needed to be on an accessible road. "James, drive faster." I kicked off my shoes and pushed the seat all the way back, propping my feet on the dash. "Oh, dear god."

The contraction surged, and I felt like I needed the bathroom.

"Call 911." James tossed his phone at Ana.

I grunted through the contraction. Ana's normally calm voice spiked with urgency in telling the operator what exactly was going on and what roads were we planning on driving.

An unfamiliar voice sounded beside me. Ana had switched the phone to speaker. "Tell me what you're experiencing."

I breathed and grunted. "I have to poo."

"Is there a safe place to pull over?" the strange voice asked.

James pulled into a parking lot and killed the engine.

"Where are you located right now?" the operator asked.

Ana gave the details while James raced over to the passenger side.

"An ambulance is on its way to you. Stay on the phone please."

"JAMES!" I yelled and curled into myself. The pressure was too much, and I pushed into it. "Oh God!" I caught my breath. "It's coming." I tried to yank off my underwear.

James beat me too it, and pulled them off, dropping them on the ground in the parking lot. "Jesus Christ, I see the head."

My right foot pressed into James' shoulder and the other against the dash. I grunted again and instinctually bared down, screaming at the top of my head.

Sirens wailed in the distance.

"The head's out," James yelled. "Oh my god. It's beautiful. So much hair."

The voice on the other end of the speakerphone spoke calmly. "Don't push. Pant as much as you can. The ambulance is almost there."

"I... need... to... push..." How in the world was I supposed to fight against an instinct?

"Ana, grab me a towel." Instantly, there was the sensation of softness pressing against my inner thigh. "Josephine, look at me."

"I... can't..."

"Yes, you can."

Inhaling sharply, I peeked at him quickly. There were tears in his eyes.

"You are doing great. Look at your baby. Our baby."

I shook my head. "I... can't... see..." Between the dress and my belly, my view was blocked. A deep pressure formed again, and I grabbed the outer part of my legs and pulled them apart, grunting loudly.

"Pant, Jo-Jo."

Like a dog, I panted although every cell in my body said otherwise. And I tried as best I could, but the urge to push was too much. I bore down with all my might until sweet relief washed over me. A deep, primal growl roared out of me.

"Oh my god," Ana whispered, squeezing my shoulders.

"It's a girl," James said, choking back the words. He wrapped the towel around the baby and lifted her up to my chest. The sweetest, softest cry came from her.

Breathlessly, I kissed the top of her dark head, and closed my eyes.

It was over. I'd just given birth. In my boyfriend's car. In a hotel parking lot.

The wailing sirens appeared, their lights flashing in all directions.

The baby cried harder, her voice growing in strength, and I tightened my hold on her, trying to keep her as warm as possible.

"You did it," James said, rubbing my thigh.

"We all did it." I inhaled and released a pleasurable sigh.

"Congrats," one of the EMTs said as he approached the passenger side of James's car. "Are you able to move? We'll get you on to the stretcher where you'll be a little more comfortable."

His co-worker was already pulling it out of the back of the

ambulance and pushing it over.

Clutching my baby to my chest, I slowly lowered my feet, one to the damp floorboard, and one onto the pavement. James reached an arm around us both, and guided me onto my feet, after kissing me and then the baby's head. With a quick easy movement, I stood, the dress falling on either side of the cord giving me a hint of modesty.

"Uh-oh." Another contraction ached.

The second EMT was quick. My dress was lifted, and a bowl was pushed between my legs like it was no big deal and this sort of thing happened all the time.

I knew what was coming and had no desire to look at it. A quick grunt and it slipped out of me and the bowl came out. My eyes slammed shut as fluids trickled down the inside of my thighs.

"I think your dress is ruined." Ana laughed. "And maybe your car too."

For a quick second, I allowed my gaze to see where I'd just given birth. Hopefully there wasn't too much blood and fluid in there.

"A good car detailer can take care of that," the EMT told James. He removed the tablecloth from the car and dropped it into the ambulance.

"Hey, James," I whispered as I one-handed myself into a more comfortable position on the stretcher. "Look where we are."

He looked around. "So?"

"The Hilton. It's where we first met." Forty weeks ago.

"But it wasn't this one." He brushed a clump of sweaty hair off my face.

"True." I glanced to the side of the brown building suddenly wondering how many guests got an unexpected show. "It's destiny though. Maybe we could call her Hilton."

"Please, no," Ana said. "Anything but that."

James radiated pride and happiness. "You are the most amazing person I know." He kissed me. "I love you so much, Josephine."

"I love you too, James."

The EMTs buckled me down and pushed me into the ambulance, James on their heels.

Little did I know attending Crystal's wedding back in October would change my life in so many ways. From the most amazing party where I'd danced my feet off with the best-looking guy on the dance floor. To a surprise pregnancy. To a slight career change.

Destiny had brought James into my life and changed it for the better.

I searched James's eyes and tightened my grip on my baby girl. "Destiny. Her name should be Destiny."

A smile spread over James's face. "I like it." He stroked his daughter's head. "Hi, Destiny. It's Daddy."

I thought I was happy before, enjoying each day as it came. But it was nothing compared to the soul-filling happiness I felt now and hoped to cherish for the rest of my life. I had the world at my fingertips. And my life felt pretty darn perfect.

Epilogue

Eight months later

*T*he key fed into the lock, and my darling boyfriend entered the apartment, a fat stack of mail in his hands.

"There's my two lovely ladies." He waltzed over and planted a kiss on my lips before kissing the top of Destiny's head.

Samson walked over, dragging his leash and sitting at the door.

James laughed. "Guess someone needs a walk?"

"Sorry, Destiny's been an absolute bear today." I pushed my bangs out of my eyes and rose, carrying our daughter, and headed into the kitchen to start preparing supper.

"Tell you what, why don't I take her with me? Give her some fresh air and give you a break for twenty minutes." James took her out of my arms. "What does my girl say? Do you want to go for a quick walk with Samson and me?"

Inside the closet, he pulled out her one-piece snowsuit and expertly dressed our eight-month-old.

I propped open her stroller; a standard contraption that pushed through the thick snow without too much trouble but wasn't considered the Cadillac model I remember the group of high-class moms using. The store employee said this was perfect for our needs and folded nicely for the inside of the closet, rather than needing its own parking spot in a garage.

"It's ready to go." I placed a blanket on the handle for James to tuck around Destiny once they were in the lobby.

"There's a wedding invite for you in the mail."

"What, really?"

Jeremy wasn't getting married for another six months, so I highly doubted it was his. Still, the intrigue piqued my curiosity and I rifled through the mail pulling out the thick, cream-coloured envelope.

"Who's it from?" Having strapped the baby into the stroller, he read the return address over my shoulder. "From Westside?"

"Yeah." I wasn't due back from maternity leave for another four months, so it was a surprise to receive any mail or communications already. Slipping my finger under the flap, I tore it open and pulled out the insert. "It's for a taste testing night."

"That's different."

"Actually, not really, if you know Meghan."

When she introduced a new flavour of steak bowl a couple of years ago, it was on a trial run basis. The results were mixed, and she ended up not adding the dish to the menu. Was she going to attempt it again? There was an inscription to come and sample ten new dishes and to chose our favourites.

Samson whined.

"Do you want to go? Could be fun." James pulled his coat on and picked the leash up off the floor. "We're going, buddy."

I cast my gaze the calendar by the door and cross checked the date. The event was in two weeks. "It's during the time Ana's here."

"And you don't think she'd love to babysit?" James cocked

an eyebrow. "It doesn't always need to be your parents, or CeCe, or Narina who babysit."

"I know and it's not that, it's just…" My gaze ran the length of my body. I still had ten pounds to lose, and the lack of sleep caused major dark circles under my eyes.

He wrapped his arm around me. "No matter what you think of yourself, you'll still be the most beautiful woman in the place."

Samson whined again and started pacing.

"You'd better go." I pushed him out the door, and after closing it, leaned against it.

It would be nice to see the gang again, especially since the invitation was addressed for Staff and Former Staff affectionately known as Family. Would Audrina and Niall be there? What about Korey and Shayne? It would be marvelous catching up with everyone, as it had been a long while since I'd seen them. Plus, I'd get to see Robin in his new managerial role. It could be a lot of fun.

I put the invitation under a magnet on the fridge and pulled the RVSP insert. Grabbing a pen from the junk drawer, I hastily scratched a checkmark beside the Yes and put a two on the number of guests attending.

For the first time in a long time, I couldn't wait to head into Westside. Now to go shopping for a dress. What do you wear to a Taste Testing?

Finish the series with the last book – SERVING UP HOPE.

Sneak Peak of Serving Up Hope
Chapter One

*W*hat a flipping waste of time," I muttered while I twisted in front of my computer screen, filling out an online dating profile. "There has to be another way."

Desperation oozed from my fingers and onto the screen where I bared way too much of my private life.

My only hope was no one I knew searched me out and discovered what I was about to voluntarily post. Online dating was supposed to make things easier and yet I was wracked with more nervousness than I would be harmless flirting with the produce manager at the market down the street. Sheesh, and the kicker was, I wasn't looking for a husband or even a long-term boyfriend, just a one-time accomplice to a wedding. And not just any wedding – my former fiancé's wedding. The one who failed to show up for *our* wedding.

As I contemplated the trajectory my life was on, I ran my fingers through my dark hair, detangling the squeaky clean, yet still damp strands.

My male friends, as in all two of them, were busy or thought it ridiculous that I even needed a date for a wedding. Especially *this* wedding.

"You don't need a date," my trusted friend and neighbour said. "However, go, be yourself and you'll show them all that you are better off without that mess in your life."

My shift manager actually thought the opposite. "Wouldn't taking a date actually hinder your chances of finding a man and having a wonderful fling?" But he was also all for going and enjoying myself to the fullest.

I cussed under my breath, daring the image of my ex to flick away rather than grow larger and stronger in my head. What nerve he had to send me an invitation. What was his reasoning behind it? Or had it all been her idea? Get some kind of last laugh at my expense?

I picked up the invitation, tracing my finger around the cream-embossed edges, wondering again if it represented some kind of sick joke. With a quiet resolve, I placed it back down and returned my attention to Mingle More's dating website. This could be the perfect opportunity to show Scumbag how leaving me at the altar four years ago on our wedding day didn't leave any lasting scars on my heart. How marrying the person I thought was my friend didn't hurt even more. It was asinine I'd even received an invitation to attend. I secretly thought it was a joke—just to see if I'd actually show up.

I'll show them.

I reread my profile, deleting the information about my employment. A fake boyfriend didn't need that information, right? All I needed was someone my age or older and good-looking, although I typed in *older, preppy-looking guy*. The guy could be a total player and a complete jerk just as long as for one night he looked like he was hopelessly in love with me.

A feeling of shallowness clouded my heart as I added a part about needing a recent photograph to accompany any correspondence, because Mr. Dreamy needed to be perfect; in looks and employment. The employment thing was key. Scumbag was not the best employee and had transitioned through numerous jobs, or at least he had when he was with me.

I clicked back and added in: *steady employment.*

Bonus points if similar in nature to a Disney Prince. I laughed out loud at that comment and took a sip of Chardonnay.

The ad was simple enough.

Single lady looking for a single male to accompany to former fiancé's wedding.
Must be willing to spend the entire day with me – three weeks from Saturday; from an hour before the ceremony (so we can meet and become acquainted) until after the cake is cut.
All food and refreshments will be covered; limited alcohol.
May provide own transportation or share with me.
Applicant must have steady employment, look great in a suit as dress code is semi-formal/business and be between the ages of 25 – 40.
Please note – I am not looking for a one-night stand or anything beyond this event. I simply need a charming date. Serious inquiries only.

There it was. I leaned back in my comfy office chair, twisting slightly, my naked feet gripping the base. I admired my dating want ad, and followed the reading with a deep groan, placing my head into the palms of my hands.

How pathetic had my life become? I owned and operated a busy restaurant, with detailed plans to open another soon, but finding a date for a wedding? Mission impossible.

Tucking my slight embarrassment into the base of my stomach, I reviewed my carefully selected words. For the fifth time.

Hmm... should I have said more? Nope. It's exactly what I was looking for. It bore a striking similarity to the want ads I placed for work, which, once I thought about it, I needed to remember to place again. Two of my staff had moved into shift manager positions, which left the door open for more entry-level jobs on the floor. At least two full-time servers were needed, and if that wasn't going to work, then four part-time ones. I jotted it down on a mile-long to do list. A low sigh rolled out of me, and I took another sip of wine. An owner's work was never done.

In the corner of my computer, the time flashed two-twelve. The late hour didn't bother me since I was a night-owl by nature, and mainly because I didn't get home from Westside until after eleven. By the time I checked my lacklustre social media pages and ran a few reports, the clock had struck one. Add to the night my foray into the online dating world, and time disappeared. However, it was late, and I had other projects tomorrow to attend to needing more of my energy.

I was almost ready to hit the submit button when I stopped. My ad was blunt and to the point, but aside from the free food and beverages, what was in it for him? What would motivate someone to spend the day with a complete stranger, especially when there would be no sex? I pinched the bridge of my nose as my thoughts climbed into a headache inducing process.

There wasn't much I had to offer as enticement for someone to give up a Saturday and hang out with me. As a workaholic, I easily logged sixty plus hours at Westside in person, not including the hours spent away from there establishing the new location I'd hoped to open in a few short months. I wasn't an avid movie goer, or up-to-date on the latest reality tv show, so chatting about the latest Star Wars movie or Marvel comic book recreation wouldn't work. At least that eliminated the nerdy types from applying.

Physically, I wasn't even much of a catch. My hair was short, but easy to take care of especially since I swam four days a week. My apartment complex had a great 25m length pool, perfect for laps, and since I was the only one who ever seemed to be there, I swam for an hour each time. My ultimate goal was to compete in a triathlon, but I'd still need to learn how to ride a bike. I haven't since I was a child of single digits. However, I refused to put that on my dating profile.

What if I added I was a total loner and lived alone? On second though, it opened the door for all sorts of hooligans to reply and put me into an awkward position. Nope, it's better I kept it off my profile.

The chardonnay touched my lips, and I swallowed down the last of the red wine, contemplating further on what interesting bullshit to add.

Giving up more personal information, I typed the words from a song sung by Neil Diamond.

If the words "When no one else would come, Shilo you always came" mean anything to you, please respond with recent photo.

That was better. A smile bubbled out. It would also narrow down a lot of applicants. For good measure, to funnel the short list even more, I added *If Captain Picard played the best Hamlet, I'd love to talk further with you.*

Still, it didn't dangle any carrots in front of would be applicants. Maybe it would be better to show up to this thing with the greatest lie I've ever told? Something along the lines of my boyfriend needed to fly over to Boston for an emergency conference for a company he was taking over and that's why I came alone. It was believable, right?

"Hah," I laughed.

If anyone accepted that as truth well… I had some ocean front property in Saskatchewan I wanted to sell them.

The wine glass beside the laptop sat empty, so my time in front of the ad was over. With a final swallow of my pride, I hit the submit button. Nothing ventured, nothing gained.

Immediately a bright red error message appeared on the screen.

"Dammit," I said, pulling my chair in closer and rubbing my temples.

Tomorrow would be better, I was sure. It was too late to be doing this, and the error was karma's way of preventing a huge mistake, according to the words the angel on my shoulder whispered. But I brushed her aside and read the error. Apparently, I needed to upload a photo. Guess appearances went both ways.

Begrudgingly I opened my phone and flipped through. There weren't many selfies at all, perhaps three. I hated the whole idea of them, hated being a part of them, and as soon as one of my friends pulled their phone out and took aim, I was out of there. Despite their reassurances to the contrary, I believed I wasn't photogenic. Like at all. I suffered from R.B.F. – Resting Bitch Face – and most, if not all the pictures I'm sporting a pissed off look, except I wasn't. It just appeared that way. My constant pout would certainly prevent guys from applying. Plus, I just wasn't model thin and pretty. I was a healthy size eight with no health issues, but it wasn't enough for a lot of guys. Obviously, or I'd have a date for the fracking wedding.

"Fuck it."

I held up my empty wine glass with one hand while I smiled into my camera. Meh, it was decent, if not a little bit goofy. Whatever. I uploaded it onto my computer.

A couple clicks later, I added it to my profile.

"Good luck."

My mouse hovered over the submit button and before I could change my mind, it clicked and sent my profile off to either be accepted or rejected. Let the chips fall where they may. Nothing could stop it now. My future lay in the hands of the internet now.

Oh crap – what had I done!

Dear Reader

Joy's story started out as a quick novella, but the more I wrote about Josephine's story, the more it all needed to be told. James truly is the jam to Jo's peanut butter, and they are perfect for each other. I hope you enjoyed the third book of the Ladies of Westside – *Serving Up Secrecy* as much as I enjoyed writing it. Now that you have read about Jade and Evanora and Joy, are you excited to read about Meghan?

As an author, it makes my day when someone shares their thoughts and gives me feedback on the characters you've invested your time with. It's because of early feedback on *Serving Up Innocence* that the rest of the stories came to be. My first beta readers wanted to know more about Evanora and Joy, and even Meghan, figuring because she's such a raging bitch, her story could be quite saucy. Share with me what you liked, what you loved, or even what you hated. I'd love to hear from you.

Contact me via email or via my website, or subscribe to my newsletter, where my subscribers get an exclusive first look at cover reveals, blurbs and early access to sales (and a free romance book every two weeks). .

Finally, I need to ask you a favour. If you are so inclined, I'd love a review or a rating of *Serving Up Secrecy*. It doesn't have to be long, even something as simple as "Loved it, looking forward to the next one" works. Reviews and ratings help me gain visibility and as I'm sure you can tell from my books, reviews are tough to come by. As a reader, you have the power to make or break a book. If you have the time, here's a link to my author page on Goodreads. Something to keep in mind.

Thank you so much for spending time with me.

Yours,

H.M. Shander

Other Books by H.M. Shander

Duly Noted
That Summer
If You Say Yes
Serving Up Innocence
Serving Up Devotion
Serving Up Secrecy
Serving Up Hope
It All Began with a Note
It All Began with a Mai-Tai
It All Began with a Wedding
Noel
Whistler's Night
Dreamers in Cheshire Bay
Return to Cheshire Bay
Adrift in Cheshire Bay
Awake in Cheshire Bay
Christmas in Cheshire Bay
Journey to Cheshire Bay
Charmed in Cheshire Bay
Second Chances in Cheshire Bay
Unforgiven in Cheshire Bay
Flirty in Cheshire Bay
Messages & Mistletoe
Living La Vida Mocha

Visit www.hmshander.com for up-to-date listings

~Acknowledgements

Gosh, it's hard to believe I am writing my eighth public thank you. It's mind boggling to me. I'm in a perpetual state of shock. A million thanks to my family – Hubs, The Teen and Little Dude – and to my parents. Where would I be without your support and endless cheerleading? Thank you for believing in me and giving me the time I needed to work on just one more chapter, and being patient with me when that stretches out into the early morning hours. Thank you for encouraging me to do what I love. Thanks for all your help with signings (especially you my little PA – you are always out there smiling beside me and helping people pick out their swag.) Love you always.

To my wonderfully dedicated critique partner – Miranda – your comments and critiques were bang on and I'm very grateful for your attention to detail in helping to pull the story all together.

To my tribe of alpha readers and beta readers. Ashley, Jill, Josephine, Lacey, Leslie, Mandy, Rebekah, and the Blind Beta Readers Club. Thank you from the bottom of my heart for all your comments and advice and wisdom and pointing out what didn't make sense and what needed to be expanded on. Thank you for falling in love with Josephine and James and seeing them through to the end.

To my cover designer – Megan – thank you for bringing the vision to life, for incorporating my themes and brand and giving the series a new life. You are a gifted designer. Thanks.

To my editor Irina – Whew, we made it just in time. Lots of changes and add ons. That last chapter! Thanks. I appreciate your quick turnaround time and the back and forth with the comments, questions and suggestions.

If I missed you, it certainly wasn't intentional. I know I couldn't stand where I am without the help of so many others. Thank you! And thank you for reading and making it all the way to the end. You all rock.

~About the ~Author

H.M. Shander knows four languages—English, French, Sarcasm and ASL—and speaks two of them exceptionally well. Any guesses which two? She lives in the most beautiful city in Canada–Edmonton, AB, a big city with a small-town feel, where all her family live within a twenty-minute drive, although her parents are contemplating moving away. As much as she'd love the beach under a blanket of stars, this is her home.

A big time coffee addict, she prefers to start her day with a mug before attending to anything pressing, like driving the #momtaxi as she shuttles her kids off to school and various extracurricular activities. Secretly she loves it as when the vehicle is empty, it gives her time to think about what crazy things those characters will do next. She is a self-proclaimed nerd (and friends/family will back this up), revelling in all things science, however, likes to be creative when there's time. Right brain, left brain? Both.

Did you know she once wanted to be a "Happy Clown" as she enjoys making people smile, but she's beyond terrified of scary clowns? How ever many different jobs she's worked, her favourite has been working as a birth doula and librarian, in addition to being a romance author. Because, let's be honest, who doesn't love falling in love?

Five things she loves, in no particular order; The Colour Blue, The Smell of Coconut & Shea Butter, Star Wars (the original three), The Ocean, and Chocolate.

You can follow her on Facebook, Twitter and Goodreads.

Thanks for reading– all the way to the very end.